PRAISE FOR

13
HANGMEN

"Fascinating tale. Ghostly fun in old Boston."
—*Kirkus Reviews*

"The book's design nicely differentiates Tony's story, set in 2009, from the past narratives. Recommend this engaging historical mystery to readers who devoured Dan Gutman's Baseball Card Adventures series and are ready for a longer, more complex adventure." —*Booklist*

"Corriveau merrily ransacks historical episodes and figures (e.g., the Great Molasses Flood, the Underground Railroad, Boston mayor John F. 'Honey Fitz' Fitzgerald) and spins, twists, and manipulates their stories to advance the DiMarco family mystery. The result is a novel that agilely balances humor and tension."
—*The Bulletin of the Center for Children's Books*

"This is an exceptionally good story, with a wry, humorous tone that has particular boy appeal. It covers baseball, history, sibling rivalry, girls, and mystery, and folds in the space-time continuum." —*School Library Journal*

13
HANGMEN

a novel by
ART CORRIVEAU

AMULET BOOKS · NEW YORK

The Library of Congress has catalogued the hardcover edition of this book as follows:

Corriveau, Art.
13 hangmen / Art Corriveau.
p. cm.
ISBN 978-1-4197-0159-7 (hardback)
[1. Mystery and detective stories. 2. Supernatural—Fiction. 3. Family life—Massachusetts—Boston—Fiction. 4. Moving, Household—Fiction. 5. Brothers—Fiction. 6. Twins—Fiction. 7. Boston (Mass.)—Fiction.]
I. Title. II. Title: Thirteen hangmen.
PZ7.C81658Aah 2012
[Fic]—dc23
2011052137

ISBN for the paperback edition: 978-1-4197-0788-9

Text copyright © 2012 Art Corriveau
Illustrations copyright © 2013 Vincent Chong
Book design by Maria T. Middleton

Printed and bound in U.S.A.
10 9 8 7 6 5 4 3 2 1

Amulet Books are available at special discounts when purchased in quantity for premiums and promotions as well as fundraising or educational use. Special editions can also be created to specification. For details, contact specialsales@abramsbooks.com or the address below.

THE ART OF BOOKS SINCE 1949
115 West 18th Street
New York, NY 10011
www.abramsbooks.com

FOR THE REAL TONY

(whose present is also jumbled up with the past)

CONTENTS

SPECIAL DELIVERY
FRIDAY, JUNE 19, 2009

Tony DiMarco kicked his sneakers off at the backdoor mat, as usual. He flung his book bag onto the kitchen table, as usual. But he didn't raid the fridge for a slice of leftover cake as usual. It wasn't an as-usual kind of day. It was Tony's last day of seventh grade at Ann Arbor Middle School—thank God—which also made it the first day of summer vacation and, therefore, the first official day of his diet. Tony's thirteenth birthday was now only three weeks away. He had totally promised himself he would begin life as a teenager twenty-five pounds lighter. The plan was to grab an orange from the fruit bowl on the counter instead.

So why was he laying his forehead against the fridge door

and *picturing* that leftover cake—devil's food smothered in chocolate frosting—tucked behind a Tupperware of spaghetti on the second shelf, left-hand side?

Because he had just suffered through a grueling two-hour final assembly at school, one that had turned out to be a love-fest for his graduating twin brothers. Not only had Mikey and Angey cocaptained the baseball team to first place—Mikey as starting pitcher, Angey as catcher—but Mikey had also been voted Class Clown, while Angey had gotten the School Spirit award. And that hadn't even been the worst. The *worst* had been when the principal had stood up and named the evil twins co-valedictorians of their eighth-grade class. Tony would never hear the end of it at dinner tonight. Who could blame him for wanting a little chocolate pick-me-up now?

The front doorbell rang.

Tony leaped away from the fridge like he had just tripped the alarm to a safe. He peered around—heart pounding—though he knew nobody else was home to catch him in his moment of weakness. His mom, Julia, had met the twins after school and driven them to the mall to buy them new dress shirts for gradu-ation. And his dad, Michael, had been in Boston all week at a history conference. Julia and the twins were probably speeding to the airport that very minute to get him. Tony grabbed an orange, then crossed the living room to the front door to see who was there.

The postman needed somebody to sign for a package. Special delivery for Anthony DiMarco.

Tony told the postman he wasn't expecting anything. Maybe he should double-check the address. It was probably a mix-up with some other Anthony DiMarco in Ann Arbor who had bought a toaster oven on eBay. The postman told Tony he *knew* his job, thank you very much; he had been doing it for twenty-two years. Tony shrugged an if-you-say-so. He balanced his orange on the arm of the sofa and signed for the box. The postman shoved it into his hands and huffed off. Tony closed the door, then double-checked the address anyway. It was right. He looked for a return address. There wasn't one. He checked the postmark. *Boston, Mass.*

It must be from Zio Angelo.

(That's what Tony called his only uncle in Boston—*zio* meant uncle in Italian—though Zio Angelo was, technically speaking, Michael's uncle and Tony's *great*-uncle. Which was why he was eighty if he was a day, and smelled like mothballs combined with cough drops.)

"That's weird," Tony said. And it was. Zio Angelo had never sent him a gift before. He always got a birthday card with a twenty-dollar bill tucked inside. (More than the twins ever got, it had to be said. Zio Angelo never sent them *anything,* even though Angey was the actual nephew named after him.) Weirder still: Tony had only ever met Zio Angelo once in his life—last Thanksgiving—when the old guy had unexpectedly turned up in Ann Arbor to spend the holiday weekend. Usually Michael just visited him in Boston, whenever his research or a conference took him there. But Zio Angelo had declared to everyone on his arrival—even more weirdly—that he had really wanted to meet Tony in person before he turned thirteen. Which led to the weirdest thing of all: Zio Angelo had insisted on sitting next to Tony at the big turkey dinner—like they were best buddies or something—so they could talk about the Boston Red Sox. The twins had immediately rolled their eyes and excused themselves from the table, abandoning Tony to suffer through a long and rambling and totally random account of how Zio Angelo had met baseball legend Ted Williams. It had happened when Angelo was a water boy at Fenway Park, back in the day.

Tony decided to open the box, even though his birthday was still ages away.

In the kitchen he grabbed a steak knife out of the drying rack. He sawed through the taped-up lid. Sure enough, there was a corny For My Nephew birthday card resting on top of something lumpy and bubble-wrapped. He opened the card.

Bummer—no cash. On the right-hand side there was a singsongy printed poem he didn't bother to read. On the left, a handwritten note in Zio Angelo's spidery old script:

Finally, your 13th birthday!
Give this the place of honor in your new room.

What new room? Zio Angelo knew perfectly well from his visit that the DiMarcos were renting a tiny two-bedroom house from the University of Michigan while Michael finished his PhD in history. Tony shared the larger bedroom with the evil twins; Michael and Julia slept in the smaller one (though they had given it to Zio Angelo for the weekend and moved onto the fold-out sofa). In actual fact, every room in the DiMarco house did double duty: The living room was where Michael kept putting off writing his dissertation, so if anyone wanted to watch TV, they had to squint through a tunnel of books. The dining-room table—which was actually in the living room because there was no dining room—was where Julia designed books freelance for the university press, which meant her computer, not Michael, sat at the head of the tablewhen the family ate dinner.

Tony pulled the bubble-wrapped lump out of the box and plucked at the tape. If *only* he did have his own room! About all he could really call his own was the shelf above his bed. And he still couldn't prevent the twins from messing with the private stuff on it: his Junior Sleuths of America trophies, his collection of murder mysteries, his Boston Red Sox memorabilia.

Speaking of the Red Sox—

Out of several layers of bubble wrap emerged a faded ball cap. The shape of the bill was old-fashioned, and the big red embroidered *B* looked a little funky. Yet for some reason Tony felt like he should recognize it. Zio Angelo's water-boy cap? Unlikely. This one was too big for a kid. He took it over to Julia's PC on the dining table. He fired up an Internet browser. He typed "vintage red sox caps" in the search box. Dozens of images came up. He scanned through them.

Time simultaneously stood still and flew by, like it always did when Tony surfed the Net.

The cap was definitely an antique, most likely from the 1930s. And judging by a similar one on eBay, it was worth a fair chunk of change. In fact, it blew away everything else on his memorabilia shelf.

Angey and Mikey burst through the kitchen door.

"Tony's on your computer again!" Mikey shouted.

Crap! Tony was not supposed to use his mom's work PC without her permission, and the twins had caught him redhanded. "Only for a second," he said to Julia as she stepped through the door carrying two department-store bags.

"I bet he's in that sketchy chat room of his," Angey said.

"Am not," Tony said. He was *for sure* not allowed to log on to his favorite website, mysterykids.com, unless Julia was present, since she was nervous about who all his online friends might actually be. (Which was kind of a drag, because that was what Tony *liked* about them: that he didn't know whether they were fat or skinny, blond or brown-haired, American or Italian or Zulu. They all just liked solving mysteries together. Plus the site wasn't sketchy—it was educational. And monitored.)

"I thought we had a deal?" Julia sighed, setting the bags down.

"He's been trying to win a trip to Chicago," Mikey said.

"Just check the browser history," Angey advised. "Like we did."

With that, they made a beeline for the fridge.

Tony went beet red. It was true—he was only a couple of clues away from winning himself a totally excellent birthday present in the site's annual competition: a trip to Chicago to play real live Clue games with kids from all over America, solving who got murdered in which room with what weapon in a gigantic mansion. It was Tony's last-ditch attempt to head off what was shaping up to be the most boring summer vacation of all time: plowing through a two-page reading list for eighth-grade English, taking more swimming lessons at the Y, and—oh yeah—*dieting*. Tony hadn't planned on mentioning the competition until he'd actually won, thereby making it harder for his parents to say no. Especially since the trip was all expenses paid, so they couldn't complain it wasn't in the family budget. (Money was always tight at the DiMarcos'. All of Julia's earnings as a freelance designer went to paying the monthly bills. Michael didn't earn a living yet as a history professor; in fact, his PhD program actually *cost* money.) Tony thought it best to change the subject: "I was only trying to find out how valuable this is," he said, holding up the cap. "Zio Angelo sent it for my birthday."

Suddenly Julia looked more startled than mad.

"What's this about Zio Angelo?" Michael said, wheeling his suitcase into the kitchen. He set his laptop on the floor and spread his arms, Vegas-style: Who-loves-you-baby?

Tony gave his dad a hug.

"Show him," Julia said.

Tony handed Michael the cap.

Michael examined every inch of it in silence. Another unexpected reaction: his eyes welled with tears. He tapped his index finger on a small 9 embroidered on the inside brim and said, "I wonder if this is, you know, *it*."

That was when it dawned on Tony: Ted Williams was number 9. Theodore Samuel Williams, a.k.a. The Kid, Teddy Ballgame. A

Red Sox legend and, arguably, one of the greatest left fielders of all time. Zio Angelo's rambling water-boy story at Thanksgiving—the one he had told after the twins had excused themselves from the table—was about how Williams had given Zio Angelo his very first number 9 ball cap as a thirteenth-birthday present during his rookie season with the Sox.

"But that would make this supervaluable," Tony gasped. "Why would Zio Angelo just up and send it to *me*?"

Michael and Julia exchanged one of those parent-to-parent glances.

"Let's not jump to conclusions," Michael said. "We need to get it professionally appraised first."

"You better tell him," Julia said.

"What are you guys whispering about?" Angey called from the open fridge.

"A piece of cake is missing," Mikey reported.

"Don't look at me," Tony said.

Everybody looked at him.

"You promised you'd have some fruit instead," Julia said.

Figures, Tony thought. Julia was slender and athletic and blond, like the twins. The three of them jogged five miles together every morning. Which was why, in Tony's opinion, she constantly sided with them. Why she was always on him about his weight. Why she was so gung ho about him losing twenty-five pounds this summer, even though the diet was actually his idea, not hers.

"But I did take a piece of fruit!" Tony said, pointing to the orange still balanced on the arm of the sofa.

"Who cares who ate what?" Michael said. Also typical. Michael was dark and round and clumsy, like Tony. In the morning, they preferred to eat a bowl of cereal and watch reruns of *History's Mysteries*. Which was why Michael was always saying he loved Tony just the way he was. Unfortunately, Michael was a total vegetarian Buddhist history professor megageek, and Tony didn't actually want to turn out like *him*.

"Actually, I ate the cake," Angey admitted. "As a midnight snack."

"*Basta!*" Michael shouted. "Enough! Enough about food, already. Everyone into the living room for a family meeting. I've got something important to tell you. Some good news and some bad news. *Andiamo!*"

Uh-oh. Michael only ever used Italian when he was seriously upset. Tony slumped back into the chair in front of Julia's PC and logged off eBay. The twins closed the fridge and headed for the living room. They helped Julia shift stacks of photocopies to the floor so they could all perch at the edges of the sofa seat cushions. Meanwhile, Michael leaned against the back of a recliner full of books. He waited for Mikey to peel Tony's orange and hand half to Angey.

"First the bad news," he finally said. "Zio Angelo is dead."

Tony stared, horrified, at the cap in his hands.

"His heart was always a little iffy," Michael reminded them. "He had that stroke—remember?—right after his Thanksgiving visit. He lost the ability to speak as a result. And he could no longer make it up and down the stairs of his house in Boston. In fact, he was completely bedridden last week, when I dropped by for a visit on the way to my conference."

Tony couldn't help but shudder. Zio Angelo had made a big point of flying out to Ann Arbor just to meet Tony. Had he known Thanksgiving might be his last chance? Tony pictured Zio Angelo scratching out that creepy For My Nephew card just before keeling over: *Finally, your 13th birthday!*

"Unfortunately, Zio Angelo took a sudden turn for the worse while I was giving my paper on Paul Revere over at Harvard," Michael continued. "It was actually the next-door neighbor who found his body and dialed 911. I immediately called your mom, of course. But we decided not to trouble you boys with the sad news—since it was your last week of school—until I could tell you in person."

Yikes! One of Zio Angelo's last acts alive *must* have been to box up Ted Williams's cap and send it off to Tony, special delivery.

"So what's for dinner?" Mikey said. "Better not be any of those lo-carb, fat-free frozen dinners—just because Tony needs to be sent to the fat farm."

"Yeah, we want regular food," Angey said. (They said *we*, not *I*, whenever they were together. One of those annoying twin things, like finishing each other's sentences.)

"We're *all* having regular food," Julia said. "I read online that those frozen things are just an expensive scam. The only diets that really work are about portion control and exercise."

"So that's it?" Michael said. "Another argument about food?"

They all sat there. They barely *knew* Zio Angelo.

"Don't you want to hear the *good* news?" Michael asked, exasperated. "I haven't even told your mom the upside yet. I've been waiting till everyone was back together."

Julia's eyebrows shot up.

"Let me guess," Mikey said. "You totally rocked your speech on Revere."

"And all the history professors went wild," Angey said.

They laughed and high-fived each other.

"Besides that," Michael said, grinning in spite of himself.

"Now you're making me nervous," Julia said.

"There was a reading of Zio Angelo's last will and testament after the wake," Michael said. "He left his house in Boston to somebody we know. Guess who."

"Nonno Guido?" Tony said. That was what they all called Michael's dad—*nonno* was Italian for grandpa—which made him Zio Angelo's brother and next-closest relative.

"Guess again," Michael said.

Stunned silence.

"You're not serious," Julia said.

"We can move right in," Michael said. "Isn't that great?"

"We do actually live here in Ann Arbor for a reason," Julia reminded him.

Michael dropped his second bomb of the family meeting. The DiMarcos would, in any case, need to move by the end of next month. Michael had gotten an email from University Housing the morning he left for Boston. He was no longer eligible to live on campus, now that he'd finished his course work. To get his PhD, he just needed to finish writing his dissertation about Paul Revere, which he could do anywhere. Like Boston, the very city in which Revere had lived and worked as a silversmith.

"Or like Ann Arbor?" Julia said. "Where I actually have work."

"You've been looking for ways to ramp up your career as a book designer," Michael said. "Boston has something like seventy-five colleges. With your portfolio and references, the academic presses will be banging down the door."

"But we're enrolled at Ann Arbor High this fall!" Mikey said.

"Its varsity baseball team is third best in the state," Angey added.

"Why would you ever want to go to boring old Ann Arbor High?" Michael said. "When you could be freshmen at Boston Latin, the oldest and most respected public school in the country? Which, in addition to boasting a *nationally ranked* varsity team called the Wolfpack, happens to be located about a block from Fenway Park."

The twins shot each other a look, not quite sure what to think.

"Bottom line?" Michael said. "No one's offering us a free place to live here in Ann Arbor. Meanwhile, there's a gigantic house just sitting empty in Boston's North End with our name on it. It's like a gift from heaven. And if we want to take advantage of it, we've got to do so before Tony's thirteenth birthday."

"Why?" Julia said.

"That's what Zio Angelo stipulated in his will," Michael said with a shrug.

They all looked over at Tony.

"I only met the guy once," Tony said—an undeniable fact.

No one knew quite where to go from there.

"So what's the North End?" Mikey said.

"The city's most historic neighborhood," Michael said. "Zio Angelo's town house is over three hundred years old."

"What's a town house?" Angey said.

"Quintessential Boston living," Michael assured him. "A brick row house that shares its walls with the neighbors on either side. Zio Angelo's is just one room wide, and two deep, but four stories tall. It's in a cobbled cul-de-sac of town houses surrounding a giant old oak. It's called Hangmen Court. How's that for a colorful address?" Michael turned to Tony. "You're awful quiet. What do you think?"

Tony glanced over at the twins. Mikey and Angey were always ganging up on him, messing with his stuff, ditching him when they went out, excluding him from their secrets. Twins should be outlawed. Or everybody should have one. "Will I get my own room?" he said.

"Funny you should ask," Michael said. "That was another weird stipulation of Zio Angelo's will: that you—and only you—should get *his* bedroom. It's the whole top floor of the house. Your own private domain."

A shiver ran up Tony's spine. So *that* was what Zio Angelo had meant in his birthday card: *Give this the place of honor in your new room.*

"Why would he do a thing like that?" Mikey said, reading Tony's mind.

"Who knows?" Michael said. "He obviously took quite a shine to Tony at Thanksgiving. Maybe you two shouldn't have excused yourselves so quickly when he started talking. Or maybe you should have rooted for the Red Sox, like Tony, instead of the Tigers." Michael turned back to Tony. "Well? Are you up for it?"

A room with a door he could slam in the twins' face, then lock?

"Totally," Tony said.

PART ONE
THE MURDER

LUCKY NO. 13
FRIDAY, JULY 10, 2009

"There it is," Tony said, pointing through the fly-specked windshield at an old-fashioned street sign off to the left:

HANGMEN CT.
DEAD END

"Finally," Julia said, throwing on the turn signal. "Note to self: Never download Boston driving directions off the Internet."

They'd been circling the North End's narrow one-way streets for a half hour. The guidebook in Tony's lap clearly confirmed it was the city's oldest neighborhood. (Originally settled by John Winthrop's band of Puritans in 1630, but changing hands often to welcome each new wave of immigrants: first to runaway blacks escaping slavery, next to whole Irish clans escaping the potato famine in Ireland, then to Jews escaping persecution in Europe, and most recently to Italian families like the DiMarcos hoping to live the American Dream.) But what Tony had seen of the North End so far looked kind of sketchy and grungy— pretty much the same as downtown Detroit.

Which was why his *very* first reaction to Hangmen Court was relief. It was exactly how Michael had described it three weeks ago: a quiet cul-de-sac of beautifully restored Colonial town houses surrounding a grassy oval planted with the largest oak tree he had ever seen. The sidewalks were laid with bricks the same color as the buildings, and an antique gas lamp sputtered in front of every stoop.

"Sweet!" Mikey said. "We're rich."

"Which one's ours?" Angey said.

Tony didn't care. The twins had done nothing but complain from the backseat since they'd all set off from Ann Arbor early the previous morning: We're too hot, turn the AC up. We're too cold, turn it down. We like this song, turn the radio up. We hate this one, change the station. Ohio is boring, how long till we get to upstate New York? Upstate is even more boring, how long till we get to the motel in Albany? This motel doesn't have a pool, let's just head for Boston. Unfortunately, Julia had been too exhausted to make the four-hour drive across Massachusetts in the dark. So they had gotten up early. And the twins had started right back in again about Denny's or McDonald's for breakfast.

It was now noon. Tony had a splitting headache. He was desperate for a pee. And he just wanted out of the car. Any of these places would do, in his opinion.

Until Julia pulled up in front of No. 13.

"Oh my God," Mikey said.

"What have we done?" Angey said.

For once, Tony agreed with them. There was no other way to put it: 13 Hangmen Court was a total dump. *Their* town house wasn't beautifully restored. It was a pile of dirty old bricks on the verge of collapse. "Must be some mistake," Tony said.

Nope. There was Michael, grinning and waving, bounding down the uneven steps of a steep front stoop. (Michael had flown ahead to meet the moving van with the family's stuff.) He didn't seem at all horrified. In fact, he seemed *pleased*. Reluctantly, Tony climbed out of the car. His dad ruffled his hair. "Pretty great birthday present, eh Tony? Thirteen must be your lucky number!"

Tony didn't reply. He was actually sort of speechless. Today *was* his birthday. But whenever he had imagined himself turning thirteen, he was always twenty-five pounds lighter. (So far he hadn't lost anywhere near twenty-five pounds. More like ten. Well, maybe eight. But if he were to be honest, that wasn't the fault of Julia's latest dieting strategy of portion control—which was basically to limit everything on Tony's plate to the size of his clenched fist: a fist-size burger patty without the bun, a fist of mashed potatoes, and a fist of peas—but, rather, the fault of all those fist-size Snickers bars he'd been sneaking on the side.) Then again, Tony had also pictured himself in Chicago, racing around a giant mansion on Lake Michigan, finding the ropes and knives of murderers in real live games of Clue with dozens of junior sleuths from all over America.

"You want us to live here?" Mikey said.

"You sure it doesn't have rats?" Angey said.

Julia didn't say anything at all. She just bit her lower lip.

Michael laughed. "C'mon, I'll take you on the grand tour. First stop, garden level!" But he didn't head back up to the weather-beaten front door. He ducked *beneath* the stoop and opened a small ivy-covered door a few steps below the sidewalk, then slipped into a part of the house that wasn't quite ground floor, wasn't quite basement.

Tony's eye caught the flutter of lace curtains in the bay window of the supernice place next door. An old man scowled down at him, then vanished.

Garden level was, as it turned out, the kitchen. Tony peered around a cavernous room of old-fashioned appliances and cupboards. Built into the giant bay window at the front was a funky little breakfast nook. Its table was laden with all the pots and pans Julia had shipped from Ann Arbor. Julia did not, to Tony's utter amazement, demand that everyone climb into the car so they could hightail it back to Michigan, where they belonged. Instead, she ran her hands over the greasy gas range—one that reminded Tony of a junkyard Cadillac—and declared she was in love. "But wait, there's more!" Michael said, beaming. He opened a door to reveal a large pantry lined with shelves. "It's called the mother-in-law room," he said. "The perfect place to set up a design studio."

"Or torture your mother-in-law," Mikey mumbled.

"Or skin a few rats," Angey added.

Tony opened the pantry's back door and peeked out. Nothing but a rotting deck overlooking a weed-infested patio at yet another level below the street. He closed it again, shuddering.

Julia and Michael didn't notice; they were too busy kissing. "And it just keeps getting better," Michael said when they finally came up for air. He opened another door to reveal an ornately carved staircase winding its way to the very top of the house. "Next stop, parlor level!" he said, leading them up to the main floor.

Parlor level wasn't, contrary to Michael's promise, much of an improvement over garden level. In the front there was a musty wood-paneled dining room (not unlike what Tony had been imagining for Chicago, he had to admit), but the Addams

Family—style table in the middle of this one had legs carved with gargoyles and was coated in dust. Michael pointed out a smoke-stained marble fireplace. "There's one in nearly every room," he said. "And they all work." He opened an empty wooden cupboard next to it and tugged on a rope. Hidden pulleys squeaked as the shelf inside began to lower. A dumbwaiter, Michael explained, for hoisting hot food up from the kitchen.

Or freshly skinned mothers-in-law.

Michael led them down a short passageway, pointing out the antique water closet on the left. That was when Tony remembered how badly he had to go. Michael warned him the toilet was pretty old-school; to flush, you needed to pull the chain dangling from a porcelain tank overhead. "I think I can handle it," Tony said. Michael laughed—very funny—and told him to rejoin the tour in the back parlor. When Tony yanked down on the chain, though, the toilet didn't flush. The chain just broke off in his hand. Tony set it on the wooden seat to wash his hands at the tiny sink. Rusty water gushed out of the tap and drenched the front of his white T-shirt with bright-orange blotches. No towels. No toilet paper, even. He had no choice but to wipe his hands on the seat of his jeans and head for the back parlor.

Why had it suddenly gone so quiet?

Everyone was staring at the tarnished brass bed in the middle of the room. Tony joined the semicircle of speechless DiMarcos. "OK, so that's weird," he said.

Michael stammered an apology. He had meant to get the bed dismantled and donated to Goodwill before they arrived. Zio Angelo had slept there after he fell ill, when it became too hard for him to make it up to his real bedroom.

"Wait," Tony said. "That isn't where the neighbor, you know, found him?"

Michael answered by *not* answering. "Check out that desk!" he said, pointing to a gigantic rolltop in an alcove over by the fireplace. "That's going straight to my new office on the second floor, which was originally the library, so it already has shelves for all my research books. In fact, let's head up there now."

Everyone trooped up to the second floor—except Tony. He couldn't take his eyes off the bed. What was that glinting under it? He stooped and tugged a small metal key—the kind Benjamin Franklin might have used to fly on his kite in a lightning storm—out of a crack between the floorboards. He pulled his wallet from his back pocket and slipped the key into an empty credit-card slot. He decided not to let anyone know he'd found it—especially not the twins—until he figured out what it opened.

Everyone was stopped at a recess in the first hairpin turn of the staircase. "Coffin corner," Michael was explaining. He darted a quick glance at Tony, then hesitated before continuing. "This little niche in the wall prevents, um, furniture from getting stuck when you're moving it up and down." No one commented. After seeing that bed in the parlor, it couldn't have been clearer what *kind* of furniture he meant.

The so-called library did indeed boast a floor-to-ceiling bookcase, though Tony worried that setting any books on the shelves might cause the whole thing to tip over on top of Michael and crush him like a bug. In the rear there was a spacious master suite that came with a gigantic four-poster bed plus its own fireplace *and* bathroom. Julia gave Michael another excited hug.

Oh, great. No chance of a mutiny now.

Tony even lost the twins as unlikely allies when they saw their two bedrooms on the next floor. Mikey immediately called dibs on the front one, because it had a wooden sleigh bed and bay window. Angey accepted, as usual, the smaller rear one containing a modest brass bed. But both rooms were connected by a full-size bathroom with a normal toilet and shower. Which caused them to high-five.

Michael turned to Tony. "Ready to check out the penthouse suite Zio Angelo saved for you?"

Tony nodded, not so sure.

He followed his dad up the final flight of stairs to a peeling door. The twins and Julia brought up the rear, discussing what colors they planned to paint their rooms.

"You go first," Michael told Tony, stepping aside. "I haven't even been up here yet myself."

Tony nodded again. Bracing himself for the worst, he turned the knob and swung the door open to discover—

The worst.

It was just an attic. Bare floors, bare walls, bare lightbulb hanging from the ceiling; no bay window, no fireplace—no bathroom! From dim wedges of daylight cast by small dormer windows at the front and back, Tony could make out— barely—an uncomfortable-looking ladder-back chair against one sloping wall, a beat-up dresser against the other, and a bookcase parked in front of some tacky laminated paneling beneath a weird slab of slate. It was a shelf, sort of, that jutted out of the wall.

"Where's the bed?" Mikey said over Tony's shoulder.

"Down in the parlor," Angey laughed.

Michael didn't deny it.

"No way," Tony said.

Michael nudged Tony into the room, reassuring him that top of the list was buying him a brand-new bed. Meantime—just for a night or two—they might need to move Zio Angelo's up from the parlor. But they would definitely toss the old bedding straight into the trash. Tony could use his own sheets and comforter from Ann Arbor.

"No way," Tony said. "I'll sleep on the floor first."

Mikey and Angey declared they wouldn't sleep in this room, *period*.

Michael suggested the twins head downstairs to the kitchen for some lunch. The fridge was stocked with hummus and tabouleh salad and pita pockets from a health-food store around the corner. He and Julia needed a private word with Tony.

"No cold cuts?" Mikey said.

"Not even any tuna fish?" Angey sighed.

"Sorry, meat wasn't the first thing that leaped to my mind," Michael said.

(Michael had, in fact, been a vegetarian since high school. He didn't mind if the rest of the family was carnivorous, but he himself wouldn't even wear leather shoes or belts. He was also a devout Buddhist, which meant that he didn't believe in killing any living creature—not even a house fly—since its soul might reincarnate into a human being one day. Though admirable, this didn't help Michael's geek factor *at all*.)

"Tabouleh tastes like kitty litter," Mikey grumbled. He clomped down the attic steps with Angey at his heels.

Michael reached over and gave Tony a side hug. "I admit it needs work," he said. "Let's face it, the whole house is a little rough around the edges. Poor Zio Angelo. He just wasn't able to look after it properly toward the end. Nothing a little DiMarco family TLC can't fix."

"Have you lost your mind?" Tony cried. "This whole place should be bulldozed to the ground!"

"It's not that bad," Michael said.

At that point, Tony melted down. It had been a very long couple of days—it was his *birthday*—and he couldn't keep it bottled up: Doors squealed open, ceiling paint drifted down on your head like snow, toilet chains came off in your hand, and water gushed orange out of the rusty tap. Hadn't anyone else noticed the amount of wallpaper stripping and floor sanding it would take to make this house even remotely livable?

Michael patted Tony's shoulder. He was positive that once Tony had run the vacuum cleaner, hung a few posters, and laid his own comforter on the bed, he would feel completely different about his new bedroom.

"Hello?" Tony said. "It's not a bedroom. It's the *attic*. Plus it feels all spooky and haunted and weird. I'm not sleeping here. Ever. That's final."

"Tony's afraid of ghosts," Mikey singsonged up the stairwell. Angey burst into a fit of giggles. They had both been eavesdropping, of course, from the third-floor landing.

Julia told them to beat it—this was a private conversation.

They clambered down the rest of the staircase to the kitchen, wailing like banshees. She rolled her eyes and advised Tony to ignore them. Which, in his opinion, wasn't at all the same as sticking up for him. Meanwhile, Michael reassured him an old house like this one had its own quirky language—creaks and groans he'd eventually get used to and stop hearing. Anyway, ninety-nine percent of all ghosts turned out to be mice in the walls.

"Not helping!" Tony said. Michael opened his mouth, then closed it again. "Seriously, Dad, what did Zio Angelo have against *me*? I was actually nice to him at Thanksgiving. Angey and Mikey were the ones who rolled their eyes at his stories. He should have made *them* sleep up here."

Michael laughed. "As weird as it might seem, Zio Angelo actually believed he was doing you a *favor* by saving you the top floor. He loved this room. He slept up here himself—ever since he was your age—and only decided to move to the parlor when he could no longer manage the stairs."

Plainly, Tony was not gaining any headway. He made one last-ditch effort. "Why don't you guys sell this place and buy a *real* house in the suburbs, someplace normal that isn't falling down around our ears?"

Julia and Michael darted each other one of their parent-to-parent glances. "Sorry," Michael said. "That's not an option."

"Why not?"

"Zio Angelo's will was actually a little complicated, but the bottom line is we're sort of stuck here for a while."

"What could be so complicated about hanging a for-sale sign?" Tony said.

Michael ruffled Tony's hair. "What do you say we grab a sandwich? Then maybe you and the twins can go out and explore the new neighborhood while your mom and I deal with the bed."

"The exercise'll do you good," Julia said.

(That was the other thing, besides portion control, she was now obsessed with. She'd been harping at Tony since school got out: stop chatting online with God-knows-who and start tagging along to the twins' pickup Wiffle ball games in the park. As if! Angey laughed at the way the thighs of his jeans scratched when he ran, and Mikey said he couldn't hit the broad side of a barn whenever he threw a ball.)

"But they *hate* me," Tony said.

"Don't be ridiculous," Julia said. "They're your brothers."

"They are totally ashamed to be seen with me, and you know it," Tony said.

Michael laughed. "They're ashamed to be seen with *me*," he said. "It's sort of normal. They're in puberty. Now how about that sandwich?"

Tony saw no choice but to follow his parents out of the room.

That's when he noticed the door didn't even have a lock. Oh, great. There was no actual way to keep the twins from bursting in. Seriously, could his birthday get any worse?

Tony stooped to tie his sneaker in front of the Paul Revere House. At Michael's insistence, he and the twins had grudgingly agreed to explore the Freedom Trail—a redbrick line embedded in the sidewalk connecting one historic site to the next. So far they had seen the Copp's Hill Burying Ground and the Old North Church. Mikey and Angey wanted to skip the house tour. They were in a hurry to get to the next stop down the line—Quincy Market—where some kid back in Ann Arbor had told them they could watch street performers outside a giant food court. Tony was secretly enjoying himself. As upset as he was about 13 Hangmen Court, he had to admit the North End itself *was* kind of great. Famous landmarks of the Revolutionary War were jumbled up with *caffès*, pizzerias, and cannoli shops. Plus there were all these other layers of history. He would never have known, for example, that hundreds of African Americans were buried in unmarked graves at Copp's Hill—back when this neighborhood was known as New Guinea because of the runaway slaves who lived here—unless he had stopped to read the plaque at the gate.

He stood back up, determined to make the twins take the tour.

They had vanished.

Tony peered around the cobbled street; they were usually pretty easy to spot. Nope, they were definitely gone. Had they gotten swallowed up in the hordes of afternoon tourists? Or had they just ditched him—as he had pretty much predicted they would—because they hated his guts? He saw no choice but to set off along the Freedom Trail, hoping to catch up. A little ways down North Street, though, the redbrick line took a sharp right onto Richmond Street. He stumbled along the uneven sidewalk for a block, until it suddenly disappeared at Hanover Street—obviously the North End's main drag. Tony swore he could be in Italy. Skinned rabbits hung in the front window of a nearby butcher shop. Grannies dressed all in black dipped their fingertips in holy water and crossed themselves as they exited a church. Old men argued in Italian over dominoes at tables set up on the sidewalk. In the middle of it all, a blind man played "That's Amore" on an accordion.

Tony decided he'd better ask somebody where the Freedom Trail went. He turned to the shop directly behind him. In the display window was a dusty jumble of furniture, vases, antique clothes, and framed maps. He glanced up at the purple-striped awning overhead: YE OLDE CURIOSITY SHOPPE, MILDRED PICKLES, PROPESS.

A tiny bell jangled as he passed through the front door. He

gave his eyes a few seconds to adjust to the gloom. The store was crammed full of old machines and mysterious mechanical devices; Buddhas and Madonnas and Shiva-the-Destroyers; rickshaws and telescopes and red-lacquered chests with dozens of puzzlelike drawers; a gilded glass case full of crystals and geodes; carved elephant tusks and a stuffed mongoose entwined with a snake. On the right, there was an entire wall of dusty leather-bound books. On the left—

Tony did a double take. Standing behind a counter of rough-hewn slate was a girl a couple of years older than him. She wore a long purple dress, a white apron, and a gathered cotton cap, though she also had punked-out black hair and a nose ring. Tony made his way over. Carved into the top of the counter was an odd spiral. Hanging overhead was a very old American flag.

As for the Colonial Maid Goth Chick, she didn't bother to look up from the book she was reading—*Astrophysics for Dummies*—until Tony cleared his throat. That was when he noticed her eyes. Not blue, and not brown. Violet. He'd never seen anyone with purple irises before. She curtly informed him the video shop was a few doors down, just past the hardware store.

"I'm guessing you're not Mildred Pickles?" Tony said. "The proprie*tress*."

"Course not," she said, then went back to her book.

Tony had every intention of asking her for directions, of

course. But that wasn't what came out of his mouth next. "You don't see many of Francis Hopkinson's quincuncial layouts these days," he said, "outside of museums." He was referring to the Stars and Stripes above her head.

That caught Colonial Maid Goth Chick's attention. "Most people think it's a Betsy Ross," she said. Her voice was surprisingly scratchy and low, like Peppermint Patty's in a classic *Peanuts* cartoon.

"Betsy Ross arranged the stars in a circle," Tony said, cribbing from Michael's lecture on flags during their last family trip to the Smithsonian in Washington, D.C. "But she was just copying someone else as a seamstress. We don't know who *created* her circular design. All we really know for sure is that Congress adopted Hopkinson's straight-across layout as the *official* American flag in 1777."

"Dude, did you *want* something?" Colonial Maid Goth Chick said. But she was obviously impressed.

"Too bad the first star in the fourth row is missing," Tony said. "If it's real, your flag would be worth a lot more money."

"It's real. But it's not for sale," she said. "Mildred's great-great-great-plus-grandmother Abigail plucked the star off when she was a girl. The ninth star represented the new state of Massachusetts—though, technically speaking, Massachusetts isn't a state, it's a commonwealth. But no one knows why, or what she did with it."

"So there *is* a real Mildred Pickles," Tony said.

"Who said there wasn't?" she said.

"You got any Freedom Trail maps?" Tony said.

"Nope."

"Can I ask you something else?" he said.

She rolled her eyes.

"Does Mildred Pickles make you dress like that to work here?"

"I don't work here," she said. She didn't elaborate.

Okeydokey, then. Tony turned and made for the door.

"Try the hardware," she called after him. "They have all sorts of tourist crap."

Tony was now drenched in sweat and totally out of breath. But he had finally found the right cul-de-sac of town houses. He'd been circling the neighborhood for a half hour—just like Julia had done with the car that morning—trying to get back to Hangmen Court. He'd given up on the Freedom Trail when the hardware store didn't sell maps either. The twins were still MIA. They had probably gorged their way from one end of that food court to the other. Meanwhile, he himself hadn't had a single snack since his hummus sandwich at lunch. Strangely, he hadn't thought once about a Snickers bar. Though now, of course, he was wondering if there were any left in the secret-stash pocket of his backpack, up in his so-called room.

"You there, boy!"

A distinguished-looking gentleman beckoned Tony over to the manicured front lawn of No. 15, where he was pruning a trellis of roses with a pair of hedge clippers. It was the same old guy who had stared out the window when the DiMarcos had first arrived.

"Hi," Tony said, extending his hand over the front gate. "I guess we're neighbors."

The old guy just frowned. "I know who you are," he said. "You're the one who owns Number Thirteen."

"Well, no, not personally," Tony said, pulling his hand back. "My dad inherited the house from his uncle, Angelo DiMarco. Did you know him?"

"*Half* uncle," the man scowled. "Your father isn't a full-blood relation."

"Sure he is," Tony said. "Our name is DiMarco, just like Zio Angelo's."

"That was Angelo's adopted name," the man said. "His real name was Saporiti."

"And you are?" Tony said, not sure where to go with *that*.

"The name is Benedict Hagmann. Double *n* at the end. I was Angelo's oldest and dearest childhood friend. So there's no point in trying to pull the wool over *my* eyes. I know a lot more than you think about the whole situation."

"What situation?" Tony said. But he edged away from the gate, just in case Old Man Hagmann—double *n* at the end—suddenly got a little wild with those clippers.

"Angelo's bizarre decision to bequeath Number Thirteen to you," Old Man Hagmann said, "a distant relative by marriage—a *child* he barely knew—as the result of an utterly unexpected and not entirely welcome visit from your father. A visit that took place, I might add, on the very morning of Angelo's sudden and quite mysterious death."

"What are you saying?" Tony stammered.

"I've already said more than I should," Old Man Hagmann sniffed. He lopped a couple of withered roses off the trellis. "But it's all highly suspicious."

"I'm, um, late for dinner," Tony said. Then he hightailed it up the front stoop to No. 13.

Crazy old fart.

Hopefully.

SURPRISES

FRIDAY, JULY 10, 2009

"SURPRISE!"

The whole family leaped out of hiding. They were wearing corny birthday hats and blowing noisemakers. They had decorated the new—well, not *new*—dining room with crepe-paper streamers. They'd hung a banner from the mantel: HAPPY 13TH, TONY!

Michael ushered the totally stunned Tony over to the seat of honor at the head of the dining table, where a small stack of presents awaited on a plate. Everyone sat, and Michael started serving up pizza out of delivery boxes. "Pizzeria Regina," he said. "The oldest in Boston, and it's just a few streets over. Zio Angelo bought after-school slices from there when *he* was a boy."

He turned to Tony and asked, "Pepperoni with extra cheese or veggie-the-works?"

"Neither," Julia said, before Tony could answer.

Right. Those twenty-five pounds that never got lost. "Just pass me the salad bowl," Tony sighed to Angey.

"That's not what I meant!" Julia said, flushing. "I meant: Not until you clear off what's already on your plate."

Oh. The presents.

"Better get busy," Michael said, squeezing Tony's shoulder. "Mine's on top."

Tony unwrapped a small flat box. Two tickets for the Boston History Mystery Tour. Tony and his dad had seen the commercial for it a million times while watching their favorite cable program over a bowl of breakfast cereal. It was sort of like the Freedom Trail, except a trolley with a real detective guide drove you around to sites of the city's most famous unsolved mysteries: Whose bones were actually under the Mother Goose tombstone in the Granary Burying Ground? Did Paul Revere really ring a handbell to wake the countryside during his Midnight Ride? Did they catch the Boston Strangler—who murdered something like thirteen people—or did they blame it on some random and totally innocent guy?

"Awesome, Dad, thanks," Tony said.

"You and me, tomorrow. Right after breakfast," Michael said.

Tony could hardly categorize his dad's behavior as suspicious. He was just acting like goofy old Michael: wolfing a slice of veggie-the-works pizza while serving the twins pepperoni-extra-cheese; teasing Angey that he needed a haircut more than Mikey, even though the twins looked exactly the same and had gone to the barbershop together; kissing Julia's forehead and complimenting her on how fast she had whipped the dining room into festive shape.

"My present next," Julia said. "It's the blue one."

Tony opened it. A cell phone. He had sort of been expecting it—the twins had both gotten theirs when they had turned thirteen—but this one was a much cooler flip model. He reached over and gave Julia a big hug.

"Sorry about the pizza thing," she whispered. "I didn't think."

"That's way too much phone for him," Mikey groused. "He doesn't even have anybody to call."

Which was when, coincidentally, the wall phone started to ring.

"The account must still be in Zio Angelo's name," Michael said, reaching up to answer it. He frowned. He covered the receiver with his hand. "Won't be a minute," he said. He stretched the cord into the hallway and shut the door.

OK, so that's a little suspicious.

"Open ours," Angey said.

Tony unwrapped the last gift on his plate. A new Red Sox cap. A supercool one, in fact, with a flat hip-hop brim. It must have set them back a few allowances.

"We bought it at Quincy Market after we ditched you," Mikey said. "So you wouldn't embarrass us by wearing that moldy old piece of crap Zio Angelo sent you." (To be fair, neither he nor Angey knew yet that it had probably belonged to Ted Williams; Michael's plan had been to wait and have it appraised in Boston by a real Red Sox expert before he got everyone's hopes up.)

"Do you like it?" Angey asked. Strangely, it sounded like he really wanted to know.

First time for everything.

Michael stepped back into the room. He hung up the phone. "Ready for a slice?" he asked Tony.

Tony nodded. He promised himself he'd eat only one. Then he really would have salad. Michael handed him a slice of pepperoni. Tony took three huge bites. He set the rest down on his plate, slightly alarmed that it was already half gone. He frowned. He couldn't get that crazy old fart next door out of his mind. "Who called?" he said.

"Nobody," Michael said. "Just the cable guy."

"Why did you step out of the room if it was only the cable guy?" Tony said.

"Terrible echo," Michael said. "Probably need to replace that phone."

"Is it true you're only Zio Angelo's half nephew?" Tony blurted without really intending to.

"Who told you that?" Michael said.

"The next-door neighbor," Tony said. "I ran into him just now. He said he was Zio Angelo's oldest friend."

Michael sat. He grabbed the half-eaten slice of veggie-the-works off his plate. He didn't take a bite, though. "Mr. Hagmann's right," he admitted, setting the slice back down. "Zio Angelo and my dad—your nonno Guido—*were* only half brothers."

"So it's true Zio Angelo's real last name was Saporiti, not DiMarco?" Tony said.

"That's right," Michael said. "Zio Angelo's own dad, Armando Saporiti, died when he was a little younger than you. His mom remarried your granddad, Antonio DiMarco." Michael went on to explain that when Zio Angelo's dad, Armando Saporiti, died of emphysema, his mom, Isabella, started running a boardinghouse at 13 Hangmen Court to make ends meet. One of her boarders, a guy named Antonio DiMarco, asked her to marry him—which she did, on condition he adopt her son, Angelo. A few years later, Isabella and Antonio had a son of their own—Guido—who was Angelo's half brother and, eventually, Michael's dad.

(Basically, families were just as complicated then as they are today.)

"I don't get it," Tony said. "Why did Zio Angelo leave *us* this place?"

"He never married," Michael said. "He never had kids. We're his closest living relatives, except for Nonno Guido. But they were never very close."

"Maybe he was gay," Angey said.

"Like you," Mikey said to Tony, cracking himself up.

"Maybe he was," Michael said. "Either of you got a problem with that? Because I've got a big problem with homophobic jokes."

They both turned red and shook their heads.

"Good," Michael said. He admitted Zio Angelo's life was a bit of a mystery to everyone. He was never much of a talker, except about baseball. He left Boston as soon as he turned twenty-one. No one really knew where he went or what he did. He only came back to live at Hangmen Court after his mother died. By then, though, he was already sort of old. Which is why he sometimes hired Michael (who was in high school at the time) to do odd jobs around the place. Michael was about the only relative Zio Angelo ever kept in touch with—not even Nonno Guido—until Tony came along. For some reason, Zio Angelo took a real shine to him.

Tony wolfed the rest of his pizza. He reached into the box and served himself another slice, though he had sworn to himself to ask Angey for the salad bowl. Avoiding eye contact with Julia, he took a big comforting bite.

Julia excused herself to fetch something from the dumbwaiter. Somehow, the pizza didn't taste very good, then.

"Is that why Zio Angelo left *me* this house?" Tony said.

Mikey and Angey both froze, mid-bite.

"Just how long did you and Mr. Hagmann chat out there?" Michael said.

Tony shrugged.

"He did," Michael said. "The house is actually yours, not mine."

"Shut up!" Angey said.

"Tony's our landlord?" Mikey said.

"Zio Angelo made me legal custodian until Tony turns twenty-one," Michael said. "So, technically speaking, I'm still the landlord."

Michael apologized for not telling Tony sooner. He and Julia had honestly thought it was best to wait until they were all a bit more settled in their new life. But as long as Mr. Hagmann had let the cat out of the bag, Tony might as well know the rest. For whatever reason, Zio Angelo had decided at the last minute to leave No. 13 to Tony—on condition he live there until he was a legal adult. So Michael couldn't sell the house, not even at Tony's request, unless it was a documented emergency. Not only that, but legally speaking, Tony sort of *had* to sleep up in the attic as another stipulation of the will.

"With all the ghosts," Mikey snickered.

"And rats," Angey said.

Michael pitched his wadded-up napkin at Mikey's head. Mikey ducked. It thwacked Angey's left ear.

"I won't miss next time," Michael said.

"Ooh, I'm scared," Mikey said.

"The Buddhist lashes out," Angey said.

"It's always the mild-mannered ones who end up going postal," Michael said, laughing.

Yikes! "So the next-door neighbor wasn't lying?" Tony said.

Before Michael got the chance to answer, Julia set a store-bought cake in front of Tony, lit with thirteen sparkler candles. "Special delivery for Tony DiMarco!" she said. The family began a rousing chorus of "Happy Birthday." But Tony was a gazillion miles away. If Old Man Hagmann was right about the first part—about Tony owning the house—was it possible he could be right about his other, um, suspicions?

Tony shot his dad a secret sideways glance.

Michael blew a party favor so hard, his eyes crossed.

The twins badgered Tony to do the candles so they could

have dessert. Tony made a wish—that Old Man Hagmann really was some crazy old fart with too much time on his hands—and blew them all out with one mighty sigh.

Tony stood barefoot in his pj's, eyeing the brass bed.

His parents had moved it to the attic and set it up in the only place it would fit—the very middle of the room. They had covered the stained and lumpy mattress with crisp white sheets. They'd laid his Red Sox comforter on top. They'd stood his two pillows against the tarnished bars of the headboard. They'd even hung a new poster of the Boston subway system—the T—on the sloping wall overhead. Tony's alarm clock was set to the correct time on top of the dresser, and his two suitcases of clothes were soldiered next to it, his boxes of trophies and books and baseball memorabilia all waiting to be unpacked by the bookcase beneath that random slate shelf.

None of it helped. Tony was still staring at the bed of a dead man.

"BOO!"

The twins burst into the room. They had draped themselves in their own sheets. Mikey leaped onto the bed. Angey flapped around Tony. Both moaned "Ton-eeee, we're going to get yooooou!"

"Out!"

Julia stood in the doorway with her arms crossed. "Now," she said. "Before I ground the pair of you *forever*."

Mikey hopped off the bed and dashed past her, wailing. Angey flapped down the staircase after him. Julia slammed the door shut.

She and Tony burst into a fit of giggles.

"It *was* pretty funny," Tony admitted.

"For God's sake don't ever tell *them* that," she said. She sat on the bed. "I came up to apologize again."

"What for?"

She patted the comforter. Tony took a seat beside her.

"The weight-loss thing," she said. "I'm not helping."

Tony wasn't sure how to answer. She was right. She was *so* not helping. "Sorry the new portion-control diet isn't working out," he said.

"I got it off some stupid website." She shrugged. "Maybe we should see a nutritionist."

Tony thought back to when he'd reached for that second piece of pizza at dinner. All those secretly stashed Snickers bars. "The problem with portion control," he said, "is you're not in control. It just makes you superanxious you're not going to get enough to eat, which makes you even hungrier." He waited for Julia to mull this over. It wasn't her fault, really. She had always been thin. She didn't have a clue what it was like. "Let's just face reality," he sighed. "I'm never going to be like the twins."

"Is that what you think I want?" Julia said, looking startled. "God, no! Two of them is enough, thanks. I just want you to feel happier about being *you*."

Surprise.

"Maybe you should try focusing on what's missing," she said. "What's creating that space in your heart you're trying to fill with food. Figure out what your *real* bliss is. For me it's art. For the twins it's sports. For your dad it's history."

"I'm not good at anything." Tony shrugged.

"You're great at solving mysteries," she said.

"That just makes me more of a geek!"

"So? I *like* geeks," Julia said. "I married one, didn't I?" She kissed Tony's forehead and stood. "Here's what I bet. I bet the more 'you' you become, the less 'you' you'll have to lose." She looked around. "Maybe you should start with this awful room. How can you make it *yours*?" She opened the door. "On that note, I need to help your father find the box with all the toothbrushes."

"Was it just me," Tony said, "or was he acting a little . . . weird . . . at dinner?"

"Weirder than usual?" she said.

Tony laughed, totally relieved.

Julia nodded over at the alarm clock. "It's eight o'clock. You were born at nine. In exactly one hour you'll be thirteen." She blew him a kiss and saw herself out.

Suddenly the room felt like an attic again.

Tony would have given anything at that moment to escape to mysterykids.com for a couple of hours. Virtual reality was so much easier to cope with most days than, well, reality. But neither Julia's nor Michael's computer was set up. The house wasn't wired for broadband yet, and the cable guy wasn't coming till tomorrow. Tony decided to unpack his clothes and put them in the dresser. He arranged his trophies and mysteries and baseball memorabilia in the bookcase. He added a *Young Sherlock Holmes* poster and a Snoop Dogg poster to the walls. He peered around. It still felt like an attic. But at least now it felt more like *his* attic.

His gaze rested on the slate shelf above the bookcase. Random! He wandered over to see if he could figure out why it was there. Gross, the top was totally coated in dust. He wiped it away with his sleeve. No way! Carved into the center was a spiraling shape, exactly like the one he'd seen at that curiosity shop.

"How weird is that?" he mumbled to himself. He placed his index finger in the center of the spiral. He felt a faint buzzing sensation, like the static prickle you sometimes got when you touched a computer screen. He ran his finger around the grooves of the spiral.

Give it the place of honor.

He jerked his hand back. He'd heard a boy's voice, echoing from some distant room. Tony told himself to get a grip. It was just Mikey or Angey, calling up the staircase, trying to freak him out. And the static was obviously from an electrical short somewhere. The room's wiring probably needed replacing.

He pulled the vintage ball cap out of his backpack. He dusted a few flakes of Snickers bar off the brim. He placed the cap on the spiral. He hovered his hand over it, just to prove to himself that his imagination was totally running wild.

Finally, your thirteenth birthday! the voice said.

Tony made a mad dash for the bed, flicking out the light.

He crawled between the sheets, pulled the comforter up to his nose. He lay there in the blue glow of his alarm clock, panting. Just past nine o'clock. He was now a teenager. He refused to look at the cap on the shelf. Instead, he stared up at the subway map of Boston, wondering if he would ever actually drop off to sleep after such a totally weird and freaky day.

Lucky thirteen, his butt.

★ ★ ★

What the heck was that?

It was now morning. And something sounded like heavy breathing, just over Tony's shoulder.

He slowly turned.

A kid his age was lying beside him, fast asleep.

Tony yelped. The kid's eyes flew open. He yelped too. They both leaped out of the bed and onto their feet.

"What are you doing here?" Tony said.

The kid squinted at him from across the mattress. He was wearing a set of embarrassing flannel cowboy pj's. He looked a lot like Tony, actually, except he was a little taller and wasn't overweight. The kid reached under the bed and pulled out a pair of horn-rimmed Harry Potter glasses, which he hooked over the backs of his tiny ears. The lenses were so thick, they made his dark eyes seem gigantic, like those of a slightly cross-eyed owl. "Sleeping," he said. "What else would I be doing at the crack of dawn? What are you doing in my room?" He had a really thick Boston accent.

"But this isn't your room," Tony said, wondering if he was having one of those dreams about having a dream.

"What are you talking about?" the kid said. He pointed down at Tony's Red Sox comforter. "That's the patchwork quilt Mama just made me for my birthday. That's the Errol Flynn poster I got at the Boston premiere of *Robin Hood*. And those are all my Hardy Boys in the bookcase."

Tony had no idea who Errol Flynn was, but the poster this kid had just pointed to was definitely of Snoop Dogg. Plus Tony *hated* the Hardy Boys. The bookcase was full of much cooler mystery writers, in alphabetical order, just the way he had arranged them last night. "Wait, who *are* you?" Tony said.

"Angelo Saporiti," the kid said. "Who the heck are *you?*"

"Oh, I get it," Tony said. "You're just some guy from the neighborhood. The twins bribed you to sneak up here as a birthday prank and pretend you're the ghost of Zio Angelo to freak me out."

"I don't know any twins," the kid said. "Is it your birthday? Mine was yesterday."

"Nabbed!" Tony cried. "Zio Angelo's birthday was in May, not July. He told me so himself last Thanksgiving." He turned and called to the bedroom door: "Nice try, guys. You can come out now." But the evil twins didn't start laughing from out on the landing. He strode over and flung the door wide open. No one was there.

"It *is* May," the kid said, shrugging. "Yesterday was May 5, 1939, the Feast of Saint Angelo—my thirteenth birthday."

Tony froze. Zio Angelo had, in fact, told him over turkey dinner that he was born on the Feast of Saint Angelo, hence his name. And Tony was pretty sure the twins had rolled their eyes and excused themselves from the table by then. He glanced over at the vintage ball cap. It was just where he'd left it, covering the spiral.

The kid followed Tony's gaze. "Ted Williams gave me that yesterday as a birthday present," he said.

Tony perched on the edge of the mattress, trying to collect his wits. He knew for a fact the twins hadn't been at the table to hear Zio Angelo's boyhood story about the cap. They didn't even know yet that it might once have belonged to Williams. Only Michael and Julia knew that. "Prove it," he said. "Tell me exactly how you came by that cap. Don't leave out a single detail."

"You still haven't said who *you* are," the kid said.

"We'll get to me in a minute," Tony said.

The kid shrugged. He sat on the other side of the mattress. "I'm a water boy at Fenway Park," he said. "Williams is number 9, a rookie left fielder for the Red Sox. But he quit halfway through a Detroit Tigers game yesterday afternoon. So I invited him home to supper—"

ANGELO

How Angelo Saved Ted Williams's Red Sox Career

FRIDAY, MAY 5, 1939

Angelo waited, like everyone else in the Red Sox dugout, for number 9, the rookie outfielder from California, to step up to home plate. It was the Sox against the Tigers in the second of a three-game series. And as usual, Williams refused to bat until the crowd stopped booing him. These standoffs could last five minutes or more.

"Good for him," said number 27, Solomon Weinberg, signaling to Angelo for a drink of water. Angelo passed him a full dipper. Angelo felt a little sorry for Weinberg, a second-string outfielder who hardly ever got to play—mostly because Williams started every game. "Number 9's the club's best hitter," Weinberg said, handing back the dipper. "He deserves a little more respect."

Williams finally stepped into the batter's box.

"So why do they hate him so much?" Angelo asked, jerking his thumb up at the disgruntled Fenway fans seated in the stands above the dugout.

Weinberg shrugged. "He's a much better ballplayer than showman, which is what the boys in the newsroom care about. He's pretty tight-lipped when it comes to giving them any copy. So they make it up. Mostly about how much he hates Boston."

Williams cracked a smart single into midfield, advancing the only man on base to third. The crowd offered a smattering of begrudging applause.

"I think he's just shy," Angelo said. "He's always nice to me. Which is more than I can say about the *rest* of the starting lineup."

Weinberg laughed. "What's your name, kid?"

Angelo told him. Weinberg looked oddly startled, then pleased. He held out his hand—his friends called him Solly—and Angelo shook it, grinning.

"I'll bet it's your thirteenth birthday soon," Solly said.

"Today, in fact," Angelo said, surprised. "How did you know?"

"You live in Hangmen Court, right?" Solly said. "Over in the North End."

Angelo nodded, mystified. Solly laughed. "My parents sold

Number Thirteen to your parents," he said. "I lived there myself when I was thirteen—when the neighborhood was still mostly Jewish. I slept up in the attic. But I haven't been back in over a decade—not since we sold the place when I was twenty-one, after I joined the team."

Angelo confessed he didn't know how much longer he'd be living there. Now that Papa was gone, Mama was always behind on the mortgage payments—even with all the boarders she took in. Solly gave his back a consoling pat. He was sorry to hear that Angelo's dad had passed. He promised to stop by the house someday soon to pay his respects to Angelo's mama.

Williams tried to steal second base. It was an amazing slide—and he was clearly safe—but the umpire ruled him out. More booing.

Williams limped back to the dugout. He took a seat on the bench next to Angelo and asked for water. Solly said, "Tough luck." Williams nodded, then shucked off his shoe to examine his ankle. It was already beginning to swell. Solly suggested Angelo fetch the team medic from the locker room.

Angelo returned with both the medic and number 4, Joe Cronin, the team's shortstop and manager. The medic took a good look at Williams's ankle and declared it a minor sprain. Williams should probably be pulled from the game so it could be packed in ice. "Just wrap it," Cronin said.

"But he shouldn't be running on that ankle," Solly said. "It's turning *purple*."

"Are you a doctor?" Cronin said. Solly shook his head. "Then keep your big mouth shut!" According to Cronin, Williams *had* to keep playing. The Sox were trailing second in the league standings after their archrivals, the New York Yankees. If they won this game against Detroit, and the Yankees lost theirs against the Cleveland Indians, they would pull ahead. And this was entirely possible. Cronin had just gotten off the phone with Eddie Collins, the Sox's general manager, who had heard from Tom Yawkey, the owner, that New York's first baseman, Lou Gehrig, had benched himself for the first time in fourteen straight seasons due to some sort of mysterious illness. So New York was suddenly very vulnerable.

"Wait, I've got an idea," Solly said. "What if Williams continues to field, but I pinch-hit and do his running for him?"

"If I wanted the opinion of an uppity Jew-boy benchwarmer, I would have asked for it!" Cronin exploded.

"That settles it," Williams said. He slipped his shoe back on, hoisted himself to his feet, and hobbled toward the locker room. Cronin demanded to know where Williams thought he was going—the medic hadn't wrapped that ankle yet.

"Home," Williams said. "I quit."

Cronin told Williams to skip the funny business: he was

under contract. That's for the lawyers to decide, Williams said. This clearly unsettled Cronin—he didn't want to incur the wrath of Eddie Collins—so he backed off. They'd do it Weinberg's way. Number 27 could pinch-hit for Williams as long as Williams played the field.

"Not unless you apologize to Weinberg first," Williams said.

"Like heck I will!" Cronin said.

Williams shrugged, then disappeared into the locker room.

Inning over. Detroit's turn at bat. Cronin whirled on Solly. "If you know what's good for you," he said, "you'll get Williams taped up and onto the field by next inning." He ordered another benchwarmer to grab his mitt. Solly headed for the locker room. Angelo noticed Williams had left his ball cap on the bench. He used this as an excuse to chase after both players—and see what happened next.

Williams undressed while Solly tried to convince him to keep playing. Nothing doing, Williams said. His favorite uncle back in Santa Barbara—the guy who had taught him how to play ball—was named Saul too. Saul Venzor, a Mexican. Williams knew all about prejudice: his *abuela*—his grandma—was born in Mexico. His mother's side of the family barely spoke English. Solly confessed he hadn't known any of that.

"Because my contract expressly forbids me from speaking to

the press about my family," Williams said. "Which is also why I never have anything to say. Which is why the Boston papers go out of their way to make me look bad to the fans. And *that's* how much I think of my contract with the Red Sox."

Angelo handed Williams his cap. Williams tossed it into his locker. It was no use, he told Solly. He wouldn't play again until Cronin apologized for his racist remarks.

"Then *I* won't play," Solly said. He opened his locker and started to undress.

"Me either," Angelo said, planting himself on the nearest changing bench. Both ballplayers laughed. Solly asked Williams what they should do with their night off. It would be Solly's treat. Williams told Solly to forget about it. What he really wanted was the one thing another ballplayer couldn't give him: a home-cooked meal.

Angelo cleared his throat. The two men looked over. "Mama's fixing me a big birthday meal when I get back to the North End," he said. "Why don't you both come? She always makes way too much food."

"It would give me a chance to see the old place and pay my respects," Solly said.

"I'm just warning you, it's not gonna be a turkey with mashed potatoes and peas," Angelo said. "We're Italian."

Williams turned to Solly. "We better hit the showers. Then you gotta wrap my ankle good and tight, Weinberg. We've got ourselves a date."

"Solly," Solly said. "My friends call me Solly."

"And I'm Angelo," Angelo said. "By the way."

The three of them were in fine spirits as they made their way past all the *caffès* and *trattorias* and butcher shops of the North End. They even stuck a dollar onto a statue of Sant'Angelo being paraded down Hanover Street to celebrate the feast day. Williams said it reminded him of Mexico.

Angelo's heart sank, though, when he led the two ballplayers into Hangmen Court. Mama was out on the front stoop of No. 13, arguing with Cyril the Squirrel again. (She called her mortgage collector that behind his back because he was short, had fat cheeks, and was always scolding her.) As usual, Cyril the Squirrel was demanding that Mama make her loan payment—it was well past the first of the month. And as usual, Mama was reminding him her boarders didn't pay *her* until the end of the week. To make matters worse, Cyril's spoiled and stuck-up son, Benny, was watching the whole thing from a limb of the oak in the center of the court.

"Most of the neighborhood is behind on their payments!" Mama shouted. "Why are you always picking on me?"

"Watch your tongue," Cyril said. "Or I'll head straight back to the bank, write out an eviction notice, and serve it on you first thing in the morning!"

Mama raised her broom and warned Cyril he'd better beat it or she'd add another lump to his ugly skull. Cyril saw that she was serious and backed away. He called to Benny to climb down from the tree. Together they strode past Angelo and the ballplayers, who were wearing their caps in spite of their street clothes. Benny's eyes bugged out when he recognized Williams. Angelo thoroughly enjoyed asking Mama, well within Benny's earshot, if the two Red Sox could join his birthday dinner.

Solly reminded Mama who he was. To Angelo's surprise, she threw her arms around his neck and gave him a big kiss hello. Williams introduced himself, apologizing for turning up at dinner empty-handed. Don't be silly, Mama said, ushering him up the stoop. His timing was perfect. She was just about to set out the antipasti.

What followed was hands down the best birthday dinner of Angelo's life—a real feast for the Feast of Saint Angelo: clams in breadcrumbs (which Solly passed on because he kept kosher), marinated artichokes, and tomato salad for starters; spaghetti in red sauce for the pasta course; roast lamb with rosemary potatoes for the main; and then a large garden salad to finish off. Just when Angelo thought he couldn't eat another bite,

Mama pulled a gigantic tiramisu out of the dumbwaiter and lit a sparkler. Antonio DiMarco, the new guy on the third floor, began a rousing chorus of "Happy Birthday." All the boarders and both ballplayers joined in. After everyone clapped, Mama began serving scoops of the tiramisu into bowls and handing them around. Angelo explained to the ballplayers that it was a classic Italian dessert, somewhere in between cake and pudding. Williams grinned when he tasted it. He said it reminded him of his Mexican grandmother's *capirotada*.

Over second helpings, Solly reminded Mama that *his* mother had had similar run-ins with Cyril's father, Chester. In fact, Solly personally blamed Chester for ruining his own thirteenth birthday. He would never forget that day as long as he lived— January 15, 1919—on account of this house, a rusty old tank of molasses, and an Irish guy named Finn McGinley. Solly glanced over at Angelo. But he'd have to save *that* story for another time, he said, when it was just the grown-ups at the table.

Angelo didn't get the chance to ask why. A commotion was brewing outside on the sidewalk. The press! They had obviously caught wind of Cronin's dugout fight with Williams and been tipped off to his whereabouts. Williams refused to budge from the table. He just asked for more dessert. And Solly helped Mama clear the dishes to the kitchen. But Angelo could plainly hear the newspapermen arguing among themselves: Even without Williams this afternoon, the Sox had managed to win against Detroit, 8–3. And the Yankees had lost against Cleveland, 2–1. The Sox were now in first place. Would Ted return to Fenway tomorrow to save the series to help the Sox win their final game against Detroit, thus sealing the Yankees' fate?

A cab screeched up. The driver climbed out, smiled for a photo, then rapped on the front door. He had an important message for Ted Williams, he said, waving an envelope in the air. He had been ordered *not* to leave until Williams got in the cab. Angelo went to the door. He told the cabbie to slide the message through the letter slot. The white envelope plopped onto the welcome mat. When Angelo brought it over to Williams, he tore it open and read what was scrawled on a single sheet of Fenway stationery. He was being summoned to an emergency meeting with Cronin, Collins, and Yawkey back at Fenway. According to Williams's contract, it would cost him a thousand dollars for every game he refused to play.

Solly collected both his and Williams's ball caps from the rack in the front hallway. He pulled a tiny scroll from behind the 27 embroidered on the inside brim of his own. He said he'd been carrying it around with him for protection since he was a boy. He took a pinch of sugar from the bowl on the table and sprinkled it over the scroll's Hebrew characters, whispering a prayer. He did this a total of nine times, counting out loud each time he started over. When he was finished, he tucked the scroll behind the 9 of Williams's brim and handed the cap over. Williams should touch the brim each time he was at bat, Solly said, for protection against his foes. And now Williams should climb into that cab and take it back to Fenway.

Williams stood his ground. Cronin's note did not contain an apology to Solly. No apology, no deal. Solly advised Williams to skip it. Solly had known since he was a kid that he wouldn't have much of a ball career—never mind why—and his chances of joining the Sox's starting lineup had anyway disappeared the minute he'd opened his "uppity Jew-boy benchwarmer big mouth" to Cronin back in the dugout. Solly turned to Angelo. "But it's all been worth it," he said, "to get the chance to celebrate your thirteenth birthday with you." He ripped the 27 off the sleeve of his jersey and placed the embroidered patch in Angelo's hand. He gave Mama a rib-cracking hug good-bye. She asked him if he was sure about what they had discussed while stacking dishes in the kitchen. He said he'd never been surer of anything in his life. Williams asked where Solly was headed. Solly said he didn't know—California maybe? He'd never been there. With that, he shook Williams's hand and ambled out the door.

Williams turned to Angelo. "What would you do if you were me?"

Angelo thought it over. "Play," he said. "I'd put some ice on that ankle tonight, wrap it good and tight, then play tomorrow. I'd play like I've never played before—not for Cronin, or Collins, or Yawkey. Not for the Boston papers or the Fenway fans. I'd play for Saul, and for Solomon."

Williams nodded. He stood. He thanked Angelo's mother for dinner. Then he turned to Angelo and made him promise always to fight for what was right. He placed his cap on Angelo's head and wished him a happy birthday. Without speaking another word, he opened the front door and, parting the crowd of reporters at the bottom of the front stoop with his silence, climbed into the waiting cab.

UNDER INVESTIGATION
SATURDAY, JULY 11, 2009

O h my God," Tony whispered. "You're telling the truth." Because there was no denying it: this kid's story matched, word for word, the one Zio Angelo had told him at Thanksgiving. "But why aren't you haunting me as an old man?"

"Haunting you?" Angelo said. "I don't even *know* you."

"Well, what were you doing in my bed, then?" Tony said.

"Heck if I know!" Angelo said. "After I finished helping Mama do the dishes, I came up here, to *my* room, to try Ted Williams's cap on in front of the mirror. It was miles too big. So I turned on my new portable radio—Mama's other birthday present to me besides the quilt—and made a couple of adjustments to the brim while I listened to the nightly news."

"And?" Tony said.

"It's true, Lou Gehrig has some sort of disease they don't know how to cure," Angelo said. "Hitler is cheesed off with Britain for guaranteeing to protect Poland. The World's Fair opened in New York to record attendance. Oh yeah, and DC gave the Batman his own comic book."

"No," Tony said. "I meant: And then what did you do?"

"Oh," Angelo said. "I gave Williams's cap the place of honor on the shelf above the bookcase. I turned off the radio. I changed into my pajamas. I climbed into bed. Next thing I knew, I was waking up beside *you*."

"So you don't want to be avenged?" Tony said.

"For what?" Angelo said.

"For your sudden and mysterious death," Tony said.

"I'm not dead," Angelo said. "Obviously."

They were interrupted by a gentle knock at the bedroom door. "Rise and shine," Michael said from the other side.

"I'm awake," Tony called out.

"Yeah, well I'm not so sure I am," Angelo said. "None of this makes any sense."

"Can I come in?" Michael said.

"Just a sec," Tony said. "Quick!" he whispered to Angelo. "Get under the bed."

"Why?" Angelo said.

"My dad's at the door," Tony said.

"I don't hear anybody," Angelo said.

"Just do it!" Tony said. "Until we figure out what's going on."

Reluctantly, Angelo climbed under the bed.

Tony let Michael into the room.

"Just thought I'd come up and see how your first night went," Michael said.

"OK, I guess," Tony said. He sat on the edge of the mattress to block his dad's view of who—or what—was under it.

Michael peered around the room. "See? I told you it would feel completely different up here with your own stuff." He wandered over to the shelf above the bookcase and pulled the cap off the spiral. He tugged at a loose stitch on the B. "Remind me to get this appraised," he said. "Wouldn't it be cool if it really was Ted Williams's first cap with the Sox?"

The sound of a doorbell echoed up the stairwell.

"Maybe that's the cable guy," Michael said, making his way over to the bed. "He promised he'd be here bright and early." He placed the cap on Tony's head, then tugged the bill over his eyes. "Get dressed. We've got a big day ahead, you and me. First we're taking ourselves out to breakfast. Then we've got some history mysteries to solve." The bell rang again, followed by someone pounding at the door. "Better get that before he wakes up the whole house," Michael said. He strolled out and made his way downstairs.

Tony pulled the cap off his head. He hung it on the brass knob topping the bedpost. He ducked his head under the bed to tell Angelo the coast was clear.

Angelo was gone.

Tony glanced around the room. No closet to hide in, no armoire to duck behind, no balcony or fire escape to crouch on. He wandered over to the slate shelf. He placed his finger in the center of the spiral. Nothing. No static hum. No echo of voices. Angelo had just plain vanished. Tony pulled on a pair of jeans and a polo shirt. Was it possible he had imagined the whole thing?

It wasn't the cable guy. It was the police.

Two plainclothes detectives. One of them was leading Michael by the arm down the stoop to a car parked at the curb. Tony stood frozen in the doorway, utterly speechless. *No way*, he thought. *This can't be happening.* And yet it was.

"What's going on here?"

Julia emerged from the door beneath the stoop, still dressed in her bathrobe and clutching a pot of coffee.

"We're taking this suspect, Michelangelo DiMarco, down to the station for questioning," said the first detective.

"Suspect for what?" Julia said.

"For the possible murder of his uncle, Angelo DiMarco," said the other detective.

"But that's completely crazy!" Julia said.

"Yeah, he's totally innocent!" Tony said. But he couldn't stop himself from glancing up at Old Man Hagmann's window. Oh great. There he was, standing right behind his lace curtains watching the whole thing.

"Don't worry," Michael said. "All of the so-called allegations against me are nothing but a series of unrelated coincidences. I can explain away every single one."

"That would be advisable," the first detective said.

"What allegations?" Julia said.

"I'm sure it'll all be cleared up by lunchtime," Michael said.

"Don't say anything!" Tony said. "Not without a lawyer present!"

The second detective told Julia that she should, in fact, contact a lawyer.

"But we just moved to Boston," Julia said. "We don't know any lawyers!"

"Call Birnbaum," Michael advised Julia. "The guy who drew up Zio Angelo's will. His card is in my briefcase." He turned to Tony. "Do me a favor? Don't mention any of this to the twins. No need to go upsetting them for nothing."

"But it's not nothing!" Julia said.

"Of course it is," Michael said. "And we'll all have a good laugh about it when I get back from the station."

"But it's not funny!" Julia said.

"This way, please," said the first detective. He opened the back door of the cruiser. His partner settled Michael into the caged backseat. They both climbed into the front, and the car roared away from the curb with tires screeching.

"Oh my God!" Julia said, clamping her hand over her mouth. She turned to Tony. "You don't think—?"

Tony glanced next door. Old Man Hagmann had vanished. Suddenly he was absolutely one hundred percent certain. "Are you *kidding*? Dad's a vegetarian Buddhist, for God's sake. He doesn't believe in killing *flies*. He won't even wear a leather belt. They've totally got the wrong guy."

"You're right," Julia said. "Sorry. I'm just a little freaked out."

"That makes two of us!" Tony said.

They just stood there.

"So what are we going to do?" Julia said.

"Get that lawyer on the phone," Tony said.

Julia flipped her cell phone shut. "Birnbaum is pretty sure the next-door neighbor called the cops," she told Tony.

They were both down in the kitchen.

"I figured," Tony said.

"Mr. Hagmann was apparently at the reading of Zio Angelo's will. He got really upset. He started making all sorts of wild accusations."

"So what did the lawyer say about Dad?"

"Birnbaum's headed over to the station now," Julia said. "He told me to sit tight by the phone until I hear from him."

The twins wandered into the room in sweatpants and T-shirts, looking like they'd just rolled out of bed.

"I guess we're not going running this morning," Mikey said, yawning.

"Who was at the door?" Angey asked. "I thought I heard voices outside."

Julia just stared at him, at a loss for words.

"Cable guy," Tony said.

"So where is he?" Angey said.

"He didn't have enough cable to wire the whole place," Tony said. "He went back to the shop for more."

"Better be coming back," Mikey said. "It'll be a long summer without HBO."

"Where's Dad?" Angey said.

Silence. Julia was still a deer in the headlights.

"He had to swing by the lawyer's to sign some papers," Tony said.

"I thought he was taking you on that history mystery thing?" Angey said.

Not anymore.

"I'd totally dog that too, if I were Dad," Mikey said. "Bor-ring."

Julia finally recovered. "Tony's meeting him at the Paul Revere House, where the tour starts. Which is why I'd better get making some pancakes. Meantime, the two of you should put on some old clothes. As soon as we've eaten, I need you to help me move all the furniture in the mother-in-law room out onto the back deck so we can pull up the linoleum. I want to start sanding the hardwood floors."

"Suddenly history mysteries aren't sounding so bad," Mikey said. He grabbed two bananas out of the fruit bowl on the counter. He handed Angey one of them. They headed back upstairs.

"Sorry," Julia said to Tony. "It's all I could think of at the spur of the moment. But now I guess you'll have to go on the tour."

"Not with Dad in jail!" Tony said.

"He's not *in* jail," Julia said. "He's *at* the jail, just for questioning. Anyway, there's nothing either of us can do until we hear from Birnbaum. We both have to believe your father is right: that everything'll be cleared up by lunch. The only way we're going to prevent ourselves from going out of our minds is by getting on with the day, as planned."

"But I couldn't even *think* about solving a bunch of lame history mysteries at a time like this," Tony said.

"Try," Julia said. "For my sake. If we ever needed a detective in the family, it's now."

PART TWO
THE MYSTERY

THE ANOMALY
SATURDAY, JULY 11, 2009

Tony headed straight next door to No. 15.

Well, not *straight* next door. First he pretended to eat breakfast with Julia and the twins. He could force down only about a pancake and a half, though, before he shoved his plate aside and declared himself late for his rendezvous with Michael over at the Revere House. He reassured Julia he would be on his new cell—just in case—and told the twins to have fun moving all that furniture. *Then* he ducked out the door beneath the stoop, climbed the steps of No. 15, and rang the bell.

A moment later, Hagmann answered.

"What's your problem?" Tony said.

"It's your father who appears to have the problem," Hagmann said.

"Yeah, because you called the cops!" Tony said.

"It was my duty as a law-abiding citizen," he said.

"To accuse him of murder?" Tony said.

"I made no such accusation," Hagmann said. "I simply alerted the authorities to what I had seen with my own eyes and heard with my own ears."

"Which was?"

"That I found Angelo stone-cold dead in his bed mere minutes after your father's so-called visit to him last month."

Tony couldn't even pretend to hide his shock.

"And that, as a result, you—a DiMarco—were suddenly named inheritor of Angelo's house, despite his solemn vow never to allow such a thing to happen."

"Why would Zio Angelo vow that?" Tony managed to stammer.

"Because the whole DiMarco clan had been shunning Angelo ever since his mother, Isabella, left Number Thirteen to him, and not her second husband, Antonio DiMarco."

Yikes! That pretty much explained, Tony had to admit, why Nonno Guido and Zio Angelo never saw eye to eye. He didn't say so to Old Man Hagmann, though. Instead he said, "But Dad made a point of visiting Zio Angelo whenever he was in Boston."

"Are you sure about that?" Hagmann said. "Or did he just say he did? Frankly, I'd never met the man until the morning of Angelo's death. Meanwhile, Angelo was pretty insistent that no DiMarco should get even a single chipped teacup of his property after he was gone. In fact, he recently asked me to type out a correction to his will changing the inheritor of Number Thirteen from your father—whom he had reluctantly chosen as the best of a bad lot when the will was first drawn up—to *me*. I strongly objected, of course. I already *had* a house and didn't need another one. But Angelo was adamant that he sign the deed of Number Thirteen over to me. I was the only one who ever visited him, who bothered to look after him now that he was ill, who actually cared whether he lived or died."

"If he felt that way about it, why did he suddenly fly to Ann Arbor to spend Thanksgiving with us?" Tony said.

Hagmann frowned. "To inform your father in person of his intention to cut all of you DiMarcos out of his will, once and for all. Angelo was convinced, on his return, that it was the stress of your father's violent reaction that brought on his stroke."

Tony had no recollection of any conflict between Michael and Zio Angelo at Thanksgiving. They seemed to get along just fine. And when was his dad *ever* violent? "If they were fighting, why would Dad bother to drop in on Zio Angelo three weeks ago?" Tony said, grasping at straws.

"Break in, more like," Hagmann said. "I began looking after Angelo full-time once he became bedridden. So you can imagine my alarm when I heard footsteps overhead in the parlor while I was making his breakfast down in the kitchen. I knew it couldn't be poor Angelo. And I raced upstairs to discover your father—a total stranger—looming over Angelo's bed in a frankly menacing way while Angelo scribbled *Trying to kill me* on the notepad he used for communicating his needs."

Tony was speechless. *That* didn't sound like his dad at all. Then again, what had he joked with the twins over pizza? That it was always the mild-mannered ones who went postal?

"I was just about to call 911 when your father introduced himself as Angelo's nephew from Michigan," Hagmann continued. "He explained away the note by reminding me that Angelo's heart medicine made him a little paranoid—which I knew to be true. He asked me if I would kindly make him a cup of tea. What could I do? Against my better judgment, I went to the kitchen and put the kettle on. When I was on my way back up with the tray, though, your father came barreling out of the parlor. He stuffed an envelope addressed to Birnbaum & Birnbaum into his coat pocket and, claiming he was late for an appointment across town, dashed out the door."

Tony's heart sank. This more or less corroborated what Michael had said: that he had dropped in on Zio Angelo just before heading over to Harvard to deliver his speech on Paul Revere at the history conference.

"To my horror, I found Angelo dead when I returned to his side," Hagmann concluded. "Which is when I called 911. And then I remembered—having recently typed out that change to Angelo's will—that Birnbaum was Angelo's lawyer. Immediately suspicious, I checked Angelo's rolltop desk, only to discover both the will and the deed to Number Thirteen were missing."

Uh-oh. Tony tried not to panic. Old Man Hagmann's allegations did sound pretty convincing. "But none of this makes any sense," he said, even though it sort of did. "Why would Dad risk the rest of his life in prison for such a falling-down heap of old bricks?"

"That's for those detectives to deduce," Hagmann sniffed. "All I know is this: that the DiMarcos have been trying to get their hands on Number Thirteen ever since Antonio tricked poor Isabella into marrying him. Why do you think he insisted on adopting Angelo as a teenager? I'll tell you! So there would be no question of the house going to him after her death. But Angelo's dear old mother confounded them all by leaving Number Thirteen to Angelo anyway."

"You have no real proof to support any of that," Tony said.

"Perhaps not," Hagmann said. "But I wouldn't get too comfortable over there if I were you. It's only a matter of time before the authorities declare your father's trumped-up version of Angelo's will to be shamelessly falsified."

"Or realize he's totally innocent," Tony said. Not knowing what to say next, he turned and strode out of Hangmen Court. As soon as he rounded the corner of Charter Street, though, he stopped at the entrance to an Irish bar to collect his wits. What were the odds those two detectives would ever buy that Michael was innocent? There was no denying how strange it was that Zio Angelo had changed his will the day he'd died, leaving No. 13 to Tony. Even stranger that Zio Angelo had tried to warn Old Man Hagmann, just beforehand, that Michael was trying to kill him. Stranger still that all this had taken place the day after Michael was notified that the DiMarcos were being booted out of university housing in Ann Arbor.

Basta! Michael couldn't possibly have killed Zio Angelo. It just wasn't in his nature. There must be some other explanation. Wait, what had Hagmann just said? That the DiMarco family had been trying to get their hands on No. 13 for generations. Could that possibly be true? Unfortunately, there was now no way for Tony to ask Michael, at least not at the moment. Nor could he call Nonno Guido without spilling the beans about the allegations against his dad. If only he could figure out a way to conjure the ghost of Angelo back and ask *him* about Antonio DiMarco. But how?

★ ★ ★

Colonial Maid Goth Chick was still reading that astrophysics book at the slate counter when he jangled through the front door. Except now she wasn't wearing that long purple dress or her gathered cotton cap. She was sporting a cutoff jean miniskirt and Bob Marley tank top. Her punked-out black hair was tied back in a ratty ponytail with a purple ribbon.

"Video shop is next to the hardware," she mumbled, turning the page.

"Can I ask you a question?" Tony said.

"Oh, it's you," she said, looking up and squinting.

"Tony," he said, wandering over. "I just moved into the neighborhood."

She stared at him.

"So what's *your* name?" he said.

"Sarah," she said. "Are you, like, stalking me?"

"I've got one of these in my room," Tony said, tapping the countertop where the spiral was carved. "Only mine's a shelf."

"It's called a pawcorance," Sarah said. "They're wicked old. Ancient Native Americans carved them centuries before the Algonquian Nation formed its tribes or the Pilgrims even thought of boarding the *Mayflower*."

"What were they for?" Tony asked. "Originally, I mean."

"Anthropologists *theorize* they marked spots where ancient

natives encountered ancestral spirits," Sarah said. "The Algonquians continued to consider them sacred, especially the more elaborate ones in the form of altars. *Pawcorance* is actually the Algonquian word for 'mockingbird.' Tradition held that the mockingbird was itself possessed by spirits, since it only ever appeared at dusk or dawn—often at pawcorances—and could sing in the voice of any animal. Dude, are you OK? You look like you're about to pass out."

Tony nodded, though he wasn't so sure.

"Unfortunately, the Pilgrims turned most of the pawcorances around New England into horse mounts, boot scrapers, door lintels, fireplace mantels—you name it," she said. "They weren't very respectful. Are you sure you're OK?"

Tony hesitated. Was he really going to go there? Sarah was, after all, a total stranger. Emphasis on strange.

Dad's in jail. OK, at the jail, for questioning. But still.

"I think my pawcorance might have conjured my dead great-uncle Angelo from 1939," he blurted. "When he was a kid. But then he disappeared again before I could figure out what was going on. I sort of need to conjure him back."

Sarah squinted at him again. "Better follow me," she said. She ducked through the purple velvet curtain behind her.

Tony checked his pants pocket for his new cell phone—just in case she skinned rats back there—but did as he was told. He was a little disappointed to find himself in an ordinary storage room crammed with more junk. Sarah busied herself filling a dented copper kettle at a small, rust-stained sink. She set the kettle on a gas camp stove and fired up the burner with a wand-like fireplace match. She reached for a teapot on a shelf above the stove cluttered with canisters and tins. "Cup of mint tea?" she said.

"Um, sure," Tony said. He'd never actually had one in his life. "So do you think my pawcorance still works?"

"How should I know?" Sarah said. She plucked two faded teacups off hooks beneath the shelf and dusted them with the black-and-skulls hanky she pulled from her pocket.

"You never conjured anyone with yours?" Tony said.

"It's not mine," she said.

"With Mildred's?" Tony said.

"Of course not!" she said.

He felt himself turn beet red. "I should probably just go," he said.

"Dude, chill!" Sarah said. "I'm not doubting your word. I'm just saying there's no reason why Mildred's pawcorance would work. I told you, they mark *sites*. We're at least fifty miles from Worcester, where this one was found."

The kettle whistled. Sarah shut off the gas and reached for one of the canisters. She placed four scoops of dried leaves in the teapot, then filled it with boiling water.

"But mine must have been moved too," Tony said. "It's now a shelf in the attic of the house I just moved into."

"Maybe, maybe not," Sarah said. "You can't rule out the possibility it was actually found at the site where your house was built, got turned into a shelf, and is therefore still more or less in its original location. A hypothesis which is supported by your claim it still works. Or am I missing something?"

Tony shook his head.

"Sugar?"

Tony nodded, figuring anything would taste better sweeter. She placed a cracked bowl on a tray alongside the steaming teapot and two cleanish cups. Tony followed her back to the main shop. She set the tray on the spiral of the countertop and poured out two cups of yellowish-looking liquid. She dropped a cube of sugar into one and handed it to Tony, telling him to park himself on a stool that looked worryingly like a stuffed rhinoceros leg. He took a hesitant sip. To his surprise, the tea was refreshing, sort of tingly and nice. Meanwhile Sarah slumped with her own cup onto the sort of lounging sofa Cleopatra might have liked. "What was your question, again?" she said.

"How to conjure Angelo back," Tony said.

Sarah frowned. She blew on her tea. "How old are you?"

"I just turned thirteen," Tony told her. "Yesterday." He wondered how old *she* was: fifteen? sixteen? It was a little hard to tell.

"Interesting," she said, not bothering to wish him a happy birthday. "And what were you doing just prior to this Angel dude's appearance?"

"Sleeping," Tony admitted.

"You didn't do anything to the pawcorance?"

Tony told her about running his finger around the spiral the night before, getting a static shock, hearing a boy's voice, placing Ted Williams's cap over the spiral before going to bed, and waking to find Angelo asleep beside him.

"In the present?" Sarah said.

"Angelo thought he was still in his own room in 1939," Tony said.

"Interesting," Sarah said again. She set her cup down on the counter and headed for the wall of books. She ran her finger along a row of tomes until she found the one she was looking for. She showed Tony its gold-stamped cover: *Of My Amazing Exploites in the New Worlde*. "Myles Standish," she said, settling back onto her sofa and leafing through the book's yellowed pages. "Militia captain for the Plymouth Colony. He was the first Englishman to explore the Shawmut Peninsula—now the city of Boston—which was already inhabited by a band of the Massachuset tribe. The band's sachem, Chickatawbut, welcomed Standish with a feast of lobsters and boiled cod. Chickatawbut promised to share this peninsula with Standish on one and only one condition. Do you know what that was?"

Tony shook his head. Of course he didn't! But he was used to these sorts of leading questions; Michael always asked them before launching into a bit of history.

"On condition that Standish's Pilgrims *never* settle near their sacred Spiraling Stone," Sarah said. "Do you know why?"

Tony shook his head again.

"Because that was where the tribe's thirteen-year-old braves held their vision quests," she said, throwing up her hands as though the answer were obvious. She then began to read a somewhat long and boring passage out of the book. It was written in a way that made the whole thing sound to Tony like Shakespeare. But he finally got the general upshot: When a boy was close to manhood—when he had lived thirteen winters and was seeking to be called a brave—he would begin his vision quest by placing an object on the carved spiral of the stone altar. This talisman needed to represent the animal totem he'd already been assigned by the tribe's sachem: a hawk feather, say, or a bear claw or porcupine quill. He then waited for a guide from the spirit world—usually an ancestor of that same totem—to appear to him in animal form. Sometimes this occurred the first night, sometimes it didn't; the conditions needed to be exactly right. Which is why the boy had the whole following year to keep trying.

"Did Angelo remind you of an animal?" Sarah asked, glancing up from the book.

Tony nodded. Angelo's thick glasses *had* made him look like a cross-eyed owl.

"You said you placed a cap on the spiral," Sarah said. "Did the cap mean anything to Angelo?"

"He had just gotten it from a famous ballplayer," Tony said.

"How did *you* come by it?" Sarah said.

"He sent it to me himself when he was an old man," Tony said. "For my thirteenth birthday, just before he died. Come to think of it, the kid version of Zio Angelo told me he also set that cap on the spiral before going to bed."

"Interesting," Sarah said.

"You think I had a vision quest?" Tony said.

"Not really," Sarah said, sipping her tea.

"Oh," Tony said. "Well, what *do* you think?"

"That ancient cultures developed rituals like the vision quest to explain naturally occurring phenomena at certain sites whenever certain atmospheric conditions came into play," she said. She strode back to the wall of books. This time she pulled out a relatively modern-looking volume. She opened it to a dog-eared page. On the left-hand side was a bunch of crudely drawn spirals.

"Petroglyphs found at prehistoric sites throughout North

America," she said. "Anthropologists have narrowed their meaning to three possibilities: the universe itself, a portal to the spirit world, or the coiled nature of time. The Massachuset language, a dialect of Algonquian, had no word for *time* before the arrival of Europeans. Nor did they have any concept of past or future. For them, everything happened—birth, manhood, marriage, death—in one long, never-ending *now*."

"You've totally lost me," Tony said.

"Ever heard of Hermann Minkowski?" Sarah said.

Tony shook his head yet again.

Sarah took him over to a round wire birdcage that was hanging from the ceiling. "In 1909, Minkowski proposed a radical new notion of time called the block universe theory. He imagined time to be spatial, existing all at once as plot points in a three-dimensional sphere—a gigantic, cosmic version of this cage—*not* a progression of events plotted along a two-dimensional line." Here she pulled the ribbon out of her hair and tied one end of it to a random wire of the cage. "Minkowski theorized it might be possible for one era to communicate with another—his explanation for ghosts and spirits—if certain atmospheric conditions forced two different points of the sphere to connect." She opened the cage and pulled the ribbon through its center. She tied it at another random spot on the opposite side. "In such a time anomaly, both moments might, in theory, take place simultaneously in a given location." She ran her finger along the entire length of the purple ribbon, then twanged it for good measure.

"So you think my pawcorance is a time anomaly?" Tony said.

"It's just one hypothesis," Sarah said. "Let's say static on the spiral is a signal the conditions are right for a thirteen-year-old to make contact with someone from another era. Let's also say that *who*—Angelo, for example—is determined by the object you place on the spiral. In this case it's the ball cap, because it is meaningful to you both, and exists in 1939 as well as 2009. Let's say the voice you then hear confirms you've chosen the right object. All you would need to do is wait for Angelo to place his cap on his spiral for an anomaly to open in the space-time continuum, and *bam!*, you're both inhabiting the same spot, simultaneously. Follow?"

Tony nodded uncertainly.

"But let's say time does indeed march on outside the anomaly. And the second either of you leaves the room—*bam!*—you find yourself back in your own era."

"But Angelo disappeared when we were both still in the room, right after my dad took the cap off the spiral," Tony said.

"Makes total sense," Sarah said. "By removing the connecting object, your dad broke the connection."

Which was when Tony suddenly remembered why he was actually there: To conjure Angelo back so he could prove his dad's innocence by ruling out a weird DiMarco family obsession with 13 Hangmen Court as a motive for murder. "You think all I need to do is put the cap back on the spiral?" he said.

"What have you got to lose?" Sarah shrugged.

Tony gulped the rest of his tea. He stood. He told her he would go straight home and give it a try. She told him to stop by again, let her know how it all went. Tony hesitated at the door. "How did you get so smart?" he said.

"I read a lot of books," she said. "Obviously."

"I guess curiosity shops don't get so busy," he said.

"People aren't all that curious," she said.

Judging by the echo of their voices, the twins and Julia were still moving furniture down in the mother-in-law room. Mikey was complaining how it was too nice a day outside to be sanding floors. Tony tiptoed up the staircase. He didn't want them to know he was back yet. He should still, technically speaking, be on that History Mystery Tour with Michael. He grabbed Ted Williams's cap off the brass knob of the bedpost as soon as he'd closed himself into his room. He took it over to the slate shelf. Before setting it on the spiral, though, he hovered his palm above the concentric rings. He could definitely feel the crackle of static electricity again, which—if Sarah's hypothesis was to be believed—meant Angelo was probably in *his* room, back in 1939. Tony closed his eyes and listened carefully. Yup, he could hear the faint echo of Angelo's voice: *I must have been having a nightmare.*

Steeling his courage, he set the cap on the spiral.

"Oh no, not you again!"

Tony whirled around. Angelo was standing near the dresser, buttoning the jersey of a Red Sox uniform.

"I can't believe you made me crawl under the bed, then left me there!" he said.

"Sorry about that," Tony said.

"Well, what do you want?" Angelo said.

"I think I know what's going on now."

"Glad somebody does," he said.

"What if I told you today's date *isn't* May 6, 1939—at least not for me—" Tony said, "but July 11, 2009?"

"Here we go again," Angelo said, sighing.

"What if I'm *not* some random thirteen-year-old named Tony. What if I'm actually your future great-nephew, the kid you'll suddenly decide to leave this house to seventy years later?"

Angelo laughed.

"And what if one of your last acts alive when you're totally ancient will be to send me Ted Williams's cap and tell me to give it the place of honor up in this room—the spiral on this shelf—so that I'll conjure you?"

"What the heck for?" Angelo said.

"To avenge your death?" Tony guessed.

Angelo held his hands over his eyes. He shuttered them open and closed. "Cuckoo!" he said.

"I'm kind of serious," Tony said. He told Angelo about his chat with goth-chick Sarah at Ye Olde Curiosity Shoppe. He explained about pawcorances and Algonquian vision quests and Minkowski's block universe theory. He described Sarah's hypothesis about how the time anomaly worked.

"Cuckoo!" Angelo said again, bending to tie his shoe. "Listen, whoever you are, I gotta go. I've only got a few minutes to change into my uniform and wolf a sandwich before I head over to Fenway for today's final game against the Tigers."

"But I'm not lying," Tony said. "I swear I'm your nephew."

"There's no way that can be true," Angelo said. "I'm an only child."

"Not for long," Tony said. He told Angelo what Michael had told *him* over pizza: that Angelo's mother, Isabella, would soon marry Antonio DiMarco, her new boarder, and have a baby boy named Guido—Angelo's half brother and Tony's future grandfather. "I'm Tony DiMarco," he concluded.

The color suddenly drained from Angelo's face. "Antonio DiMarco asked Mama out at breakfast this morning. To the movies, to see *Gone with the Wind*. She said yes. I couldn't believe it. Papa's only been gone a year."

"Antonio is actually the reason I conjured you back just now," Tony said. "I was wondering if you had any idea whether he *really* likes your Mama, or if he's just hoping to marry her and adopt you so he can get his hands on this house."

"I barely know the guy," Angelo shrugged. "He's fresh-off-the-boat Italian. But I'm liking him less and less by the minute. What makes you think he's after the house?"

Tony saw no choice but to come completely clean. "The police hauled my dad down to the station on suspicion of murdering you. Your lifelong best friend claims he saw Dad forcing you to sign this house over to me an hour or so before you died. He says the DiMarco family has been obsessed with owning Number Thirteen since Antonio was a boarder here."

"Which lifelong best friend?" Angelo said.

"Benedict Hagmann," Tony said. "He lives next door at Number Fifteen."

"Are you kidding?" Angelo said. "I *hate* Benny Hagmann. He's probably my worst enemy in the whole world!"

SOMETHING FISHY
SATURDAY, JULY 11, 2009

Tony's cell phone hooted once, like a cuckoo clock. (He hadn't quite figured out the ringtones yet.) "Hang on a sec," he said, pulling it out of his pocket and flipping it open. Julia had sent him a text: *No update on Dad. How's tour? Solving any crimes?* He thumb-typed her back: *Working on it.*

"What are you doing?" Angelo said.

"Sending a quick message," Tony said, holding up his phone.

"I don't see anything," Angelo said.

Oh right. Angelo couldn't see Tony's comforter or Snoop Dogg poster either. "Never mind," Tony said, shoving the phone back into his pocket. "Where were we?"

"How much I hate Benny Hagmann."

"Yeah, well at some point the two of you bury the hatchet

and become best buddies," Tony said. "Because he eventually ends up looking after you in your old age. Which is why you decide, at one point, to leave him this house."

"Not in a million years," Angelo said.

"Why not?" Tony said. "People change."

"Not the Hagmanns," Angelo said. "Benny and his friends call me Hootie instead of Angelo on account of my glasses, and *Wop*oriti instead of Saporiti because they hate all the Italian kids at school."

Tony refrained from commenting that Angelo had also reminded *him* of an owl, animal totem—wise.

"Plus Benny's father also happens to be Cyril Hagmann, Mama's mortgage collector."

"Cyril the Squirrel?" Tony said.

"Who made a special trip back here this morning to serve that eviction notice on Mama. And Benny tagged along, just so he could see my face. According to Cyril, if Mama chose to cook for half the Red Sox rather than pay her bills, she deserved to lose this house. He said the police would soon be escorting her off the premises, the bank would be putting Number Thirteen up for public auction, and he would be snapping it up himself for a bargain price. But nobody gets the best of Mama. She just turned the tables on him."

"How?" Tony said.

According to Angelo, Mama merely held the eviction notice up to Cyril's face, tore it to shreds, and showered it over his head like confetti. She reached into her apron pocket, pulled out a wad of cash, and slapped it into Cyril's hand. All paid up, she said. See you next month. By the way, your kid's fly is down. She then slammed the door in both their faces. After a good laugh, Angelo asked Mama where she suddenly got the money. Solly Weinberg, she said. He pulled her aside in the kitchen during the birthday dinner. At first she refused to take it. She didn't believe in charity—that was why she ran a boardinghouse—but Solly insisted. He'd made a pact when he turned thirteen never to let Cyril's father, Chester Hagmann, get his hands on the place. Mama would be doing him a favor by accepting a loan. He just hoped she and Angelo would make the same vow never to let a Hagmann set foot in the house. Which was exactly what they did then and there.

"So there's no way I would just up and give it to him," Angelo concluded. "Ever."

"That's weird," Tony said. "Old Man Hagmann made this big point earlier of telling me he didn't even *want* Number Thirteen, since he already owned the house next door."

"My foot," Angelo said. "If any family is obsessed with getting its greedy paws on the place, it's the Hagmanns."

"There's something fishy here," Tony said.

"Very fishy," Angelo agreed.

"I wonder why," Tony said. "I mean, it's not *that* nice."

"You think maybe Solly knows?" Angelo said. "I could ask him when I get to Fenway this afternoon. Wait, no I can't. He's probably on a train headed for California."

Tony wandered over to the pawcorance. He stared at Ted Williams's cap, still resting on the spiral. "Maybe there's another way to ask Solly."

"What? Conjure him up like you did with me?" Angelo said.

"Didn't he tell you he lived here himself till he was twenty-one and joined the team?" Tony said.

Angelo grinned. "I guess I'm going to be a little late for the game."

"I wouldn't want to get you in trouble with Cronin," Tony said.

"More trouble, you mean," Angelo said. "The press found Williams at my house."

"So how do we do it?" Angelo said. "Conjur up Solly, I mean."

"We need an object that connects him to you."

"What about this?" Angelo said. He tapped the 27 on the right sleeve of his jersey. "Mama sewed it on for me last night, but it would be easy enough to pull it off."

"Let's give it a try," Tony said.

As soon as Angelo had plucked off the patch, Tony suggested he place it on the spiral next to the cap—since he had the most direct connection to Solly. This Angelo did. They both looked around the room. Nobody.

"Wave your hand over the spiral," Tony said. Angelo did. "Feel any static electricity?" Angelo shook his head. "Hear any voices?" Nope.

They both took a seat on the bed.

They waited. They waited. They waited. Nothing.

"So if you're from the future, I guess you already know whether Williams agrees to play in today's game against the Tigers."

Tony nodded. "You told me yourself last Thanksgiving."

"What did I say?"

"The Sox swept the whole series. They took the lead over the Yankees. But it didn't help much. The Yankees came right back, even without Gehrig. At the end of the season, the Sox still ended up second, trailing the Yankees by something like seventeen games."

"What about Williams?"

"He was the team's star player, leading the league in RBIs," Tony said. "In fact, he played for the Sox his entire career—the Boston fans ended up loving him—and he turned out to be one of the greatest players of all time. Two-time Most Valuable

Player of the American League, two-time winner of the Triple Crown, inducted into the Hall of Fame in 1966. To this day he holds the record for the highest career batting average of any player with five hundred or more home runs."

"And Solly?" Angelo said, obviously impressed. "Is it true he never ends up having much of a baseball career?"

Tony confessed he had never even heard of Solomon Weinberg.

"What about me?" Angelo said. "Do I ever play professional ball?"

An awkward moment of silence. Tony didn't know *what* Zio Angelo ended up doing once he moved away from Boston at the age of twenty-one. But he was pretty sure it wasn't pro ball. Otherwise Zio Angelo would have told Tony all about it at Thanksgiving. It wasn't exactly the sort of thing you kept secret.

Angelo sighed. "It's because of my glasses, isn't it?" he said. "They get so darned fogged up when I run."

"At least you're not too fat to play," Tony said. "My brothers Mikey and Angey call me Ton-of-Bricks. They're twins."

"I used to be just as fat as you," Angelo said.

"How did you drop the weight?" Tony said.

"I stopped eating so much," Angelo said.

"Easier said than done." Tony sighed.

"Tell me about it," Angelo said. "Mama's constantly shoving

food at me. It's how Italian mothers show their love. I always ate whatever she put on my plate, without even thinking about it."

"So what did you do?" Tony said.

"I just started thinking about it," Angelo said. "I realized the trick is to stop eating as soon as you no longer feel hungry. If you wait until you feel full, you've already eaten way too much."

Tony pondered this. In truth, he never stopped eating until he felt *pain*.

"Plus you gotta exercise. Do calisthenics and stuff. That's what the Sox do to trim down during spring training," Angelo said.

"Like jumping jacks?" Tony said.

"And sit-ups and squat thrusts," Angelo said. They lapsed into a silence. "Too bad there's *nothing* I can do about my eyesight." Angelo sighed.

Tony wandered back to the pawcorance. He jiggled the 27 patch on the spiral. Still no static. Still no voices. Nothing. Something wasn't right.

His phone cuckooed with another message. He pulled it out. Julia again: *Dad update. Head home asap!* He texted back: *On my way.*

"You're doing it again," Angelo said.

"Sorry," Tony said. "I've got to go. Mom's got news about Dad."

"Just as well," Angelo said. "The later I am, the madder

Cronin is going to get. Should we try again when I get back from Fenway?"

They both decided to leave the cap on the pawcorance, to make it easier to connect with each other as they came and went.

"I guess I'll see you later," Tony said, heading for the door.

"Like in about seventy years," Angelo said.

They both started giggling like idiots.

Tony tiptoed down to the foyer. He could hear Julia's voice echoing from garden level. She was telling the twins to roll up the linoleum flooring in the mother-in-law room while she heated up the leftover pizza for lunch. He slipped out the front door. He had a good ten minutes to kill to make his walk home from the History Mystery Tour at all plausible to the twins. He wandered over to the grassy oval in the center of Hangmen Court. That was one ginormous oak tree. He wondered if he'd ever be thin enough to climb it. All sorts of graffiti had been carved into its trunk: lovers' hearts with people's names inside, *Don't Tread on Me!*, swear words, *Save the Union!*, people's initials, *Stop Hitler!*, years of graduating classes, *U.S. out of Vietnam!*, peace signs, *U.S. out of Iraq!*, smiley faces. Tony's eye caught on one heart in particular: *Antonio + Isabella. Vero amore.* His Italian wasn't great, but the heart sort of said it all.

Benedict Hagmann was full of it.

★ ★ ★

"I'm home!" he called, letting himself in the front door.

"We're in the kitchen," Julia called back.

Tony headed down there. Lunch was indeed leftover pizza and salad. Julia made room for him next to her on the bench in the eating nook. Even though she was trying to act normal, Tony could tell by the line between her eyebrows that it was only an act.

"Where's Dad?" Angey said.

"At the lawyer's," Tony lied. "The paperwork wasn't quite ready when he got to Birnbaum's office this morning. He decided to go on the tour with me first, then circle back. He said he'll text Mom when he's done."

Julia handed him a paper plate with two slices of pizza on it.

"Just one," Tony said. "And some salad."

"Too many Snickers bars?" Mikey snorted.

"You *want* me to stay fat, don't you?" Tony said. "Because it makes you feel all superior. Well, sorry to disappoint you."

Angey looked over, surprised.

"How about we try to have a meal that doesn't involve a fight?" Julia said. She nonetheless squeezed Tony's knee under the table. "How was the tour?"

Tony didn't get a chance to answer. The front doorbell rang.

"I'll go," Angey said. He ducked out the door beneath the stoop to see who it was.

"Nice job, by the way, weaseling out of moving all that furniture onto the back deck," Mikey said. "Don't worry, the real fun begins this afternoon with floor sanding."

Angey returned with the cable guy.

"Finally," Mikey said. "What took you so long?"

The cable guy stared at him blankly.

"Why don't you two show him which rooms need data ports?" Julia said to the twins. "You're almost finished, and Tony just sat down."

"Follow me," Angey said to the cable guy.

"I hope you brought plenty of extra cable this time," Mikey said.

Together they led him up to parlor level.

Finally Julia was able to give Tony a quick update. The police had let Michael make one phone call at noon. He'd told her he'd spent the entire morning being interrogated at the station, first by one detective, then the other. But they were not letting him go until both detectives met with the coroner who had examined Zio Angelo's body and signed his death certificate. Meantime, Michael was still being held in the interrogation room for further questioning. Birnbaum was trying his best to find him a good criminal lawyer, since he only did estate planning himself.

"Shouldn't we tell the twins?" Tony said.

"Your father was absolutely convinced they would let him go

once they'd read the coroner's report," Julia said, sighing. "He insisted he'd be home by supper, latest. Meantime, he just wants you and me to keep acting normal. Whatever *that* means."

"Mind if I skip the floor sanding after lunch?" Tony said. "Old Man Hagmann collared me on my way out the door this morning. He gave me an earful about all his allegations against Dad. I'm pretty sure I can prove most of them are wack."

"Just don't do anything dangerous," Julia said.

The twins trooped back into the kitchen.

"Best the cable guy can promise is to get the first and second floors wired today," Mikey told Julia.

"He said we should look into Wi-Fi for the top two floors," Angey added.

"I'll talk to your father about it," Julia said, vaguely.

Speaking of which. Tony pulled out his phone, pretending he'd just gotten a message. "It's Dad," he said. "He wants me to meet him at the lawyer's office. He says I have to sign some of the paperwork myself, since I actually own this place."

"Don't even tell me you're dogging us with all the sanding," Mikey said.

Angey swiped the phone out of Tony's hand. "He's totally lying. His phone didn't even ring."

"I set it on vibrate," Tony said, hoping it wouldn't start to cuckoo.

"I don't see any texts from Dad here," Angey said. "Just a couple from Mom."

"That's because your father took my phone this morning," Julia said. "His was out of juice. I'm charging it now."

"Oh," Angey said, disappointed. He handed Tony's phone back.

Tony took a bite of pizza, followed by a forkful of salad. Angelo had suggested he stop eating as soon as he no longer felt hunger. But it wasn't going to be easy for him to guess when that was, since he hadn't felt hungry for lunch to begin with.

Uh-oh. Benedict Hagmann straight ahead on Hanover Street, blocking the way to Ye Olde Curiosity Shoppe. The old man appeared to be lost in concentration, comparing the ingredients on two different bottles of bug spray at a sidewalk stand of gardening supplies out in front of the hardware store. Tony dove behind a clearance rack of seeds a few feet away. What was Hagmann toying with around his neck? Some sort of charm on a silver chain. No way! Three interconnected spirals, carved out of white stone or bone.

Hang on! Could it actually be the pawcorance the Hagmanns were after—so they could do a little time traveling of their own?

Hagmann's face suddenly froze in horror. He fingered the entire length of the chain. He patted his shirt. He checked his pants pockets. He stooped forward and began searching the sidewalk for whatever he'd lost. Tony seized his chance. He tiptoed behind Hagmann's back and ducked into the curiosity shop next door.

"Hello?"

The place appeared to be completely empty.

"Sarah?"

No answer. He wandered over to the wall of books. *Secrets of the Lost Civilization of Maya. Quantum Mechanics for Better Living. Hatha Yoga and You. White Witchcraft Made Easy.* He wondered, not for the first time, if Mildred Pickles—whoever she might be— was a complete lunatic. Then he reminded himself: He had just spent half the morning hanging out with his dead great-uncle.

A whole section of the bookcase suddenly opened. Tony had to jump out of the way to avoid being flattened like a cartoon character. Sarah wafted out of a narrow passageway containing a rickety staircase that led up to the floor above. She was eating a piece of sushi from a bento box with a pair of purple chopsticks. "Sorry about that," she said. "Want a shumai dumpling?"

"I'm good," Tony said.

"So how did it go with the pawcorance? Was my hypothesis correct?"

"Not a hundred percent," Tony admitted. "I was definitely

able to reconjure Angelo with the ball cap. But then we tried to conjure this other kid named Solly with the arm-patch number from his Red Sox uniform. He never turned up."

"How old was Angelo in 1939?" Sarah asked. "Exactly, I mean."

"Thirteen," Tony said. "And a day. Why?"

"And how old was this Solly you were trying to conjure?"

Tony shrugged. "Twenty? He didn't live in the house after that. His family sold it when he was twenty-one, as soon as he joined the team."

"Follow me," Sarah said. She led him over to the slate counter. Setting the bento box aside, she reached for a gigantic leather-bound book resting on the spiral—*The Compleat Numerologist*—which was already open to the first page of Chapter 13. "It struck me—after you left this morning—that your anomaly was probably triggered somehow by the interaction of the numbers thirteen and nine," Sarah said. "So I decided to brush up on some basic numerology. I'm pretty convinced your pawcorance can only connect thirteen-year-olds to each other."

Sarah explained: The number thirteen had *always* been troublesome when it came to time. That's because there were thirteen lunations—full moons—to a solar year, and so far no culture in the history of humankind had ever been able to divide a year into a nice neat thirteen-month calendar without a few pesky minutes and seconds left over. The twelve-month Gregorian calendar used today was totally inaccurate. When you did the exact math, a year was 365.2422 days long. Almost a quarter of a day had to get lopped off at the end of most years, with an extra day added back to February—a leap year—every fourth year. (Same was true of the Jewish calendar, by the way, even though it was actually based on the thirteen lunations; the Sanhedrin still had to add the occasional leap month to sync everything up.) The Aztecs had probably come the closest with an eighteen-month calendar of twenty-day weeks, cycling over fifty-two years. But even *they* had had extra time left over— which, they believed, was responsible for that tiny bit of chaos in ordinary existence they called *change.* "In other words," Sarah concluded, "I think the number thirteen is an anomaly in itself. It probably keeps time marching forward—causing change as it does so—but, in the process, also creates anomalies in the space-time continuum."

"For thirteen-year-old boys," Tony said.

"Or girls," Sarah said. "Just because you've only conjured a boy doesn't mean you couldn't, in theory, conjure a girl."

"Noted," Tony said.

"Here's something else," Sarah said. "The prime thirteen inhabits that transitional space between single- and double-digit numbers."

"What about eleven?" Tony said. "That's also a prime."

"Except that eleven's chief characteristic, mathematically, is to stay the *same*. Eleven times two is twenty-two. If we're talking about change, here, thirteen is totally that awkward age between childhood and adulthood. The perfect moment, really, to enter an anomaly. All very scientific, when you think about it."

Tony wouldn't have gone *that* far. But he did see Sarah's point. "So let me get this straight," he said. "If I want to conjure Solly, it'll have to be when he's thirteen. But to do that, I'll need to find an object that connects him to thirteen-year-old Angelo."

"I'd start with an object that contains the number nine," Sarah said.

"Why's that?" Tony said.

"It's all right here in Chapter Nine," she said, flipping to a dog-eared page closer to the front of the book. "The symbol for nine is, in fact, a simplified spiral. And mathematically, nine does the same thing—it turns in on itself." She drew it out with a purple pencil as she explained: Whenever you multiply nine by any number other than zero, the sum of the digits in the total is always nine ($9 \times 2 = 18$, $1 + 8 = 9$; or $9 \times 13 = 117$, $1 + 1 + 7 = 9$). "Bottom line?" Sarah said. "Nine can't help but seek out and return, time and again, to its own nine-ishness."

"Wow," Tony said. "That's intense."

"No doubt why the anomaly only connects thirteen-year-olds

in years ending in nine," Sarah said, closing *The Compleat Numerologist* with a satisfied thwack. "And probably why the object being used to establish the connection between two thirteen-year-olds needs to contain the essence of nine."

"Like the number on Ted Williams's baseball cap!" Tony said.

The front door jangled. Tony's heart leaped to his throat. What if Old Man Hagmann had spied him through the display window? It wasn't him. It was just some random guy with crazy white hair zigzagging out of his head like lightning bolts.

"Video shop's a couple of doors down," Tony said.

"I don't want to rent a video," Zigzag said. "I'm here to look at snow globes with Boston scenes inside."

"They're over next to the geodes," Sarah said. "I'll be right there."

"I have one more question," Tony said. "Are pawcorances supervaluable?"

"If you're Algonquian, I guess," said Sarah. "As a curiosity, they're only worth a couple of hundred bucks. They aren't very rare. Hundreds of them are still scattered across New England."

"But mine still works," Tony said. "Do you think *that* would make it valuable enough to, say, murder someone for it?"

"Only if you're thirteen," Sarah smiled. "Otherwise, it's just a slab of slate carved with a spiral, right?"

"I guess," Tony said.

"Why do you ask?"

Tony quickly told her about the Hagmanns and their obsession to own 13 Hangmen Court. As far as he could tell, though, there wasn't anything even remotely special about the town house, apart from the pawcorance in his room. But all the Hagmanns who seemed to want the place were way over thirteen.

"Interesting," Sarah said. "Mildred has an excellent genealogy book on Boston. I'll skim through it as soon as I get rid of the tourist."

Tony told Sarah he would give her his cell phone number so they could update each other. He pulled one of Mildred Pickles's business cards from the holder on the counter. He flipped it over and wrote out his number on the back. He tucked another card into his wallet, just in case. "Where *is* Mildred Pickles?" he said. "How come I've never seen her?"

"She's here most of the time," Sarah said, shrugging. "*I'm* usually at my real job."

"Where's that?" Tony said. If she had a real job, did that mean she was sixteen?

Before she could answer, Zigzag wandered over. "That's a great flag," he said, pointing to the Stars and Stripes above Sarah's head. "Good ol' Betsy Ross. Is it for sale?"

Tony and Sarah rolled their eyes at each other.

Tourist.

★ ★ ★

Angelo was lying on the brass bed when Tony let himself into the attic. "I'm listening to the end of the game on my new radio," he said. He wasn't dressed in his uniform now. He was wearing a pair of Levi's and a checked shirt. "Ted Williams is playing, just like you predicted. He just hit a home run, even though his ankle's all taped up. The Sox are ahead by a mile."

"Why aren't you there?" Tony said.

"Cronin fired Solly last night for dragging Williams away from the game. And he fired me today, as soon as I got to Fenway, for giving them a place to hide. Cronin told the press it was a loyal Sox fan—Cyril Hagmann!—who tipped him off as to Williams's whereabouts. Cyril claimed he grew concerned when he saw number 27, Weinberg, filling Williams's head full of Commie-Jew notions of equality by showing him an immigrant slum in the North End."

"Ouch," Tony said.

"No wonder you've never heard of Solly," Angelo said. "Cyril the Squirrel gets him blackballed from the major leagues."

"Jerk," Tony said.

"So what's the news on your dad?"

"Not good," Tony said. He explained what Julia had told him at lunch—that Michael was being held at the station, pending further investigation. Which was why they really needed to try conjuring Solly again—*thirteen-year-old* Solly—so they could get to the bottom of why it was the Hagmanns, not the DiMarcos, who were desperate to own No. 13. Tony told Angelo about his most recent chat with Sarah, and how they needed to find a new object with nine-ish energy.

"Hey, how about that prayer scroll?" Angelo said. "The one Solly tucked into Ted Williams's cap at my birthday dinner? He said he'd been carrying it around with him since he was a kid."

"What's nine-ish about that?" Tony asked.

"Just before he tucked it into Williams's cap, he sprinkled it with nine pinches of sugar—remember? He said some prayer in Hebrew nine times."

Tony crossed the room and grabbed the cap off the pawcorance. He checked behind the 9 of the inside brim. The scroll was gone—

And so was Angelo.

Panicked, Tony placed the cap back on the spiral. Angelo materialized on the bed before his very eyes, grinning like the Cheshire cat. "How spooky was that?" Angelo said.

"The scroll's not there anymore," Tony said.

"I know," Angelo laughed. "I was just telling you when you disappeared. I took it out. It kept scratching my forehead while I was trying to make the cap fit better." Angelo unscrewed the brass knob of the right bedpost. Out of it he pulled a small,

rolled-up piece of parchment. "Solly told us it was for protection," he said, sheepishly. "And you've got to admit this room is
awful creepy. At least now I know why."

"Go ahead and place it on the spiral," Tony said.

Angelo hoisted himself off the bed and joined Tony at the
pawcorance. He set the scroll next to the cap. They both hovered their hands over it. Tony's palm began to itch. He could
tell by Angelo's grin that he too could feel the static electricity.

"I think it must be working," Tony said. "Can you hear the
echo of a boy's voice?"

Angelo nodded. "It's faint, though. I can't make out what
he's saying."

"Maybe Solly is too far away," Tony said.

"What do we do?" Angelo said.

"Wait for him to hear *our* voices, I guess," Tony said.

"Prayer scroll!" Angelo shouted. "On the spiral! Now."

Nothing.

"This could take ages," Angelo said. "How should we kill
the time?"

Tony had an idea. But he could feel himself going red at the
very thought of it.

"What?" Angelo said.

"You told me the Sox did weight-loss exercises as part of their
spring training," Tony said. "Maybe you could teach me a few."

"Why not?" Angelo shrugged.

"Let me just change into a pair of gym shorts and a tank top," Tony said, relieved. "It's kind of hot up here."

"Not for me," Angelo said, flopping on the bed. "So far it's been a pretty rainy May." He started tossing the brass knob with one hand, catching it with the other. "What's wrong?" he said when he noticed Tony hadn't moved.

"Aren't you going to step outside?" Tony said.

"What for?" Angelo said. "I spend half the afternoon watching the Red Sox get dressed and undressed—well, until today, that is."

"I'm kind of shy," Tony admitted. "The twins give me a pretty hard time about my weight."

"You think *I'm* going to make fun of you?" Angelo said. "I used to be way fatter than you."

Tony pulled off his polo shirt and dropped it to the floor.

"Go on," Angelo said. "Time's a-wasting."

Tony shucked off his jeans.

"Underwear sure hasn't changed much," Angelo said, yawning. "Hang on a sec—where did your clothes go?"

"They're right there," Tony said, pointing.

"More spookiness," Angelo said. "I can't see your shirt or your jeans anymore."

"Try taking off your T-shirt," Tony said.

Angelo did. It vanished. "Very weird," Tony said. He went to the dresser and pulled his favorite tank top out of the second drawer. He tugged it over his head. "Can you see what I'm wearing now?"

"SpongeBob for President?" Angelo laughed.

"Maybe all we can take into the anomaly is the clothes on our backs," Tony said. He fished the cell phone out of his jeans pocket. "Which is why you can't see this."

"See what?"

"It's a phone," Tony said. "They're wireless in my time. Everybody has one. We take them with us wherever we go. It's what I was fiddling with earlier."

"Rats!" Angelo said. "I'd love a look at one of *those*."

Tony pulled on a pair of basketball shorts. "Apart from each other, we only seem to be able to see stuff from our own times."

"So how come we can both see this bed?" Angelo said. "And that dresser, and the bookcase over there?"

"I don't know," Tony said. "Because I can't see the quilt your mama made *on* the bed, any more than you can see my Red Sox comforter. You can't see my murder mysteries, and I can't see your Hardy Boys books. Maybe all we can see is stuff from the house that exists for both of us."

Angelo hopped off the bed and had a look through the dresser drawers. "You're right," he said. "It's just my own socks and underwear inside."

"I guess that's why we can both see Ted Williams's cap," Tony said.

"I wonder why you can also see Solly's prayer scroll," Angelo said. "It wasn't in the cap by the time you got it."

"It must belong to the house somehow," Tony said.

They both glanced over at the pawcorance. Still no Solly.

"Ready to sweat?" Angelo said.

"I guess," Tony said.

Angelo taught Tony several old-school calisthenics. First jumping jacks, then sit-ups, then push-ups. Tony got winded pretty fast. After ten squat thrusts, he suggested they take a break. They both sat on the floor, leaning against the foot of the bed. Tony noticed Angelo's glasses had fogged up. "I almost forgot," he said. He grabbed his jeans, which were still lying on the floor. From the back pocket he pulled the page he had printed off the Internet. (By the time he got home from Ye Olde Curiosity Shoppe, the cable guy had finished installing broadband in Michael's new office, and Julia had set up Michael's laptop and printer so they could all check emails.) He unfolded the printout and offered it to Angelo.

"Um, I don't see anything," Angelo said.

"I guess I'll just read it to you," Tony said. "It's the history of contact lenses."

"What're they?" Angelo said.

"Like tiny eyeglasses you wear directly on your eyeballs," Tony said.

Angelo laughed.

Tony told him he was totally serious. All the big sports stars would eventually wear them. According to Wikipedia, Angelo would only have to wait another decade before scientists invented hard lenses.

As soon as they did, Angelo should get a pair. He'd never fog up again.

"Do they hurt?" Angelo said.

"You'll barely notice they're in your eyes," Tony said. "Especially when soft lenses come out in the 1970s."

"What's Wikipedia?" Angelo said.

Tony didn't even begin to know how to explain the Internet. Luckily, he didn't have to. They were interrupted by a voice:

"What's going on here?"

A kid their age was standing at the pawcorance. It was Solly, of course. But as a thirteen-year-old. He was dressed in a black wool suit, there was a yarmulke pinned to the back of his head, and his face was framed by long brown curls. Tony thought they looked a little like ram horns and wondered if the ram was his animal totem.

"Solomon Weinberg?" he asked.

Solly nodded, startled.

"Hurray!" Angelo said. "It finally worked!"

"Who are you, and what are you doing in my room?" Solly said. He had an unexpectedly thick Yiddish accent, one he would obviously lose by the time he became a benchwarmer for the Sox.

Tony introduced himself and Angelo. He explained they were both from the future—well, sort of. Tony was actually sitting on the floor of his attic bedroom in 2009, whereas Angelo, here, was in his *own* bedroom in 1939. That was all because of an anomaly in Minkowski's block universe. Tony launched into an explanation of how the top floor of 13 Hangmen Court acted as a weird sort of time machine—

Solly strode over to the door and opened it. "Scram!" he said.

"Wait, I can prove it," Tony said. "You just turned thirteen, didn't you?"

Solly nodded uncertainly.

"And you just set a prayer scroll on the spiral, right?"

"That doesn't prove you're from the future," Solly said. "It just proves you've been spying on me. Why? I swear I don't know anything about that molasses!"

Molasses? Who said anything about molasses?

Tony explained how the prayer scroll would eventually end up in the brim of that baseball cap on the shelf, a present to Angelo from a Red Sox outfielder. Angelo—who was actually Tony's great-uncle—would give that cap to Tony for *his* thirteenth birthday. Setting both the cap and the scroll on the spiral was how they were all connected, why they were all in the attic at the same time. See?

"No," said Solly. "Any more than I see a Red Sox cap."

"Ted Williams doesn't exist for him yet," Angelo whispered to Tony. "Like your cell phone doesn't exist for me. The best way to prove we're from the future is to say something that's going to happen."

"You know him better than I do," Tony said.

"Scram!" Solly said. "Now. I mean it."

"Wait, I know!" Angelo said. "Something happened to you today, on your birthday, something you'll never forget because of this house, a rusty molasses tank, and some guy named Finn McGinley."

Solly suddenly went very pale. He closed the door. "Who told you that?"

"You did. On *my* thirteenth birthday. By then you're an outfielder for the Sox, though to be honest, your career gets sort of ruined at my party."

"Is Finn OK?" Solly asked. "I'm waiting for word from him."

"I have no idea," Angelo admitted. "The press arrived before you got the chance to finish your story. All I know is that a Hagmann is involved somehow. *Chester* Hagmann."

"Which is actually why we conjured you," Tony said. "We've both got serious issues with our own Hagmanns over this house."

"It's all because of my big mouth," Solly sighed, taking a seat beside the other boys on the floor.

"What is?" Angelo said.

"Chester Hagmann has just double-crossed Finn into selling him this house. Otherwise the Irish mob will make Finn a pair of cement shoes and sink him to the bottom of the Charles River, all on account of that worthless molasses. Unless, that is, Finn really *does* know a way to beat Hagmann at his own game."

"Hang on, hang on," Tony said. "Start from the beginning."

"I should have known what kind of day it would turn out to be, just by the crazy weather outside," Solly began.

SOLLY

How Solly Saved 13 Hangmen Court with a Ring

WEDNESDAY, JANUARY 15, 1919

Solly actually began the morning of his thirteenth birthday in good spirits. There was still a week left of winter break from school, it was a beautiful springlike day—very unusual for mid-January in Boston—and he was off to the synagogue to memorize the Torah passage he would be reciting for his bar mitzvah Saturday morning.

He just had one slightly unpleasant errand to run first.

Solly found Finn McGinley, the owner of the run-down town house his family rented—13 Hangmen Court—exactly where Mameh said he would: in the boarded-up pub at the corner that used to be called One-Eyed Jack's. And just as Mameh had predicted, Finn was perched on a stool at the end of the grimy bar, smoking a cigar and reading the *Boston Globe*. His makeshift office. Solly's only surprise was the slumlord's age; Finn couldn't be much more than twenty-five.

"I'm here to pay the rent on Number Thirteen," Solly said.

"About time," Finn said without looking up. "It's two weeks late."

"I've only got half," Solly admitted. "It's been slow at the deli where my mother waitresses—on account of the holidays. What little tip money she made had to go to the doctor treating my baby sister's polio. Plus my father hasn't been shipped back yet from the trenches in France, where he's been fighting the Germans. And his soldier's pay seems to be lost in the mail."

"You know how many hard-luck stories I hear a day?" Finn said.

Solly exploded with anger. "Shame on you!" he shouted. "You grew up in the North End. Have you already forgotten what it was like for *your* folks to start a new life in a new country? It's a *shanda*, I say—a shame." Solly instantly regretted his outburst. Mameh was always chiding him for making things worse with his sass.

Surprisingly, Finn didn't get angry. He looked up from his paper and started to laugh. "If it isn't Solly Weinberg," he said.

Solly nodded, mystified. Why would Finn know his name?

"Your thirteenth birthday must be coming up."

"It's today," Solly said.

"Time flies," Finn said, shaking his head. "Tell your mam she can pay me the rest when she's ready."

"I—I don't understand," Solly stammered. "Why the change of heart?"

"I *haven't* forgotten," Finn said. "I lived over at Number Thirteen myself when I was your age—back when the North End was still known as Little Dublin. I slept up in the attic, just like you. And I wanted to play ball for the Sox, just like you, back when they were still called the Pilgrims. Hadn't you better be getting to bar mitzvah practice?"

Solly nodded. How did Finn know all this?

"Well, off you get, then. You don't want to make the rabbi angry, or he won't let you plant that tree tonight."

Solly turned to leave, utterly baffled. It was as though this young Irishman could read his mind. On his way out, he nearly collided with Chester Hagmann, who was just swinging through the saloon doors. What was *he* doing here? Hagmann was the owner of Purity, a factory behind the synagogue that distilled molasses into fuel for munitions. He was also Finn McGinley's rival slumlord in the North End—owner, in fact, of No. 15 next door. Everyone knew the two men couldn't stand each other.

Solly stooped and pretended to tie his shoe so he could eavesdrop.

"Where's the rent on my tank?" Hagmann said to Finn. "It's two weeks late."

"You've got some nerve," Finn said. "Every drop of molasses in it is worthless, now the armistice has been signed and the demand for munitions has vanished. *You* won't even buy the stuff off me, and the tank is sitting in your yard."

"Not my problem," Hagmann said. "Next time read the *Globe* instead of the racing form before making an investment." He pulled a document out of the breast pocket of his suit jacket and laid it in front of Finn. "It's a deed transfer. You know very well you can clear your debt with a single signature."

"I won't sell you Number Thirteen and that's final," Finn said.

"We'll see about that," Hagmann said, repocketing the document. "You have until the end of the day to pay up—or else." He strode out of the pub.

Solly thought it best to follow.

Except that Finn's body went completely rigid. His eyes rolled back in his head. He flopped face-first onto the zinc countertop. Solly raced over. Was the Irishman dead? No, he was still breathing. What was more, his eyes were darting back and forth beneath their lids. Solly tried to shake Finn awake. He merely shuddered and mumbled as though he were dreaming. Solly wasn't sure what to do next—fetch a doctor?

Finn sat bolt upright. "Where's Hagmann?"

"Gone," Solly said.

"Did he see me keel over?"

"I don't think so," Solly said.

"Close call," Finn said. "I made a pact with a bunch of child-hood buddies, see, never to sell Number Thirteen to a Hagmann. And I'm a man of my word."

"Are you OK?" Solly said.

"Fit as a fiddle," Finn said. He could plainly see, though, that Solly wasn't so sure. "I just fall asleep sometimes, all of a sudden like." Finn explained the technical name for it was narcolepsy. He'd been having sleeping fits ever since he was a boy. Doctors all told him the same thing: it was hereditary, there was no way to wake him, there was no cure. The fits were brought on by stress, Finn said. And he was under a great deal of that at the moment. A few of his recent ventures hadn't panned out. Plus he'd had a couple of unlucky afternoons at the track.

Solly didn't know how to respond. Why would Finn—a complete stranger—be telling *him* all this?

"Lucky for me, I have a plan," Finn said, winking. He tapped the *Globe*'s front-page headline: *Congress to Ratify Prohibition Tomorrow.* "Because as a matter of fact, I *do* read more than the racing form."

Before Finn could elaborate, another man strode into the bar.

Solly recognized him immediately. Frank Wallace, leader of the notorious Gustin Gang—the Irish mob that now terrorized all the Jewish business owners of the North End.

"Surprised you're not taking one of your little naps," Wallace said, grinning and slapping Finn on the back. He turned to Solly. "I've known this guy since he was your age. Always sleeping on the job."

"I've got a little business proposition for you, Frank," Finn said.

"Was a time you were too good for the Wallaces," Frank said.

"Times have changed," Finn said.

Wallace jerked his thumb at Solly. "Who's the kid?"

"My new errand boy," Finn said, flashing Solly a grin. "He's OK."

New errand boy? Since when?

"Well, spit it out," Wallace said. "I ain't got all day."

"When Prohibition gets ratified by Congress tomorrow, it'll be illegal to make or sell another drop of booze after exactly one year's time," Finn said.

"So?" Wallace said.

"So you should buy up every drop of the molasses I've got stored in a tank over at Purity and turn it into cheap rum. You'll make a fortune over the next twelve months. I'd even consider reopening One-Eyed Jack's and letting you sell it here—for a small taste of the profits, of course."

"I'm listening," Wallace said. He perched on a bar stool while Finn gave him the particulars: how much molasses was actually in the tank, what sort of discount Finn would be willing to offer the Wallaces per gallon, who in the North End would have the equipment to distill it. Frank pulled out his wallet and handed Finn a wad of cash. Would this do as a down payment? Finn counted it out. Yup, that'd do nicely. The two men shook. Wallace departed, whistling.

Finn looked surprisingly sad. "That was a bitter pill to swallow," he said to Solly. "When I was your age, I secretly helped Boston's future mayor put Frank Wallace's brother Stevie behind bars—back when the Gustin Gang was still known as the Tailboard Thieves. But I've *got* to pay Hagmann before the end of the day."

"What's this about being your new errand boy?" Solly said.

Finn pulled a small duffel bag out from behind the bar. He stuffed the cash into it. He slid the duffel across the countertop to Solly.

"Make this one delivery on your way over to the synagogue, and your mother can consider last month's rent fully paid," Finn said. "Whaddya say?"

★ ★ ★

Solly waited in a chair outside Chester Hagmann's office. His stomach had been growling since he'd gotten to Purity; the entire factory smelled like homemade cookies. And lunch was still a long way off. He checked his pocket watch again. He was late for bar mitzvah practice. And Finn was right: he *didn't* want to make Rabbi Zuckerman angry. Not only was today Solly's birthday—the fourteenth day of Shevat, 5679, by the Jewish calendar—tomorrow was the holiday Tu B'Shevat, the New Year for Trees. Which is why the rabbi had picked Solly especially to plant a sapling in the synagogue's front garden at tonight's sunset ceremony.

How had Finn known that?

Hagmann's secretary told Solly to step inside. Solly found the factory's owner behind a gigantic oak desk at the far end of a long, wood-paneled room.

"You again!" Hagmann frowned.

"Special delivery from Finn McGinley," Solly said, setting the duffel on his blotter. "Should be all there." He turned to leave.

Hagmann told him to take a seat. He didn't trust Finn McGinley any more than he trusted a Jew-boy. He would need to count out every penny. Reluctantly, Solly perched on the edge of a chair and watched while Hagmann sorted bills into piles.

"McGinley is only delaying the inevitable," Hagmann muttered. "It's just a matter of time before he loses everything at Suffolk Downs—including Thirteen Hangmen Court."

For some reason, Hagmann's smugness got Solly's goat.

"I wouldn't count on it," Solly blurted. "As soon as Congress ratifies Prohibition tomorrow, Finn will be rolling in dough."

"What makes you think that?" Hagmann said.

"He just sold every drop of his molasses to Frank Wallace," Solly said. "He's going to turn it into cheap rum and sell it. Finn's going to reopen One-Eyed Jack's."

A slow, hideous grin spread across Hagmann's face, one that gave Solly a chill. "All's well that ends well, I guess," he said. "The rent's all here. You can go."

Solly made his way through a forest of rusty holding tanks in Purity's yard. The synagogue was just over the fence. He felt a sudden pang of guilt. Though Finn hadn't explicitly told Solly to keep his plan a secret, it certainly wasn't Solly's place to blab it to Hagmann. Especially not after Finn had given Mameh a break on the rent. Why couldn't he ever keep his big mouth shut? He saw no other choice but to return to Finn's office after bar mitzvah practice and confess what he'd done. Hopefully Finn would still be there—though he wasn't looking forward to how the Irishman might react.

Some birthday this was turning out to be!

★ ★ ★

Finn was still there.

But so was Chester Hagmann. And he was once again setting that deed transfer in front of Finn to sign.

"Didn't Solly deliver the duffel bag?" Finn said.

"He did," Hagmann said.

"Then I should be all paid up," Finn said.

"You are. That's not why you're going to sign Number Thirteen over to me."

"So why would I do that?"

"Consider it a fair trade for my help out of your current dilemma," Hagmann said.

"What dilemma?" Finn said.

"When I suggested you read the *Globe*, I meant beyond the headlines," Hagmann sneered. "As soon as Prohibition becomes law, only *existing* rum producers will have a year to phase out their operations. It will become a federal crime for anyone new, like Frank Wallace, to make rum—or for you to reopen this bar."

Finn went very pale.

"So I'd say your dilemma is fairly obvious," Hagmann continued. "If you tell Wallace the molasses he just bought is worthless, you're likely to find yourself in a pair of cement shoes at the bottom of the Charles. If you don't tell him—and he blithely starts making rum—I'll be forced to inform the authorities, seeing how the holding tank is actually mine and I wouldn't want to be implicated, whereupon you'll both likely end up behind bars. You could, of course, give Wallace his money back. Except that it's now sitting in my bank account. Lucky for you, it's the exact amount I'm willing to pay for Thirteen Hangmen Court." Hagmann handed Finn the fountain pen out of his pocket.

"Who told you about my deal with Wallace?" Finn said.

Hagmann pointed over to Solly.

Finn's eyes rolled back in his head. He dropped the pen. His arms and legs went completely rigid. He flopped face-first onto the bar.

"What's wrong with him?" Hagmann said, alarmed.

"It's a sleeping fit," Solly said.

"Well wake him up!" Hagmann said.

"I can't," Solly said. "No one can. He told me it's a rare condition. It's brought on by stressful situations. Who knows when he'll wake up?"

Hagmann tugged the deed transfer out from under Finn's nose. He wiped off the drool, then tucked it back into his pocket. "Tell him to bring me the deed to Number Thirteen by the end of the day, or else." He turned to leave.

"You're nothing but a dirty double-crosser!" Solly shouted.

"Do you think a little double-crossing would stop me?" Hagmann laughed. "My family has been waiting for *generations* to get back what is rightfully ours. I suppose I have you to thank for making that possible." He strode out.

A moment later, Finn woke up. Solly immediately began babbling an apology. It was all his fault. Now Finn would be forced to break that pact with his childhood friends. Now he'd have to sell 13 Hangmen Court to a Hagmann. And now a Hagmann would surely turn Solly and his family out onto the streets.

Finn laid a consoling hand on Solly's shoulder. "I should never have done business with a Hagmann in the first place," he said. "It's *my* fault for thinking I could outwit this day. But here it is anyway. At least I know exactly what I need to do to get the best of Chester Hagmann."

"What?" Solly said. "I'll help!"

"You can start by taking the same oath against the Hagmanns that I did," Finn said. He pulled a gold band off his finger—two hands clasping a crowned heart—and slipped it onto Solly's. "Swear by this ring. It binds one Irishman to another by the heart of love, the hands of friendship, and the crown of loyalty. My brother Paddy gave me this one on *my* thirteenth birthday."

"But I'm Jewish!" Solly said. "I'm not allowed to swear by false idols or symbols."

"Just promise," Finn said. "One day you'll understand why."

Solly promised he would never let a Hagmann own No. 13—the least he could do for having just ruined Finn's life.

"Good lad," Finn said. "Now you're assured the luck of the Irish. This very ring saved Paddy from a different Wallace and foiled a different Hagmann."

And he launched into the tale of how.

Solly interrupted. "Sorry, but what are we going to do to get the best of Chester Hagmann? We only have until the end of the day."

Finn told him to listen very carefully. He should go straight to the giant oak in the center of Hangmen Court. He should circle the base of its trunk until he spied a hollow formed by its gnarled roots. Tucked into that hollow he would find a wrought-iron door knocker bearing the same symbol as the ring he was now wearing. He should rehang the knocker on the door of No. 13, in its original holes. Any neighborhood cop or fire-man—they were all Irishmen in Boston—who saw the knocker would think an Irish family still lived there, and would do his best to protect the house from harm.

"Harm? What kind of harm?" Solly said.

"Just hang that knocker and everything should be fine," Finn said. "Then wait up in your room. Neither you nor your mam should answer the door for anyone."

"Until when?" Solly said. "Until I hear from you?"

"That may take a while," Finn said.

"What about Tu B'Shevat?" Solly said. "The ceremony is at sunset."

Finn tugged at one of Solly's curls. "With any luck, you'll still get to plant that tree," he said. He checked his pocket watch. "I'd better go. I don't have much time."

"For what?"

"Trust me," Finn said. "You'll know soon enough." He escorted Solly to the door. He shook his hand and wished him *mazel tov!* on his birthday. He strode down Charter Street without looking back.

Solly glanced at the upper right-hand corner of the doorpost. He had already found the knocker. He'd dusted it off. He'd fitted it into its original holes in the door—ones he'd never really noticed before—so it looked as though an Irish family lived at No. 13.

Except for the mezuzah in the upper-right corner.

Should he take it down? Did he dare?

He knew from his bar mitzvah studies that moving a mezuzah was against Talmudic law. The whole point was to proclaim that Jews lived within who believed in the one true God. The mezuzah case was inscribed with the Hebrew letter *shin*, the first letter of the *Shema Yisrael* prayer. *Hear O Israel...*

Trust me. That's what Finn had said.

Solly pried the mezuzah out of the rotting wood with his penknife. He opened the case. He pulled out the prayer scroll inside it and tucked it into his pocket, knowing the mezuzah was now deconsecrated. At least this way, whatever happened, he would be carrying his faith with him wherever he went. Out of his back pocket he dug the handful of sugar he'd taken from the bowl in the kitchen. He placed a pinch inside the case instead, and chanted a Hebrew prayer for protection against his foes, one Mameh had taught him from the Old Country: *In the name of Abraham, Isaac, and Jacob . . .* He repeated this eight more times. He slipped Finn's ring off his finger. He couldn't possibly wear it to the tree planting. Instead, he placed it in the case for safekeeping. Now it was a supersugared mezuzah-Irish-good-luck-charm double whammy. He looked for a place to hide it near the front door. He spied a loose brick where the stoop joined the building. He scraped at the crumbling mortar with the knife until he could pull the brick away. He shoved the case into the cavity, then chipped off the back of the brick so there would be room to slide it into place.

He headed up to his room in the attic.

Now he must wait to hear from Finn. He decided to change into his best suit, just in case he got to go to the tree planting. *Prayer scroll.* He took the scroll out of his other pants pocket—God forbid Mameh should wash it with the weekly laundry!—and looked around for a place to keep it. *On the spiral. Now.* When he set it on the slab of slate, he got a faint static shock, heard the echo of a boy's voice. *This could take ages.*

He turned to discover two strange boys sitting on the floor, watching him.

What a terrible, awful *shanda* he'd made of his thirteenth birthday.

UNNATURAL CAUSES

SATURDAY, JULY 11, 2009

"Wow, did you hear that?" Angelo said to Tony. "Not only have the Hagmanns been after this place for *generations*, but they think it rightfully belongs to them, and they're not above a little double-crossing to get it back."

"Like, say, accusing my dad of forcing you to sign Number Thirteen over to me," Tony said. "But now I'm wondering something else."

"What?" Angelo said.

"If it was Benedict Hagmann *himself* who murdered you, then framed the dirty deed on Dad."

"Murder?" Solly said.

Tony filled him in on Hagmann's allegations against Michael.

"There's something I don't understand," Angelo said. "If it's true that Number Thirteen once belonged to the Hagmanns, why would Finn make a pact with friends *not* to let them get it back?"

"Not only that, but Finn made Solly swear the same thing on his ring," Tony pointed out.

"Who then asked Mama to make the exact same promise at my birthday dinner," Angelo added.

They both turned to Solly.

"Finn didn't say why he made the pact," Solly said. "He just said I'd understand one day. He wouldn't even tell me how he planned to get the best of Chester Hagmann."

The house suddenly rumbled and shuddered. Tony and Solly ducked for cover.

"What's wrong?" Angelo said. Obviously, he hadn't felt a thing.

"I think we're having an earthquake," Tony said. He grabbed his cell phone and scrambled to his feet.

"In Boston?" Angelo said.

"It sounded more like an explosion," Solly said, jumping up as well.

Solly and Tony dashed out the bedroom door. All Angelo could do was sit tight till they got back. Both boys had vanished into their own times as soon as they reached the stairwell.

★ ★ ★

At garden level, Tony peered out the door of the mother-in-law room. Whoa, the back deck was no longer there! Nor was any of the furniture Julia and the twins had moved onto it. He spied the three of them on the weedy patio below, toeing the rubble of rotted timber, smashed chairs, and broken glass.

"What happened?" Tony said.

"Isn't it obvious?" Julia said.

"Mikey and me were on that deck a minute before it went," Angey said.

"Good thing *you* were at the lawyer's, Two-Ton," Mikey said, "and not on the deck with us. We'd be goners, for sure."

"Better get down here," Julia said.

"How?" Tony said. "The stairs fell with the deck."

"Through the basement," Julia said.

"Basement?" Tony said. "I thought garden level *was* the basement." So there *was* another floor below the street.

"Look behind the door at the bottom of the staircase," Julia said.

Tony took a rickety old staircase down to a dank cellar. The place was coated in dust and festooned with cobwebs. There were *definitely* rats down there. No wonder Michael had left this level off his welcome tour.

Gingerly, Tony made his way past stacks of faded Christmas decorations, filing cabinets spilling over with paperwork, a gigantic furnace, and a workbench covered with rusty tools. Finally he reached the welcome shaft of light streaming through an open bulkhead door.

"Where's Dad?" Mikey said as soon as Tony had climbed the steps and joined them on the patio.

"He, uh, went to look at beds," Tony said. "For my room."

"Maybe you better call him," Angey said to Julia.

Julia burst into tears. "I don't know how much more of this I can take!" she wailed. "I knew moving here was a terrible idea. I just knew it! Why did I ever let your father talk me into it?" She rushed into the house, sobbing.

"Wow," Angey said. "She *never* cries."

"This is all your fault," Mikey said to Tony.

"How is this *my* fault?" Tony said.

"If you hadn't sucked up so much to Zio Angelo at Thanksgiving," Mikey said, "he would never have left you this death trap. We would all still be living in some nice rental in Ann Arbor. Me and Angey would be training for freshman soccer. And you'd be out of our hair at some fat camp on the Upper Peninsula."

Tony bit his lower lip. Secretly, he sort of agreed: Life would be a heck of a lot easier in Ann Arbor. Plus Mikey didn't even know the *half* of what was going on. "How about we clean up this mess?" Tony said. "Getting into a fight right now is definitely not going to do much for Mom's stress level."

"He's right," Angey said to Mikey.

Mikey stared at Angey in disbelief. But as soon as Angey began stacking rotted timbers, Mikey pitched in by piling broken bricks. Meanwhile, Tony tried to puzzle together which arms and legs went with which chairs. A moment later, his cell phone cuckooed with a message. Who could *that* be? Julia was upstairs bawling her eyes out, and Michael was still being interrogated by the police. He checked the display screen. *New Message from: Pickles.* He called up the actual text: *Update. Stop by shop.*

"Who's that?" Mikey said. "You don't have any friends."

"Wrong number," Tony said, stowing the phone.

That was when Julia wandered back out, dabbing her eyes with a tissue. Tony gave her a hug; she definitely looked like she could use one. "Pity party's over," she said. "Thanks for holding it together, you guys."

"Did you call Dad about the porch?" Angey asked.

"He must be out of satellite range," Julia said. Placing her hands on her hips, she peered up to where the deck used to be. "That's not going to be cheap," she said.

"Maybe we could rebuild it ourselves," Mikey said.

"We made that tree house with Pablo and his dad last summer," Angey reminded her. "And it came out great."

"Appreciate the handyman spirit," Julia said. "But this definitely looks like a job for a professional. The problem is finding one. We don't even have a copy of the Yellow Pages yet."

Tony knew very well they could now look up handymen online. But he took full advantage of the fact his mom was blanking on the cable guy's visit by telling her about the hardware store over on Hanover Street. The corner hardware back in Ann Arbor had a bulletin board at checkout with the business cards of all the local carpenters and plumbers—remember? Maybe this one did too. He'd be happy to run over and check.

"You're just trying to weasel out of more work," Mikey said.

Actually, I'm trying to get to Ye Olde Curiosity Shoppe.

"Couldn't hurt," Julia said. "Besides, we need a tarp or something to cover up the holes where the deck separated from the wall. It looks like it might rain."

"*We'll* go," Mikey said.

"We haven't had a break all day," Angey said.

"But you don't even know where it is," Tony said.

Julia suggested all three of them go. Her heart had definitely gone out of sanding the floors of her new studio. About all she could manage right now, while she waited for their father to get home, was a long hot bath.

Crap! Now how am I going to get that update?

"I'm still on the cell," Tony reminded Julia. "You know, just in case—"

"In case what?" Julia said. "A miracle happens?"

★ ★ ★

Tony totally ditched Mikey and Angey at the hardware store. As soon as the twins had plucked a few business cards off the handyman bulletin board, he suggested they grab a tarp and some bungee cords in Building Supplies while he priced rat traps for the cellar over in Pest Control. But he immediately looped back up Plumbing and ducked outside. Served them right. They were always ditching *him*.

Crap! The front door of Ye Olde Curiosity Shoppe was locked, the CLOSED blind drawn, the purple awning rolled up. Tony checked his watch. Just past six. He peered into the darkened display window, just in case Sarah was waiting for him behind the counter. All he could see, though, was his own reflection. Did his face look thinner? Maybe a *little* thinner.

An odd plink on the sidewalk behind him.

An old-fashioned key on a purple ribbon. Tony looked up. No one was there, but a second-story window was open. He tried the key in the door. It worked! He let himself inside. Empty. But a book was lying open on the slate counter. He took a peek at the front cover: *Balthazar's Comprehensive Guide to Historic Boston*. He scanned the page Sarah must have been reading. Sights of Interest in the North End. His eye caught a paragraph subtitled "Hangmen Court":

Possibly the North End's most notorious Colonial address. In Puritan times, the magnificent oak in its courtyard was used to hang horse thieves, murderers, and witches. When the original homestead burned to the ground, a labyrinth of taverns and inns sprang up around the tree to cater to spectators, making Hangmen Court the preferred lair for pirates and smugglers. These were razed in the mid-18th century and replaced with brick town houses. In the 19th and 20th centuries the court served variously as a tenement district for fugitive slaves, Irish clans, persecuted Jews, Italian immigrants—

The wall of books opened. It wasn't Sarah who emerged from behind it. It was a woman Julia's age. But that was where the similarity ended. Julia looked like a regular TV mom, whereas this woman looked like she couldn't decide whether to be a punk rocker for Halloween or an evil witch. She was dressed in a purple-and-black plaid miniskirt, black army boots, black stockings, black T-shirt with a purple peace sign, and black leather jacket. And her hair, which was severely bobbed with razor-straight bangs, was dyed so black it looked, well, purple. Plus she was eating a grape Popsicle.

"You must be Tony," she said. "I'm Mildred Pickles."

"Proprietress," Tony stammered.

"I see you got my text," she said.

"*Your* text?" Tony replied. "Where's Sarah?"

"She had to leave for her shift at work," Mildred said. "But I'm totally up to speed: You've got a hot pawcorance over at Thirteen Hangmen Court that conjured your dead uncle Angelo. You need a nine to fire the thing up, but you have to be thirteen to use it. No grown-ups allowed. You're wondering why the old dude next door—Hagmann—is jonesing for the house so bad."

That was pretty much it, in a nutshell. Tony decided to trust her.

"I think Hagmann might even have *killed* Angelo to get his hands on the place," he said. "He got my dad hauled down to the station on a bunch of trumped-up murder charges, but I'm pretty sure it was to cover his own tracks. This other kid I conjured, Solly, says the Hagmann family has been after Number Thirteen for generations."

"Wouldn't surprise me," Mildred said. "They've certainly been involved in some pretty sketchy behavior for generations—thirteen, to be exact. But not always under the name Hagmann."

"You lost me," Tony said.

"It doesn't strike you as odd?" Mildred said, tapping the page Tony had just read in *Balthazar's*. "The similarity, I mean, between Hagmann and hangman?" She reached under the counter and pulled out another book. *Payne's Compendium of the First*

Families of Boston. "I did a little down-and-dirty genealogy this afternoon, when I got back from Wiccan practice. Turns out, the Hagmann family of Boston only traces back to the mid-1700s, having moved to the North End from Worcester. Before that, there's no trace of the name. There was, however, *another* family living in the North End called Hangman, dating all the way back to the first Puritans to settle Boston. Three guesses where they lived and what the family business was."

"You mean the Hagmanns were literally hangmen?" Tony said. "Like with hoods and nooses?"

"Coincidence? I don't think so," Mildred said.

She filled Tony in on what she had learned from *Payne's Compendium* just before her Popsicle break: The very first hangman of Boston didn't even have a last name when he set foot on American soil. He was just some orphaned street urchin named Abel, indentured to John Winthrop. (Winthrop was, of course, leader of the group of Puritans who established the settlement of St. Botolph's Town—soon to be shortened to Boston—on the Shawmut Peninsula in 1630.) One of Winthrop's first orders of business was to get Abel, along with every other able-bodied male, to start clearing land for the Massachusetts Bay Company. This work crew met with very little resistance from the local Massachusets, mainly because eighty percent of them had died from the smallpox Myles Standish had given them a decade earlier—including their sachem, Chickatawbut. In fact, one of Winthrop's first acts as governor was to condemn Obbatinewat, Chickatawbut's son, for practicing heathen rituals on what was now Christian land. As the colony didn't yet have a professional hangman, Winthrop had Abel perform the gruesome task using the oak in front of a *curious stone altar*. The rest of the heathens were duly banished from the peninsula, and Winthrop awarded the land around the altar to his second-in-command, Jebediah Pickles.

That's right, Pickles.

Fast forward to 1639. Jebediah's oldest daughter, Mildred, was accused of witchcraft because she was visited by "demons" on her thirteenth birthday. Winthrop instructed Abel Hangman—as he was now known—to string Mildred up from the oak in her own front yard. Though Mildred and her family managed to escape to Salem, Abel identified the midwife, Margaret Jones, as a member of Mildred's evil coven. She was properly tried and hanged for sorcery, and Abel was rewarded with the now-vacated Pickles home for his service to the community.

The Hangmans prospered at Hangmen Court until the witch trials of Boston drew to their spectacular close in 1689. That's when Ethan Hangman was convicted of falsely executing innocent women for sorcery in order to confiscate their property. Which was when the Hangmans took flight in the middle of the night to escape their own noose. Which was also when a family named Hagmann turned up in Worcester and opened a rope factory. "But all they had really done was shift an *n* from the middle of their name to the end," Mildred concluded.

"They were chased out of Boston for murder?" Tony said.

"Not before falsely accusing my very own great-great-great-plus-grandmother of witchcraft," Mildred said. "Want a Popsicle?"

"I'm on a diet," Tony said.

The door jangled. In walked Sarah, dressed in her Colonial-maid getup. "Hi, Tony," she said. "Hi, Mom."

"Hi, sweetie," Mildred said. "How was work?"

Mom? Sarah is Sarah Pickles?

"Tourists," Sarah said, sighing. She turned to Tony. "Did Mildred give you the skinny on the Hagmanns and Hangmen Court?"

"Tony thinks one of them iced his uncle and pinned it on his dad," Mildred said.

"Better call the cops," Sarah said. "Any Popsicles left?"

"I still don't have a motive," Tony said.

"Isn't it obvious?" Mildred said. "The Hagmanns are wicked desperate to get the Hangman family homestead back."

"Even though they stole it from *our* family to begin with," Sarah said.

"But the original house burned down," Tony said, tapping *Balthazar's* as a reminder. "And then whatever inn or tavern took its place was flattened by the city to build the town houses that are there today. What difference would it make to Benedict Hagmann or any of his ancestors whether they own Number Fifteen or Thirteen?"

"He's right," Sarah said.

"Dang," Mildred said. "You want grape or cherry?"

Tony's pocket started cuckooing. "Sorry," he said. "I just got this thing. I haven't quite figured out how to get it to vibrate." Julia calling. "I gotta take this," he said. "Mom might have news about Dad."

While Tony answered his phone, Mildred opened the bookcase and went upstairs. Sarah slumped into the Cleopatra lounging sofa, pulled off her white cap, and fanned her face with it.

Julia didn't have news. But the twins were all freaked out about losing him. They claimed to have tried calling and texting him a half dozen times (which was true), but he hadn't answered (also true). Where was he? Tony admitted he had just finished chasing a dead-end lead. Julia told him to hoof it back to the house, pronto. She was out of excuses about where Michael might be for dinner. She saw no choice but to come clean to the twins; and she wanted Tony to be there, for moral support. He told her he was on his way.

"I gotta go," he said to Sarah.

"I'll text you if we dig anything else up," Sarah said. "Unfortunately, I've got another shift tomorrow. Sunday's a big day for us."

"Where exactly *do* you work?" Tony said.

"I'm a tour guide at the Paul Revere House," Sarah said. "Volunteer. They can't pay me till I turn sixteen in August. But I don't care. I'm way into history. And heavy metal. And beagles."

That explained her Colonial-maid outfit. And her age.

"Me too," Tony said. "Well, the history part, anyway."

"Then you should stop by the museum sometime," she said. "I'll give you a behind-the-scenes tour."

"That'd be great," Tony said. "Sometime."

When I'm not so busy trying to save my dad by catching a murderer.

Oh, great. Old Man Hagmann was out in his front yard spraying his rosebushes with whatever toxic chemical he'd bought at the sidewalk sale. Now that Tony was trying to avoid him, he couldn't swing a cat without hitting him. He pulled out his cell phone and pretended to be deep in conversation.

Hagmann stepped directly into his path. "So?"

Tony said he'd call right back—as if he knew anyone in Boston except, maybe, the Pickleses—and snapped his phone shut. "What?" he said.

"So have they officially charged your father with Angelo's murder yet?"

"Back off, Benny," he said. "You may have everybody else fooled, but not me. I've got my eye on you."

"What are you talking about?" Hagmann said, startled.

"My dad's so-called motive, for one," Tony said. "Antonio DiMarco married Isabella Saporiti for love. And my dad loved Zio Angelo. The only family that's been trying to get its hands on Number Thirteen—for *generations*—is the Hagmanns. So what's *your* alibi?" Oops. He hadn't at all meant to lose his cool and tip his hand. But it had been a long day.

"How dare you!" Hagmann sputtered. "Angelo *wanted* me to have Number Thirteen out of thanks—because I was the only one who bothered to look after him once he fell ill. Not your grandfather Guido. Not your father."

"Yeah, well, obviously you didn't do such a hot job," Tony said. "So like I said, back off." To avoid going off on the whole hangman thing, he stepped around the old man, stomped up the steps of his own front stoop, and began fumbling for his keys.

"Come back here," Hagmann said. "I demand to know who has been filling your head with these lies."

Tony slammed the door in his face.

A BIG
MISUNDERSTANDING
SATURDAY, JULY 11, 2009

Tony was still shaking with rage when he entered the attic. He found Angelo sitting on the bed, teaching himself how to juggle with three of the four brass knobs he'd unscrewed from the bed frame.

"You look like you've just seen a ghost," Angelo said.

"Very funny," Tony said, taking a seat beside him.

"What the heck happened?" Angelo asked.

Tony explained how the back deck had collapsed; how he had had to help clean up the mess; how he'd ditched the twins at the hardware store and sneaked off to Ye Olde Curiosity Shoppe instead; how he'd learned from the Pickleses that the Hagmanns of Boston were actually dirty rotten ruthless hangmen from way back; and how he'd then had a fight with Benedict Hagmann on the way up here.

"Jeepers, no wonder you've been gone so long," Angelo said.

"I've only got a few minutes to talk," Tony said. "Mom's going to tell the twins about Dad at dinner. I promised I'd totally have her back when she did. But I wanted to sneak up here first to hear what Solly's explosion was about."

"Haven't seen him yet," Angelo said. "He must still be back in his own era, outside this anomaly thingy. But I've got a pretty good idea—if what Mama just told me at supper is true."

Before Angelo could elaborate, Solly himself burst into the room. "You are never going to believe what just happened," he said. He motioned for Tony and Angelo to shove over on the bed.

"You're covered in soot," Tony said.

"And you smell like cookies," Angelo said.

"Molasses," Solly said. "A gigantic tidal wave of oozing, sticky molasses, burbling down Atlantic Avenue, wrecking homes, lifting trolleys off their tracks, snapping telegraph wires, starting fires, injuring hundreds. Women screaming and crying, men rioting and fistfighting, kids pillaging and looting."

"The Great Molasses Flood of 1919," Angelo confirmed with a nod.

"Molasses?" Tony said. "From where?"

"That's exactly what I asked an Irish fireman sandbagging the entrance to Hangmen Court," Solly said. "The fireman told me a holding tank at the Purity factory had exploded. No one knew why for sure, but it looked deliberate. The police had now barricaded off most of the Jewish quarter around the factory, he said. They weren't letting anyone in to save their homes or search for lost relatives while they investigated the crime scene. Meanwhile, members of the fire brigade were trying to keep the flood from spreading to the rest of the neighborhood— wherever they saw the Irish symbol of two hands clasping a heart—even though their own station had been flattened in the blast."

"It becomes known as a claddagh," Tony said. "I knew an Irish exchange student back in Ann Arbor who wore the same kind of ring."

"Well, it's a good thing you put that claddagh knocker up on your door," Angelo said to Solly, though he pronounced it more like *cladder*.

"Not just me," Solly said. "Suddenly they were everywhere I turned: drawn with soap on windows, hanging on flags from doorways, chalked onto the sidewalk out in front of stoops. Which was why the fire brigade was sandbagging Hangmen Court first."

"Sounds like claddaghs saved the day," Angelo said.

"Then what happened?" Tony said.

"I started looking for Finn," Solly said.

He wasn't at the pub. He wasn't at the deli on Hanover Street, though Mameh was safe. None of the shopkeepers in the neighborhood had seen him, nor any of the renters at his other buildings. Claddaghs everywhere, but no Finn. There was only one place left to look: Purity.

Solly sneaked past the police barricade and headed for the synagogue—the fastest way to get to the factory. Thank God the synagogue was still standing, though its roof was ablaze and men from the temple had formed a bucket brigade to douse the flames. Solly did a double take. Standing in line next to the rabbi was a soot-and-molasses-covered Finn McGinley. Solly called out to him. Finn looked over and grinned. "So you can still plant that tree today!" he shouted. Solly froze in terror. Coming up the street from the barricade was a furious-looking Frank Wallace with a half dozen goons from his gang. Coming down the street from the factory was Chester Hagmann, leading a half dozen cops toward the synagogue. "Run!" Solly shouted to Finn. When Finn saw why, he waved a sad goodbye and vanished into the crowd. Solly took Finn's place in the bucket brigade. They soon got the fire under control. But the tree-planting ceremony was definitely canceled. So was his bar mitzvah on Saturday.

"Wow, you really *did* have a terrible birthday," Tony said.

"Do you guys think Finn blew up his own tank?" Solly said. "No molasses, no way for Frank Wallace to make illegal rum. No way for Chester Hagmann to blackmail Finn into selling Number Thirteen. No need for my family to start packing."

"I've got some good news and bad news," Angelo said.

"You know what happened to Finn?" Solly said.

Angelo nodded. "At supper, I asked Mama if she ever heard of a guy named Finn McGinley. Turns out he's sort of a North End legend."

"So neither Wallace nor the cops nab him?" Solly said.

"That's the good news," Angelo said. "Hagmann tried to blame him, of course. He reported to the police that Finn rented the holding tank from him, owned all that molasses, was desperate to get rid of it. But there was no way to prove it. All of Purity's accounting ledgers were destroyed in the flood. Needless to say, Frank Wallace denied knowing anything about the tank, or what the molasses might have been for. In the end, the police blamed the explosion on unseasonably warm weather: rapid expansion of the molasses inside the tank, too much stress on the rusty seams."

"So all's well that ends well," Tony said, slapping Solly's back.

"Not exactly," Angelo said. "I haven't got to the bad news yet."

The bedroom door flew open. The twins! Tony clutched the edge of the bed, terrified. How was he going to explain what Angelo and Solly were doing in his room?

"I can't believe you ditched us," Mikey said. "Mom went mental about us not looking after you and sticking together and stuff."

"Why are you sitting up here alone, talking to yourself?" Angey said.

"What's wrong?" Solly asked Tony.

"Look, the door's open," Angelo said. "Maybe somebody came into Tony's room during his time."

"I don't see anybody," Solly said.

"Aren't you getting a little old for imaginary friends?" Mikey said to Tony. "Then again, they're probably the only ones you'll ever make."

Angey didn't laugh. He checked behind the door.

Tony breathed a sigh of relief. Clearly, the twins couldn't see or hear Angelo or Solly any more than either thirteen-year-old from the past could see or hear the twins. "What makes you two think you can just barge in here whenever you like?" Tony said, pointedly.

Angelo informed Solly that Tony must be talking to his twin brothers.

"Dad's home," Mikey said. "Dinner's in five minutes."

I knew he was innocent!

"I wouldn't be grinning, if I were you," Mikey said. "He didn't buy you a new bed. He gave up when Mom called him about the back deck. Can't afford it now. So it looks like you're stuck with this one." With that he waltzed out.

Angey didn't follow him. Nor did he add his usual two cents. He just stared at Tony. Tony pretended to address him, but really he was tipping Angelo and Solly off about what was going on. "Dad's home? So what's for dinner?"

"There must be a break in the case," Angelo said to Solly, "if the police have released Tony's dad from jail." He told Tony to eat fast and report back. Meanwhile he'd give Solly the lowdown on Tony's afternoon. After he gave him the bad news, that is.

"Seriously," Angey said. "Who *were* you talking to?"

"I got a cell phone for my birthday," Tony said. "Duh."

"But it's over there, on the dresser," Angey said, pointing.

Crap! Tony hopped off the bed, grabbed the phone, and made for the stairs. "Let's go," he said. "I'm starving." *Not.*

"You really are as crazy as Mikey said," Angey declared. But he peered one more time around the room before closing the door behind him.

It was a totally weird dinner.

Julia kept hugging Michael and squeezing his arm and

kissing his forehead. She served macaroni and cheese straight out of a box with packaged frozen peas—she *never* bought prepared food—while Michael and Tony made up stuff about the History Mystery Tour they hadn't actually taken. Portionwise, Tony had no problem refusing seconds; it was all he could do to choke down the first pasty, fist-size lump of macaroni stuck to his plate. Then, as Michael scooped frostbitten ice cream onto slices of leftover birthday cake, Julia gave him the update on the back-deck fiasco. The twins had gotten the names of several local contractors from the hardware store. She had called a guy named Eddie Wong, who would be stopping by tomorrow to give them an estimate for rebuilding it. Meantime, she and the twins had hung a temporary tarp over the holes in the back wall in case it rained. Tomorrow they would definitely need to finish sorting what was salvageable from what needed to be hauled to the dump. To everyone's surprise, Tony passed on dessert. Finally the twins headed upstairs to check emails on Michael's computer, insisting that Tony clear the table all by himself since he hadn't lifted a finger all day.

Tony leaped up and gave his dad a big hug. "They set you free!"

"That's the beauty of being innocent." Michael grinned. "Thanks, by the way, for covering for me."

"He was a total rock star," Julia said.

"What finally convinced them?" Tony said.

Michael told Tony and Julia the whole story:

At about half past six, the two detectives had released him from the interrogation room with their apologies. They had just interviewed the coroner who had examined Zio Angelo's body. There wasn't a shred of evidence suggesting foul play. In fact, the coroner could cite only one minor irregularity—barely worth mentioning: that Zio Angelo had stopped taking his daily dose of heart medicine at some point. There wasn't a trace of it in his bloodstream at the hour of his death. Unfortunately, old people living on their own often forgot their meds, so even *that* wasn't all that unusual. As far as the detectives were concerned, the reason for Angelo's death remained natural causes. Which was a moot point, as it turned out, since the eyewitness who had insisted they undertake their investigation to begin with had just telephoned the station to drop all charges. Case closed.

"Wait, Old Man Hagmann dropped the charges?" Tony said. "What about all his allegations?"

"Don't tell me you've been talking to *him* again!" Michael said.

"He's not so easy to avoid," Tony said. "He told me he caught you breaking into Zio Angelo's house the morning of his death."

"I've had a key since high school," Michael said, laughing.

"Whenever I visited him, I usually knocked. This time I just let myself in, since I knew that he'd moved most of his stuff into the parlor because it was hard for him to get up and down the stairs. But I didn't know he was completely bedridden. And I was utterly surprised when Mr. Hagmann came racing up from the kitchen, waving his own key. He explained how he'd been looking after Zio Angelo round the clock since he'd had another stroke the day before, and I actually remember feeling relieved that Zio Angelo had such a good friend living right next door."

Hagmann has a key? Angelo swore never to let him into the house.

"What about the envelope for Birnbaum & Birnbaum?" Tony said. "The one Hagmann said you stole from the desk? The one he saw you tuck into your pocket before rushing out the door?"

"Zio Angelo handed me that envelope himself to send off. I just popped it into the nearest mailbox on my way to the T, since I was already running late for my conference. I had no idea it contained a will. I didn't even know who Birnbaum *was* at that point—not until he contacted me to attend the reading of the will."

"How about that missing deed?" Tony said.

"Mr. Hagmann didn't leave much out, did he?" Michael said. "Still missing. Who knows what Zio Angelo did with it, or if he ever even had one? Birnbaum said there were plenty of other ways—like back taxes—to prove he owned the place."

"And that note Zio Angelo wrote?" Tony said. "The one that said 'Trying to kill me'?"

"Oh my God!" Julia said.

Michael frowned. "He *did* scribble something like that on his pad. But Zio Angelo had told me in Ann Arbor his heart medicine sometimes made him paranoid. When I explained this to Mr. Hagmann, he agreed we shouldn't take it seriously, and he offered to make us all a cup of tea."

"And then he called the cops on you!" Tony said.

"Obviously, Mr. Hagmann has some issues with the fact that Zio Angelo decided to leave this place to us instead of him," Michael said.

"Birnbaum told me he had a meltdown at the reading of the will," Julia said.

Michael confirmed this. It was a small gathering: Michael, Nonno Guido, two distant cousins from the Saporiti side, and Benedict Hagmann. Just as Birnbaum was about to announce who would get the house, Hagmann stood up and declared he possessed a more recent version of the will—with an addendum he had personally typed out for Angelo himself—changing the original inheritor from his half nephew, Michelangelo DiMarco, to himself, Benedict Hagmann. Birnbaum was happy to concede that Angelo's signature on the addendum was authentic. But it wasn't the will's *most recent* change. Birnbaum then showed everyone the will Michael had unwittingly sent off to him a few days earlier. It also included Hagmann's addendum. But Zio Angelo had crossed out Hagmann's name in ballpoint pen. In the margin, he had scribbled a few spidery lines declaring he now wished to award the house to his great-nephew Tony, who would one day understand why. Meantime, his nephew Michael would serve as custodian until Tony reached the age of majority. There were also two odd stipulations: that Tony sleep in the attic, and that the house not be sold to anyone—including Benedict Hagmann himself—unless there was a documented emergency. At that point, Hagmann flew into a rage. He didn't want or need another house. It was the principle of the thing. He definitely smelled a rat here, especially regarding those two stipulations. He had seen evidence of foul play with his own eyes, and he would be alerting the authorities. Angelo's death would be avenged if it was the last thing he did. "We were all sort of stunned," Michael concluded. "But Birnbaum assured me the changes to Zio Angelo's will were ironclad, and that I should just ignore Mr. Hagmann's threats."

The doorbell rang. Michael said he'd get it. He headed up to the front hallway.

"Maybe he's just a complete lunatic," Julia said to Tony.

"Maybe," Tony said. *Or maybe he's a murderer, like half his ancestors.*

"Look who's here," Michael said, returning to the kitchen.

Old Man Hagmann, and he was holding a bouquet of yellow roses.

"I've come to apologize," he said. "And welcome you all to Hangmen Court." He handed Julia the flowers.

"Are you kidding?" Tony said.

Hagmann hung his head. "I know we haven't gotten off on terribly good footing," he said. "But I've been in a total state since Angelo's passing. Overcome with grief. I was looking for someone to blame. I see that now. It's time to accept Angelo's final wishes and move on."

"Are you *kidding*?" Tony said again.

"My only hope is that we can put this terrible misunderstanding behind us and become good friends as well as good neighbors."

"Of course we can," Michael said, beaming. But he would. He was a Buddhist.

"Wrong foot, *my* foot," Tony said.

Julia shot him a cool-it glance. She asked Old Man Hagmann—a bit uncertainly—if he would like a glass of lemonade. Hagmann said that would be delightful. Julia said she'd just put the roses in water. Were they from his garden? Hagmann told her they were a prize-winning hybrid tea called Golden Peace.

Tony could not believe his ears.

Michael offered Hagmann a seat in the breakfast nook,

apologizing for the stuffiness of the kitchen. But it was still the only room free of boxes. Unfortunately the back deck, where they might have caught a breeze, had collapsed earlier that afternoon.

"I noticed," Hagmann said, perching on the bench. He accepted a glass of lemonade from Julia. "A pity Angelo let the place go so badly." He took a sip. "I rather suspect that porch is just the tip of the iceberg."

"God forbid," Julia said, rapping the table.

"Inheriting a free place to live hasn't turned out to be all that free," Michael said.

"If I were you, I would be tempted to cut my losses," Hagmann said. "Sell the house. Buy someplace more suitable for a growing family."

"Except we can't," Michael said. "Not even to you, according to those final stipulations in Zio Angelo's will. Not until Tony, here, is a legal adult."

"I forgot about that," Hagmann said. "Unless there's a dire emergency."

"God forbid," Julia said again, knocking on her head this time.

Hagmann set his unfinished lemonade on the table. He stood. He said he didn't want to impose on their evening. "By the way," he said, "I seem to have misplaced a small black key, one that must have fallen off the silver chain I wear around my neck." He pulled it out by that odd triple spiral, the one Tony had spied at the hardware store. Up close, it looked really, really old. "I've searched my own house from top to bottom. I must have lost it while making one of my morning visits to Angelo. It's not valuable, just a family keepsake every first Hagmann son gets on his thirteenth birthday. But if you or one of the boys finds it, would you please let me know?"

Michael and Julia promised they would.

"So all is forgotten?" Hagmann said to Tony, grimacing with his long yellow teeth.

Tony shrugged. He knew exactly where that key was. He had tucked it into his wallet after finding it wedged between two floorboards under the bed in the parlor.

"All's well that ends well," Michael said, ruffling Tony's hair.

"Excellent," Hagmann said. "I'll just see myself out."

Tony cleared the rest of the table while Michael did the dishes and Julia stowed leftovers in the fridge. Michael said they might as well take the high road with Hagmann; his apology had seemed sincere enough, and no real harm had been done. Julia agreed they had bigger fish to fry, anyway. How on earth were they going to come up with the money to fix that back deck? They couldn't just leave the holes in the wall, and most of their savings had already been used up by the move cross-country.

"I'll just have to find a summer course to teach," Michael said. "Maybe you could start calling around for some freelance work."

"And where exactly am I supposed to do it?" Julia said.

"The dining table?" Michael winced.

Tony tuned out. He wondered instead what he would say to Angelo and Solly when he got back upstairs. It was now official: Angelo had died of natural causes. Hagmann had dropped all charges. Michael had been released from the station. Just a big misunderstanding. Everyone was letting bygones be bygones. He stopped at the second-floor coffin corner to text Sarah Pickles an update: *Dad free. No murder. Hagmann sorry. Case closed.*

Case closed. Right?

TWEAKING HISTORY
SATURDAY, JULY 11, 2009

So all's well that ends well, I guess," Tony concluded. Both Angelo and Solly stared at him, dumbfounded.

"Except that I get murdered by Benny Hagmann," Angelo said. "And he gets away with it, scot-free."

"The coroner swears you died of natural causes," Tony said.

"You don't believe that for a second," Angelo said. "And neither do I."

"Plus Cyril Hagmann is going to ruin my major-league base-ball career by calling me a communist," Solly said.

"Not to mention the fact that his father, Chester Hagmann, causes Finn McGinley to disappear forever," Angelo added.

"Forever?" Tony said. "What do you mean, *forever*?"

"That's the bad news I was just about to tell you when your

brothers barged into the room," Angelo said. "No one ever saw Finn again after he dashed away from the bucket brigade at the synagogue. Some said he fled Boston and started a new life under an assumed name, so his wife could declare him dead on all his insurance policies and pay off his debts. Others said he was secretly bumped off by Frank Wallace for selling him millions of gallons of molasses that ended up on the cobblestones of the North End rather than in rum bottles. But no one knows for sure."

Gloomy silence. A murder, a ruined ball career, and a total disappearance—all at the hands of the Hagmanns.

Tony's face brightened. "Maybe none of that ever has to happen," he said.

"Huh?" Angelo said.

"We know the Hagmanns are desperate to own Thirteen Hangmen Court, right? We also know they're prepared to do a bunch of rotten things to get it. So why not just sell it to them before they do?"

"Because we all hate the Hagmanns," Angelo said.

"So?"

"But Finn made a pact with friends *not* to," Solly said. "Then he made me swear the same thing. And I'll eventually make Angelo swear it too."

"Which is probably why I end up stipulating in my will that

you can't even sell the place to a Hagmann—or anyone else—until you're a grown-up," Angelo pointed out.

"So?"

"What are you getting at?" Angelo said.

"Say we decide to turn back time a little more," Tony said. "Say we conjure Finn with the pawcorance—when he's thirteen, like us, and still living here. Say we find out why he's made that pact against the Hagmanns and convince him *not to*—bury the hatchet, let bygones be bygones—since his grudge will only end in tears for all concerned. And say grown-up Finn is free to sell Number Thirteen to Chester Hagmann as soon as he officially owns the place. Suddenly everybody's happy! Finn won't have to disappear, Solly's career with the Red Sox won't get ruined, and best of all, Angelo won't get bumped off. So what if none of us ever gets to live here? It's not *that* nice a house. In fact, by the time Angelo leaves it to me, it's falling down around my family's ears and we can't afford to fix it."

"You mean change the course of history?" Angelo said.

"Just tweak it a little," Tony said. "All we need is an object that connects Solly to thirteen-year-old Finn."

"What about the claddagh ring?" Solly said. "When Finn slipped it on my finger, he said his brother Paddy gave it to *him* when he was thirteen."

"Does it have anything nine-ish about it?" Tony said.

"I'm Jewish," Solly said. "What do I know about Irish jewelry?"

"You hid it in the mezuzah case, right?" Tony said. "For safekeeping? Sneak down to the front stoop and bring it back, so we can have a good look at it."

Solly said he couldn't do that. Mameh was home from the deli now. She was standing out on the front stoop with all her friends, fretting about who hung the Irish knocker on the front door, wondering if it would cause even more tension between the Irish and the Jews. Angelo said he couldn't go either. Mama's bedroom was right above the front door. She was sure to hear and call the cops, thinking it was a robber. Only Tony himself was free to go down and see if the ring was still there after all these years.

In the weak glow of the sputtering gas lamps, Tony squinted at the knocker on the front door. He had never really noticed the heart-and-hands design, probably because the whole thing had been painted over a half dozen times. He glanced up to the right doorpost. He could just make out four tiny paint-filled holes where the mezuzah must have been before Solly pried it off. Next he crouched to examine where the building met the stoop. He spied the brown brick from Solly's story. Sure enough, the mortar around it had all but crumbled away. He tugged until it slid out. He reached into the hollow behind and grabbed a small rectangular metal case, imprinted with a Hebrew character. He pocketed it, slid the brick back into the hollow, and stood up.

Blinding white light.

"*Now* what are you doing?" Angey asked, beaming a flashlight into his eyes.

"Sleepwalking?" Tony said.

"You've been acting totally weird since we moved here," Angey said.

"That's what you always say about me," Tony said, trying to brush past him.

"I'm serious—why are you out on the front stoop? It's getting late."

"I thought I heard a noise," Tony said.

"Me too," Angey said, extinguishing the flashlight. "Wouldn't surprise me one bit if it *was* a ghost. This house totally creeps me out."

Tony didn't know how to answer. If Angey only knew! He just said good night and headed up the stairs. He didn't look back until he got to his room, though he could feel Angey's eyes on him the entire way. God, he wished he could lock his door!

Both Angelo and Solly could see the mezuzah in Tony's hand as soon as he walked into the room. Unlike his cell phone, it was obviously part of the house for all of them. Solly took the case and shook out its contents: an hour-glass trickle of sugar followed by a gold ring. Tony and Angelo examined the ring while Solly poured the sugar back inside. Next, Solly grabbed the prayer scroll off the spiral and—disappearing for a moment—tucked it back inside the mezuzah. He reappeared as soon as he set the case on the spiral. Meanwhile, Tony showed Angelo an inscription engraved on the ring's inner surface: *P McG 9/9/89*. Plenty of nine-ishness. He handed the ring to Solly, who set it on the spiral next to the restored mezuzah and cap. Tony then hovered his hand over everything. A faint static hum, but no voices yet.

"Say something to conjure Finn," Tony advised Solly.

Solly thought for a second and then said, "Put the ring on the ring."

They waited. Still no voices.

"It took a little time to conjure Solly," Tony reminded them.

They all sat on the bed. Tony turned to Angelo. "So it actually works," he said. "This whole not-eating-unless-you're-really-hungry thing. I had, like, half as much at dinner as usual and I skipped dessert." He turned to Solly to explain. "I'm trying to lose some weight. Angelo was actually teaching me a few Red Sox calisthenics before you turned up."

"I'm a water boy at Fenway," Angelo said.

"I tried out for that job," Solly said. "They told me no Jews allowed, even though I had the best throwing arm of anybody."

"Mine's only so-so," Angelo admitted. "I'm a better catcher."

"Well, mine's nonexistent." Tony laughed.

"It's all in the wrist," Solly said. "I'll show you. You got a ball?"

"Nope," Tony said. Actually, he did. It was on his memorabilia shelf—signed by every Red Sox player of the 2004 World Series–winning team. But there was no point in saying so, since he knew neither Solly nor Angelo could see it.

"Sure we do," Angelo said. He unscrewed the brass knob of the right bedpost. He tossed it over to Solly. Solly gave Tony a few pointers, then handed him the knob. Tony crossed the room and threw the knob back. Not bad for a first try.

Solly froze. He shouted something in Yiddish at the door, then switched to English so the others would understand. "What is it, Mameh?" He cocked his head to listen. "No, I don't want any supper. That burned-cookie smell in the air is making me a little queasy. I think I'll just crawl into bed." He relaxed. "Coast clear," he said. "Try again." He tossed the knob back to Tony.

The three boys practiced for most of the night. It was amazing how much Tony's aim improved as the hours passed. He even got the hang of a curveball, sort of. He had just needed somebody to show him the *right* way, instead of making fun of him for doing it the wrong way.

"It's almost breakfast time," Angelo said, winging the knob over to Solly. "And still no Finn. Should we try a more nine-ish object?"

Tony yawned. He told Solly to check for static on the claddagh ring. Solly threw Tony a wicked knuckleball and hovered his hand over the spiral. "Wait, I hear a kid's voice!" he said. "It's saying something about the luck of the Irish."

The twins burst into the room. Again.

"Wake up," Mikey said.

Startled, Tony dropped the brass knob on the floor.

"Why are you already up and dressed?" Angey said.

"Who cares?" Mikey said. "We need to take the tarp down before that contractor gets here, so it's all hands on deck."

"But those are the same clothes he was wearing yesterday," Angey said.

"I thought I told you guys to quit barging in here!" Tony said, signaling to Angelo and Solly he was no longer alone in the room.

"Not your brothers again!" Angelo sighed, rolling his eyes.

"What in the name of Jesus, Mary, and Joseph?"

Everyone but the twins looked over at the pawcorance. A redheaded kid now stood there with his hands on his hips.

"I take it you're Finn McGinley?" Solly said.

The kid didn't reply. His eyes rolled back in his head, his arms and legs went rigid. He toppled to the floor.

"That's him, all right," Solly said.

"Now what do we do?" Angelo said.

Tony and his family all stood around while Eddie Wong, a hip young guy in his twenties, scratched at the crumbling mortar between rows of bricks with his penknife. Over the side fence, Old Man Hagmann whistled softly and swept the pristine patio of his own backyard. It couldn't be more obvious he was snooping. Meanwhile, Eddie pulled a loose brick away. He sniffed the space behind it. He shook his head and checked a few more boxes on his estimate sheet.

"Not good?" Michael said.

"There's nothing to bolt a new deck *to*," Eddie said. "Most of this back wall needs to be repointed."

"What does that mean?" Julia asked, biting her thumbnail.

"All the mortar needs to be chiseled out—it's crumbling away—then a fair number of bricks need to be replaced before I can remortar, and *then* I can rebuild the deck." Eddie made a few last notes on his sheet, totaled it up, and handed it to Michael.

Michael literally gasped like he was an extra in a cheesy horror film. He handed the sheet to Julia. She just went very, very pale.

"I totally understand if you want to get a couple more bids," Eddie said. "But whatever you do, don't cheap out on that repointing. Every time it rains, you're getting more and more water damage behind those bricks. You can smell the mold."

Michael nodded. He told Eddie he appreciated the honesty. Eddie was no doubt right about the repointing. But they would have to get back to him. It was a heck of a lot of money.

"What are we going to do?" Julia asked, as soon as Eddie had shown himself out.

"Maybe we can take out a home improvement loan," Michael said. "Based on the value of the house."

"I doubt it," said Old Man Hagmann. He was now hanging over the fence. "I was president of the Charter Street Bank before I retired. I know a bank's lending policies. The house is too far gone. You'll have to apply for a loan based on your family income."

"Well, *that* wouldn't go very far," Michael said.

"If ever there was a time to invoke the emergency clause of Angelo's will, it would seem to be now," Hagmann said.

"What? Put the place up for sale?" Michael said. "Who would buy it?"

"I might," Hagmann said.

"Sold!" Mikey said.

"We grown-ups would have to talk about the price, of course," Hagmann said, smiling with all his long yellow teeth. "But I'm sure we could agree to something mutually advantageous."

"It's not actually my decision," Michael said. "The house belongs to Tony."

All eyes turned to him.

Tony tried to get his tired brain around the situation. On the one hand, why not? He was already trying to convince Finn McGinley—as soon as he woke up—to sell the house to a Hagmann. Why shouldn't he invoke the emergency clause now and make Benedict pay for something he would anyway inherit from Cyril once all the thirteen-year-olds upstairs had tweaked history? Talk about the ultimate double cross! On the other hand, what if Finn *didn't* agree to dissolve his anti-Hagmann pact? History would play out exactly the same way, the Hagmanns would ruin countless lives, ol' Benedict would literally get away with murder, *and* he'd own Zio Angelo's house, just like he wanted, in the bargain. It all depended on whatever Finn decided when he woke up.

"I need to think about it," Tony said.

"Are you *crazy*?" Mikey said. "What's there to think about? Sell it!"

"Tony's right," Michael said. "And Mr. Hagmann would also need to weigh the decision very carefully. Restoring this house to its former glory won't be cheap." Michael crossed the patio to show Eddie's estimate to Old Man Hagmann.

Hagmann waved it off. "I don't want to restore it," he said. "I just want to tear it down so I can expand my rose garden."

Stunned silence.

"Oh," Michael said. "Well then, in that case we'd have to say no."

"Why?" Mikey cried. "Who cares what he does with it?"

"Zio Angelo," Michael said. "He loved this house. I know he wouldn't have wanted it to be torn down. With all due respect to Mr. Hagmann, that's probably why he decided, in the end, to leave it to Tony."

Hagmann's face darkened into a scowl. "I wouldn't be so hasty to refuse my offer," he said. "You might be very sorry in the end."

"I am sorry," Michael said. "I know I just said it was Tony's decision. But as legal custodian of Zio Angelo's estate until Tony reaches the age of majority, I have to step in and refuse your offer."

A rumbling noise. No. 13 shuddered and groaned. At garden level, a section of the wall around the door teetered forward and crashed to the patio in a cascade of bricks and broken glass.

Hagmann laughed—a weird, high-pitched hyena cackle. "Oh, you'll be sorry," he said. "Very sorry indeed." He collected his broom, opened his own back door, and disappeared inside, still cackling.

Mikey poked his finger in Tony's chest. "You idiot!" he said. "Why did you hesitate? Now he'll never buy this dump. Or anybody else. And we'll get stuck here until you're twenty-one. And more and more chunks of it will just keep falling off until it collapses around our ears, anyway. And we'll never be able to afford HBO, or new laptops for school, or baseball clinics, or vacations, or *anything*."

Angey pulled him off. Mikey wrenched free of Angey's grip. He huffed out the back gate to the service alley, slamming the iron fence. Angey hesitated, then followed after him. Michael laid his arm across Tony's shoulders. "Something will work out," he said. But it was pretty clear he didn't believe that any more than Mikey.

Finn was still asleep when Tony got back to the attic. Angelo was still crouched over him, scrutinizing his face. "He sort of looks like a sleeping fox," Angelo said.

Maybe that's his animal totem, Tony thought. Angelo's was obviously an owl. Solly's was a ram. He suddenly wondered what his own totem was. Should he ask Angelo? What if it was something embarrassing, like a hamster? Or worse. "Did you try waking him up?" he asked instead.

Angelo nodded. "He wouldn't budge."

"Where's Solly?" Tony said.

"He went down to the backyard to use the outhouse," Angelo said. "He's never actually seen a flush toilet. He says they're the latest gadgets for rich people."

Tony took a seat next to Angelo. "We really, *really* need to convince this kid to make up with his Hagmann and sell the place. Otherwise, my parents are headed straight to the poorhouse." He filled Angelo in on everything that had just happened down on the back patio: Eddie Wong's estimate to fix up the house; Hagmann's offer to buy it just so he could put in a rose garden; Michael's refusal to sell; the collapse of the back wall before their very eyes.

"Wait—Benny Hagmann just wants to tear the place down?" Angelo said. "That doesn't make any sense."

"Less and less all the time," Tony said, sighing.

A moment of silence.

"Sorry I end up leaving you such a death trap," Angelo said. "Guess I'll never turn out to be very handy."

There wasn't much else to say. They needed to wait for Finn to wake up before they could actually *do* something about it.

"What do you keep looking at?" Tony said.

"He's so handsome, it's sort of scary," Angelo said. "Don't you think?"

"The twins are pretty handsome." Tony shrugged. "But they're total jerks."

"Life is so unfair," Angelo said. "Some people get all the breaks."

"He's a *narcoleptic*," Tony said.

"You got a girlfriend yet?" Angelo said, totally out of the blue.

Tony shook his head, though his mind flashed to Sarah Pickles. "You?"

"I'm not really on that page yet," Angelo said.

Tony suddenly remembered that Angelo would never marry, never have children.

"Maybe you never will be," Tony said. "On that page, I mean."

"Hang on," Angelo said. "Aren't you jumping the gun a little? I'm only thirteen."

The bedroom door blew open. But this time it wasn't the twins. "Mama!" Angelo said, startled. "No, I'm fine. I just lost a button. I'll be right down." The door swung closed again. "I forgot all about breakfast," he whispered to Tony. "On Saturday mornings she makes a late *colazione*—eggs over polenta and spinach—for the boarders. Be back as soon as I can."

To keep from nodding off, Tony pulled the wallet out of his back pocket and contemplated the little key in the credit-card slot. It wasn't big enough to open a door. (Not that any of the doors in this place actually locked.) So what did it open? And what difference did it make if Hagmann planned to level the place, anyway? Tony put the key back and pulled out his new phone. Should he call Ye Olde Curiosity Shoppe and pick the Pickleses' brains? He saw there was a return text from Sarah, sent last night: *Case closed? Doubt it. N still in Hangman. Just in different spot.*

Suddenly Finn sat up. "Paddy?" he said.

"He's not here," Tony said, stowing his phone. "I'm Tony."

Finn scrambled to his feet. "Where's Paddy? Did Stevie Wallace send you?"

"You're probably not going to believe this," Tony said, "but—"

"I gotta go," Finn said. He bolted for the bedroom door. But when he swung it open, Angelo suddenly materialized.

"Oh, hi," Angelo said, stepping into the room. "Glad you're finally awake."

Finn backed away, terrified.

"What did I miss?" Angelo said, turning to Tony. "Did you ask him about his pact against the Hagmanns yet?"

"I must still be in the middle of one of my—" Finn said, then broke off.

"No, you're awake," Tony reassured him. He launched into his explanation about how they were from the future—he was getting pretty good at that part—and wrapped up by explaining how the ring on the spiral had conjured him, a baseball cap had conjured Angelo (though Finn probably couldn't see it), and a mezuzah had conjured Solly (who Finn couldn't see either, since he was in the outhouse). And just in case Finn didn't believe they *were* from the future—neither Angelo nor Solly had at first—Tony could prove it by revealing a couple of secrets about Finn that they as total strangers couldn't possibly know. That's because Finn himself would actually tell those secrets to Solly—who would be right back—in about a decade.

"What secrets?" Finn said, edging toward the door.

"That you pass out in narcoleptic seizures brought on by stress," Tony said.

Finn froze in his tracks. "Nobody knows about that except One-Eyed Jack," he said. "The doctor only just explained to me what these sleeping fits were this afternoon."

"That today is your thirteenth birthday."

"Christmas Eve, 1909," Finn whispered.

"That Paddy, your older brother, gave you his claddagh ring—the one with two hands clasping a heart that you set on the spiral before you fell asleep—inscribed with his initials and his date of birth: September 9, 1889."

"If you really are from the future, like you say, you'll be able to tell me what's about to happen to Paddy," Finn said.

"I don't know," Tony confessed.

"Then I gotta find him," Finn said. "It's past dark. He should be home by now."

"Solly might know what happened to Paddy," Angelo offered.

Tony glanced out the window. It wasn't even noon yet for him, Angelo, and Solly. Not only was Finn in a different month of a different century, he was also in a different time of *day*. Boy, were things getting complicated!

Angelo continued, "You mentioned something about Paddy to him when the grown-up version of you gave him the ring on *his* thirteenth birthday. The fastest way to find out would be to wait for Solly to get back from the outhouse."

Finn hesitated, then sat on the edge of the bed.

"Meantime, maybe you could tell us why you made a lifelong pact against the Hagmanns with all your friends," Tony said.

"What pact?" Finn said.

"Uh-oh," Angelo said. "We got him too early. He hasn't made it yet."

"Mind you, I truly hate Cedric Hagmann," Finn said.

"Well let's start there," Tony said.

"For some reason, he's just desperate to get his hands on this house, even though he already owns the Charter Street Bank, the rental house next door, and a giant mansion on Garden Court Street," Finn said. "That's why he's always asking Mam to marry him, even though she's his housecleaner and an Irishwoman. But Mam keeps saying no. She swore to all us kids she'd never betray the memory of our da like that, no matter how desperate things got. Until today, that is. Cedric Hagmann just told me how he plans to blackmail her into becoming his bride."

"How?" Tony said.

"By threatening to turn her in to the police for harboring criminals in the attic."

"Is she?" Angelo said.

"No, but Paddy is." Finn sighed. "Don't ever believe what you hear about the luck of the Irish," he said. "This has been the most *un*lucky birthday of my life."

"Hang on—you'd better start from the beginning," Tony said.

Finn started over. At dawn he had helped Mam carry her buckets and mops over to Garden Court Street so she could clean Cedric Hagmann's house for Christmas. When he got back to Hangmen Court, though, he couldn't get into the attic bedroom he shared with Paddy. Though the door didn't have a lock, it was barricaded shut with a chair. Finn begged Paddy to open up; his boots had holes in them and his socks were now wet. Suddenly the door flew open. Finn found himself staring down the barrel of a revolver, aimed by a hoodlum who told him to reach for the sky.

All went black. When he finally came to, he was lying on the brass bed with Paddy hovering over him. Turns out the hoodlum was Paddy's new boss—Stevie Wallace, leader of the notorious Tailboard Thieves. Stevie had hijacked a delivery truck of whiskey earlier that morning. The police had raided the Wallace family home on Gustin Street, and Stevie had narrowly escaped out the back window. Until the heat was off, the gang would now be meeting at 13 Hangmen Court—at four o'clock that very afternoon, in fact. Finn begged Paddy to quit the gang. Paddy assured him he'd like nothing better; but it was the only way he could think of to keep the McGinleys together. Mam was trying her best to make ends meet. But with Da gone, she was a short step away from the poorhouse. Paddy made Finn swear on his ring not to tell Mam about the gang. It would kill her to know he was working for the Irish mob. He left to catch up with Wallace.

Finn decided then and there to drop out of school. If he found himself a decent-paying job, maybe Paddy could quit the gang. He hit the streets, in spite of his wet socks. The first HELP WANTED sign he came to was in the window of a pub at the corner, called One-Eyed Jack's. He walked straight through the saloon doors to apply for it.

Which is when the *real* trouble began . . .

FINN
How Finn Helped Honey Fitzgerald
Get Reelected as Mayor

FRIDAY, DECEMBER 24, 1909

In the gloom, Finn spied a half dozen Irishmen standing at the bar. The one with his back turned was arguing with the elderly black bartender with snow-white hair. "What do you mean, you don't serve my kind here?" the Irishman said.

"You heard me," the bartender said, polishing a pilsner glass.

"You should feel honored I've even stooped to coming in," the Irishman said. "And the only reason I *have* is because I'm waiting for my new man to catch up with us. So pour me a whiskey."

"Plenty of other places in the North End sell whiskey," the bartender said.

"Don't get uppity with me, Sambo!" the Irishman said. "I want to speak with the owner."

"You are," the bartender said. "Now get out."

That was when Finn noticed the patch over the bartender's left eye. One-Eyed Jack.

"Lucky for you I got pressing business," the Irishman said. "But I'll be back for a double. And you'll be giving it to me on the house." The Irishman turned to leave. It was Stevie Wallace—Paddy's new boss—the hoodlum who had pointed the revolver at Finn up in the attic.

All went black again.

Finn was lying on the zinc countertop when he woke. The bartender was mopping his forehead with a damp dishrag. Up close, Finn could see he was really old—eighty, at least. But there was an energy about him that made him seem much younger.

"Thanks," Finn said.

"Jack Douglass, at your service."

"Sorry about earlier," Finn said, sitting up.

"What for?" Jack said. "You helped me get rid of him. I've never served his kind—hoodlums—and never will. You must be Dolly McGinley's boy. I'd recognize the color of that hair anywhere."

"I go by Finn," he said, surprised. "You know Mam?"

"I sold her your house," Jack said.

Even more of a surprise. There weren't very many Negroes left in New Guinea, now that the Irish had moved into the neighbor-hood and renamed it Little Dublin. Not unless you counted the ones in the Copp's Hill Burying Ground.

"I hope you're not here to tell me your mammy's gone and married Cedric Hagmann?" Jack said.

Finn shook his head. How did he know about that? "I'm here for that dishwashing job," he said.

"How old are you, son?"

"Sixteen," Finn lied. "I'm just small for my age."

Jack laughed. "I don't happen to have a job for a sixteen-year-old," he said. "But I might just have one for a twelve-going-on-thirteen-year-old."

Finn grinned. "I turned thirteen today."

"Right on time," Jack said. "I guess you're hired."

"When do I start?" Finn said.

"Right now," Jack said, handing him the dishrag. "One-Eyed Jack's is open every single day of the year. Happy birthday."

Finn's first morning of work was surprisingly busy. There were dozens of glasses to polish, all the tables to wipe clean, floors to sweep, and a mountain of potatoes to peel before the lunch shift. By noon One-Eyed Jack's was packed with a raucous group of well-heeled, middle-aged Irishmen, and Finn was up to his elbows in suds, with dirty plates and mugs towering around him. In spite of his age, Jack seemed to be everywhere at once, doing the work of two men. Soon Jack told Finn to stop washing and start waiting tables. He shoved a plate of fish-and-chips into Finn's barely dry hands and instructed him to set it in front of the loudest man in the saloon. This Finn did. To his horror, a piece of battered cod toppled off the top and plopped into the loud man's lap. He didn't make a fuss, though. He just popped it into his mouth, saying, "That'll fix it for trying to swim away." The table roared. It was only then that Finn realized who the man actually was: Honey Fitzgerald, Boston's former mayor and the Democratic challenger in January's mayoral election.

"Cat got your tongue?" asked Honey-Fitz.

"Lad's just wondering what you're doing in a place like this," Jack called from the table he was serving nearby.

"Having my lunch," Honey-Fitz said. "What are you doing here?"

"I wash dishes for Jack," Finn stammered.

"Used to be my job," Honey-Fitz said. "When I was your age."

"You?" Finn said. "Here?"

"That's right, in a Negro establishment," Jack said.

"Some people in this town don't think much higher of the Irish," Honey-Fitz told Finn. "Or the Italians, which is what the guy to my left is. Or the Jews, the guy to my right. But it's really only the difference of a few ships who got here first, isn't it?"

Finn grinned.

Honey-Fitz addressed the table: "Call me color-blind if you must, but I *like* how jumbled up with races and colors and creeds my dear old North End is. It was my dearos, don't forget, who first got me voted into office. So I reckon this is the perfect place for my unofficial reelection campaign headquarters."

Finn glanced around the table, startled.

"Fear not," Honey-Fitz said, chuckling. "Only half these guys are Beacon Hill politicians. The other half are Royal Rooters for the Boston Pilgrims. On game days we meet at a joint called Third Base at the ballpark. The rest of the time we meet here."

Back in the kitchen, Jack confirmed that the former mayor wasn't entirely full of his so-called Fitzblarney. He had made it his mission to battle prejudice throughout his career. As a state senator Honey-Fitz had helped get Columbus Day declared a public holiday for the Italians. As a congressman he'd convinced President Grover Cleveland to veto a bill deporting any immigrant unable to read the U.S. Constitution.

"So why did he lose his last election for mayor?" Finn asked.

"Oh, he's not perfect by a long stretch," Jack admitted. "He got himself into a lot of hot water creating government jobs for all his so-called dearos: tea warmers, tree climbers, rubber-boot repairmen, watchmen to supervise the watching of other watchmen. Boston will be ready for the likes of Honey-Fitz again only if he can prove he's for reform. Which is why his big campaign promise is to bring Stevie Wallace and the Tailboard Thieves under control by New Year's Eve. Too bad he didn't stop by this morning, eh?"

Finn felt himself going red. Stevie Wallace was now using the attic of 13 Hangmen Court—the very house One-Eyed Jack had sold Mam—as his headquarters. To hide his shame, Finn hustled a tray laden with apple pie out to the saloon.

The conversation had turned serious. How *was* Honey-Fitz going to turn this campaign around? He was trailing Mayor George A. Hibbard substantially in the polls, and there was little over a week left until election day, after the New Year. Did he have a plan?

Honey-Fitz turned to Finn. "What do *you* think I should do?" The men around the table chuckled. "I'm serious," Honey-Fitz said. "What does the man on the street say?"

Finn stopped serving pie. He thought about it for a moment. "Maybe you need a rallying song," he said. "Like how the Royal Rooters sing 'Tessie' at Pilgrims games."

The table roared.

"Go on, then," Honey-Fitz said. "Give us a song."

"Me?" Finn said.

"Never let that stop you from helping a friend in need," Honey-Fitz said.

The table chanted for Finn to give them a song.

Finn started to sing "Sweet Adeline," a tune Mam sometimes hummed to herself while she was boiling up the cabbage for dinner. His voice cracked a couple of times—he really wasn't much of a crooner—but he didn't give up. The longer he sang, the more silent the room grew. Respectful. Thoughtful. Honey-Fitz himself joined Finn at the final chorus. The politician had an amazingly sweet tenor voice. By the end, there wasn't a dry eye. A cheer went up. Everyone ruffled Finn's hair and slapped his back, slipped him a nickel. The table began to chatter in earnest about how Honey-Fitz should get straight into his car and drive around to every Boston neighborhood, reminding voters how he was one of them, not just some stuffed shirt at city hall.

Honey-Fitz pulled Finn aside and asked him how he could return the favor.

"Recommend a good doctor," Jack piped up from over Finn's shoulder. "The boy needs a physical examination."

Honey-Fitz pulled a business card out of his pocket and scribbled a note on the back before handing it to Finn. His own doctor on Beacon Hill. If Finn handed Doc O'Leary this card, he'd put the exam on Honey-Fitz's account.

"But I'm fine!" Finn said. "Honest!"

"Can't very well have you falling asleep on the job," Jack winked. "You better head on over there now, son. He might be closing early for Christmas."

★ ★ ★

Finn returned to One-Eyed Jack's in a slight daze. It was the first time in his life he had ever been to a doctor's office. He hadn't been prepared for all the poking and prodding with scary metal instruments. But at least now he could name what he had: Narcolepsy. Cataleptic fits. No one knew what caused them, according to Doc O'Leary. He couldn't be woken from them. So far, there was no cure. Finn should get plenty of sleep at night and avoid stressful situations. And whenever he did topple over, his family and friends needed to move him out of harm's way. Apart from that, there wasn't much Finn could do—except take comfort in the fact that his condition put him in pretty good company. Harriet Tubman was narcoleptic. And Louis Braille. And Thomas Edison.

With all this occupying his thoughts, Finn was far from expecting what awaited him when he entered through the saloon doors: a cash register drawer gaping open, two empty whiskey bottles beside it, a half dozen shot glasses smashed on the floor—and Jack lying hog-tied and gagged in the sawdust behind the bar.

Finn cut Jack loose and helped him over to the nearest booth. Suddenly, Jack seemed very old and frail—smaller, even. He dashed to the kitchen for a damp dishrag to clean the nasty cut above Jack's good eye. Jack waved him away. "The Tailboard

Thieves decided to pay me another visit," Jack said. "Turns out they had Christmas presents to buy and were a little short on cash." Stevie Wallace had demanded Jack open his register for them. Jack refused. Stevie smacked Jack across the face, and then his younger brother, Frank, trussed him up. The rest of the Tailboard Thieves broke into the register and cleaned it out, then poured themselves a little holiday cheer, on the house— and onto Jack while he lay at their feet.

Finn hung his head in shame. "My brother Paddy wasn't with them, was he?" he asked. "He's a carrottop, like me."

Jack nodded. "He didn't touch me, though. He just stood guard at the door."

Finn didn't know what to do next. He had sworn on Paddy's ring to keep quiet about the Tailboard Thieves. Yet Jack was the only person who had ever taken his sleeping fits seriously enough to get him to a doctor. Hang on! He had only sworn not to tell Mam about the Tailboard Thieves. He wouldn't actually be breaking his promise by telling Jack. "They're meeting up in the attic of Number Thirteen," Finn said. "It's where they now plan their heists. Paddy hates working for the Wallaces, but he doesn't see any way out. If only I could eavesdrop on them somehow. I'd tell Honey-Fitz all about their next caper—after warning Paddy to stay away—so he could catch them red-handed."

"Maybe there *is* a way," Jack said. "I lived up in that attic myself when I was a runaway slave. I know of a secret place to hide. When are they meeting next?"

"Four o'clock," Finn said.

"Mind the bar for me," Jack said, hoisting himself to his feet. He winced and clutched his side. "Feels like a couple of cracked ribs," he gasped. "You'd better walk me over to Number Thirteen, so I can lean on you a bit."

At the front door of Finn's house, Jack grabbed hold of the knocker. (Finn had never noticed that it bore the same heart-and-hands design as the ring Paddy wore.) Jack splayed each wrought-iron hand—with a rusty squeal—away from the heart. Next he pulled the tarnished crown out of its resting place above the heart and inserted it into a slot below. Attached to the heart was the door rapper itself. Jack cranked this nine times to the right, wincing with each hard-won turn. Suddenly the iron heart popped entirely out of the knocker, revealing itself to be an odd sort of hook.

Jack rested his head against the door, teetering as though he might faint. "Feeling my age," he said.

"Just tell me where that hiding place is," Finn said. "You'll never make it up three flights of stairs in your condition."

"Appreciate the offer," Jack panted, pocketing the heart hook. "But I can't do that. I promised not to, on account of a Hagmann. One day you'll understand." Jack asked Finn to head back to the pub. Honey-Fitz would be turning up for his end-of-the-day pint of birch beer. (The former mayor was, in fact, a teetotaler.) Finn should ask Honey-Fitz to wait there till Jack got back. He should then hide behind the old oak in the middle of the court until he saw the Tailboard Thieves leave. That way he could help Jack back to the saloon as soon as he came out.

With that, Jack disappeared inside the house.

And not a moment too soon. Stevie Wallace and his gang rounded the corner of Charter Street and strode up Hangmen Court. Finn pressed his back against the door so they wouldn't notice the heart missing out of the middle of the knocker. Paddy scowled and told Finn to beat it. Wallace said the kid might as well stand guard—make himself useful—as long as he didn't fall asleep. The rest of the gang chuckled, then followed Wallace up the stairs, Paddy with them.

There was Honey-Fitz. Finn raced off to meet him at the front door of the pub. He ushered the politician inside, opened him a birch beer, and handed him the racing form. Finn needed to leave for a moment but would be back with news of the Tailboard Thieves' next heist. Honey-Fitz's face lit up. Finn wasn't pulling his leg, now? There was only a week left to make good on his campaign promise, and he was trailing worse than ever in the polls. Finn crossed his heart, then dashed over to the old oak.

Cedric Hagmann was already hiding behind it, holding a potted poinsettia.

"What are *you* doing here?" Finn said. "Why aren't you at the bank?"

"I was going to leave this on the stoop for your mother," he said. "A surprise Christmas present. But I see she already has other admirers."

"It's not what you think," Finn said.

"Doesn't matter what I think," Hagmann said. "What matters is what the police will think when I tell them Dolly McGinley is harboring known criminals."

"She has no idea they're there," Finn said. "She's at your house, cleaning it."

"Your older brother certainly knows they're there," Hagmann said. "And if she wants to keep him out of jail, she'll have to marry me to buy my silence."

"But that's blackmail!" Finn said. "That's no way to win someone's love!"

"Who said anything about love?" Hagmann said, sneering. "I would do just about anything to get my hands on that house."

"Why?" Finn said. "What do you want with another run-down old building? You live in a huge mansion!"

"Stupid little Mick," Hagmann hissed. "You could never in a

thousand years imagine what sort of treasure lies hidden within those walls!"

Before Hagmann could elaborate, though, they heard Wallace and the gang laughing and stomping their way down to the front stoop of No. 13. Hagmann shoved the poinsettia into Finn's hands and strode quickly out of the court.

Finn hoofed it back to the stoop just as Wallace emerged from the front door. Now Finn *had* to help Honey-Fitz catch Stevie Wallace. Not only would it save Paddy from a life of crime, it would save Mam from the blackmailing clutches of Cedric Hagmann. Wallace did a double take at the poinsettia. "I was just having a pee behind the tree," Finn said. "Look what I found." Wallace laughed and flipped him a quarter. He advised his gang to get a move on; the caper they were about to pull would make them all rich as the Three Wise Men by dark. Panicked, Finn watched Paddy fall reluctantly into step behind the rest. How could he warn Paddy that he was headed straight into a trap, one that his own little brother was helping Honey-Fitz to set?

Finn gasped. He dropped the poinsettia. His eyes rolled back in his head. His arms and legs went rigid. He toppled to the sidewalk. Paddy dashed to his side. "Not again," Wallace said. "Wake him up!" Paddy said he couldn't. There was nothing he could do until the fit passed. "Just leave him there," Wallace said.

"The kid'll wake up eventually." Paddy told Wallace he would carry Finn up to his room. He wasn't about to leave him alone in the street. Wallace would surely do the same for his own little brother, Frank. Wallace relented, saying Paddy knew where they were headed. The gang ambled up Hangmen Court without him.

Paddy slung Finn over his shoulder like a sack of potatoes and toted him up the stoop. While Paddy fumbled with the lock, Finn opened his eyes a crack. To his relief, he spied Jack slipping out the kitchen door beneath the stoop. Jack pantomimed that he would wait until they were up in the attic before heading back to the pub to meet Honey-Fitz. But he looked terrible. His face had gone very gray, and it was covered in sweat. Finn vowed to check on him as soon as he could.

The moment Paddy laid Finn on the bed, Finn opened his eyes. He admitted to his brother that he had only been faking a sleeping fit. He'd seen no other way to save Paddy from getting arrested along with the other Tailboard Thieves when they were nabbed by the cops at their next heist.

"Who tipped the coppers off?" Paddy asked, alarmed.

What could Finn tell him without implicating Jack or his secret hiding place? "That snooty banker, Cedric Hagmann," he lied. "I caught him spying on you guys from behind the old oak. He told me the cops knew all about your new hiding place. One of your own gang members is a secret stool pigeon."

"*Hagmann* knows about the heist?" Paddy said, jumping up. "Then it must be true. I've got to warn Stevie."

"Why?" Finn said. "Just let them get caught."

"I can't," Paddy said.

"But they robbed and beat up One-Eyed Jack!"

Paddy flushed with shame. "I swore an oath of loyalty to the gang on my ring. And a man's only as good as his word." Paddy twisted the ring off his finger. He dropped it into Finn's palm. "But I swear to you now—with this very same ring—that I will quit the gang as soon as I've done my duty by Stevie. Meantime, wish me the luck of the Irish. I'm going to need it." Paddy dashed out the door.

Finn hurled the ring across the room. It ricocheted off the wall and landed on top of the slate shelf with a clank. Loyalty, be damned! Men like Stevie Wallace should earn the trust and respect of others, not just expect it because of some stupid ring! Finn climbed off the bed. There was no way he could just lie there. His loyalty wasn't to any symbol, it was to his brother! He went to collect the ring off the spiral. In doing so, he got a static shock. And he heard the echo of a voice: *Put the ring on the ring.*

"I take it you're Finn McGinley?"

Finn whirled around. Paddy? No, three boys his own age. Kids he'd never seen around the neighborhood before.

He went rigid and toppled over, fast asleep.

CONDEMNED
BY A HANGMAN

SUNDAY, JULY 12, 2009

The bedroom door swung open. Solly materialized and strode in. "Sorry," he said. "Mameh pulled me aside to show me a *Globe* article about what they've already called the Great Molasses Flood. They're definitely blaming it on the warm weather." He did a double take when he saw Finn sitting on the bed. "You're awake," he said.

"I take it you're Solly," Finn said.

Solly nodded. "Did I miss anything good?"

"There's a treasure," Angelo said. "And it's hidden somewhere in the house!"

"Where?" Solly said.

All eyes turned to Finn.

"I have no idea," Finn said. "I don't even know what it is.

All I know is Cedric Hagmann will do anything—including blackmail my poor mam into marrying him—to get his filthy paws on it."

"I guess that explains why ol' Benedict couldn't care less about tearing the place down," Tony said. "He's not after the house. He's after what's hidden *in* it."

Finn stood. "I don't know who this Benedict is. And right now, I don't care. I need to rescue my brother."

Tony turned to Solly. "Didn't grown-up Finn say something about how the ring saved Paddy from the Wallaces when he gave it to you?"

"He's OK, then?" Finn said.

"He's fine," Solly said. "You told me so yourself when you gave me his ring."

"What did I say?" Finn asked, anxiously.

Solly told them all: By the time Paddy finally caught up with Stevie Wallace, it was five minutes too late. The Tailboard Thieves were already inside the Charter Street Bank holding it up. That's right: Wallace's next caper was actually to rob Cedric Hagmann's bank! All Paddy could do was watch from the nearest street corner—having tried his best to warn them—as the police wagon roared up and half the precinct spilled out. Leading the charge up the front steps was the captain, who shouted into a bullhorn that the Tailboard Thieves were all under arrest.

Honey-Fitz, who was right behind the captain, grabbed the bull-horn from his hands and shouted—loud enough for all the boys in the press to hear—that Wallace might as well come out with his hands up. There would be no more shenanigans from the Tailboard Thieves this holiday season. Wallace was giving the good, honest, hardworking Irish citizens of Boston a bad name.

Paddy watched Frank Wallace climb out a side window and dash away, as Stevie Wallace and the others came out the front doors with their arms raised. The cops slapped them all into handcuffs. "Boston hasn't heard the last of the Wallaces," Stevie cried as he was being led to the wagon. "Meantime, we're leaving the good Irish folk of the North End something to remember us by—"

Which was when the bank's safe blew up! The side window Frank had just crawled through shattered, and a cascade of bills fluttered out—mostly twenties—several handfuls of which Paddy himself was able to pocket in the mad scramble. That minor mishap didn't stop Honey-Fitz from holding a huge campaign rally at Faneuil Hall the day after Christmas. He'd proved to all of Boston he was indeed for reform by locking the Tailboard Thieves behind bars before New Year's Day, as promised. And he reminded all his dearos he was one of them by singing a rousing chorus of "Sweet Adeline"—thereby clinching January's mayoral election by a landslide. As for Paddy, he simply set off for Hanover Street with a pocketful of twenties on Christmas Eve, to buy his family presents. He was, in fact, safely home and decorating a surprise tree by eight o'clock.

"The luck of the Irish!" Finn grinned.

"Plus that song was your idea," Angelo said, slapping Finn on the back. "If it hadn't been for you, Honey-Fitz would never have gotten reelected."

"And if that hadn't happened," Tony added, "his grandson, John F. Kennedy, might never have become the thirty-fifth president of the United States."

"So why's that such a big deal?" Angelo said.

"Hey, I think that's Paddy now," Finn said, interrupting. "Sounds like he's letting himself in the front door. I'll just pop down and check." He strode out of the room, disappearing into the early evening of his own time.

Tony heard the front doorbell ring. He ignored it. Michael or Julia or one of the twins would just have to get it. He was in the middle of a situation, here. "Now what do we do?" he asked Angelo and Solly. "It isn't going to be all that easy to convince Finn his mam should marry Cedric Hagmann, just so the dirty blackmailing creep can find whatever treasure he's talking about and leave the rest of us alone."

The doorbell rang again. Where *was* everybody?

"Yeah, but look what happens if we don't," Angelo said.

Whoever was at the door started pounding. Probably the cable guy, ready to finish installing the broadband. Tony said he'd be right back. Meanwhile Angelo and Solly should brainstorm what to do about Finn.

It wasn't the cable guy. It was two men in shirts and ties and hard hats. Looking over their shoulders, Tony saw an official-looking van parked at the curb: CITY OF BOSTON HEALTH & SAFETY UNIT. *Uh-oh.* They declared they needed to speak with Anthony DiMarco, the owner of the building. Tony raised his hand, guilty as charged.

Michael pulled up in the family car. They all watched him pop the trunk and pull out two more tarps and a fistful of bungee cords. "Can I help you?" Michael asked, joining them at the stoop.

"We're safety inspectors for the city," said the one who looked like the boss. "There's been a complaint from a concerned citizen—one of your neighbors—about the condition of this building."

Uh-oh.

Michael admitted they were having a little trouble with the back wall. But he had put a call in to a local contractor. It should only be a matter of days before the guy started in on the necessary repairs.

"There's a bit more at stake here than that," the chief said. "We've come to perform an emergency inspection of the entire building. We need to determine whether this town house poses a health or safety hazard to its inhabitants and immediate neighbors. We would like to begin in the basement, please."

"Um, sure," Michael said. "Right this way."

Uh-oh.

As soon as everyone was standing among the stacks of Christmas decorations, the chief informed Michael they would need to check the main chimney flue for obstructions. They all peered around. His assistant finally located it behind an old metal cabinet. Could Michael and Tony move it aside? Both he and his boss had bad backs. Tony and Michael huffed and puffed the cabinet a few feet to the left. The doors swung open, spilling an avalanche of dusty folders and yellowed paperwork onto the floor. Michael suggested they deal with it later. Because the inspectors had already begun to examine a gigantic old fireplace, framed in rough-hewn slate slabs.

"Probably the original kitchen hearth," the chief inspector guessed.

"I wonder what happened to the mantel," his assistant said, frowning and noting a long crack in the mortar on his clipboard.

Tony couldn't help but wonder—after everything he'd learned at Ye Olde Curiosity Shoppe the day before—if

Jebediah Pickles hadn't salvaged the slate for both this hearth and the shelf in his room—the missing mantel—from Obbatinewat's pawcorance.

The inspectors shone their flashlights up the flue. Michael peered over their shoulders and asked how everything looked. Tony poked his toe at the pile of paperwork on the floor. Utility bills. Tax forms. Canceled checks. *Wait, what's that?* A photo of a handsome blond man in his early twenties, standing at the beach. Cape Cod? The man was windswept and tan, dressed only in one of those embarrassing old-fashioned bathing suits. Grinning and waving at the camera, like he wasn't used to getting his picture taken. Tony turned the photo over. *Anders Fogelberg* was scrawled in pencil across the back in Zio Angelo's spidery script. Next to it was added a date in ballpoint pen: *d. June 8, 1979.*

Who the heck was Anders Fogelberg?

Tony shoved aside a stack of dog-eared travel brochures, looking for clues. He unearthed an old photo album. The cover was embossed with the initials *A. D'M.* He took a quick peek through its yellowed pages. Photos, ticket stubs, postcards, luggage tags, exotic stamps, foreign coins. A scrapbook. Most of the pictures seemed to be of Angelo posing in front of random monuments and tourist sites at different stages of adulthood: the Eiffel Tower, the Grand Canyon, the Taj Mahal, the Great Wall of China, the Golden Gate Bridge. Tony wedged the photo of Anders Fogelberg into the album and tucked it under his arm so he could have a closer look later. Meanwhile, the chief inspector strongly advised Michael not to use *any* of the fireplaces until the chimneys had been properly cleaned by a certified sweep.

"Time to check out the boiler," said the assistant.

"Get a look at *that* dinosaur," said the chief. "I doubt it's ever been replaced."

And that's pretty much how it went as Tony and Michael followed the inspectors around the rest of the house. At garden level they were not at all pleased to see the hole in the back wall or the missing deck. By parlor level it was clear the electrical wiring was a potential fire hazard. On the second floor, the inspectors found strong evidence of termite damage—*that* wouldn't be cheap—and on the third floor they discovered none of the gas-lamp jets had ever been properly capped, and a few were even leaking. Big problem.

Tony fumed as the assistant scribbled an alarming number of notes on his clipboard. It couldn't be more obvious that Benedict Hagmann was the concerned citizen who had called Health & Safety—trying to psych the DiMarcos out, no doubt, so they would end up begging him to take No. 13 off their hands for a song.

The inspectors asked to see the attic. If the stains in the

ceiling plaster were any indication, the roof was leaking and would need to be replaced.

Tony's heart leaped to his throat.

Michael led everyone up there. He opened the door on Angelo and Solly, sitting on the bed. Nobody freaked out, though. Michael just sat in the ladder-back chair. The inspectors started poking at beams, taking floor measurements, knocking on walls.

"What's wrong?" Angelo said to Tony. "You have this weird look on your face."

"How long is this going to take, *Dad*?" Tony said, telegraphing he was not alone.

"Gotcha," Angelo said. "We'll just sit tight until you give us the all clear."

Meanwhile, Michael gave Tony a your-guess-is-as-good-as-mine shrug. "What's that under your arm?" he asked, nodding at the scrapbook.

"Oh, just something I found in the basement," Tony said.

"What?" Angelo said. "Is there a break in the case?"

"I'll tell you about it later," Tony said to both boys and Michael at once. He shoved the album into the bookcase.

"Angelo and I figured out a plan," Solly said. "Finn's mam doesn't need to marry Cedric. Finn should just never, *ever* make any pacts with childhood friends. Nor should he go to the horse races as a grown-up, or do any business with a Hagmann—with one important exception: selling Number Thirteen to Chester the very first time he makes an offer. Otherwise, he'll end up disappearing forever in his twenties."

"I *what?*"

The boys all whirled around. Finn was standing in the door-way. "Paddy's down in the parlor," he said. "Decorating a tree loaded with presents—just like Solly said. What do you mean I disappear forever?"

"Oops," Solly said. "Me and my big mouth."

Meanwhile, oblivious to how crowded the room was getting, the chief inspector turned to his assistant. "That's odd," he said, frowning. The assistant agreed.

"Now what?" Michael said.

"The interior dimensions of this floor fall short of the exterior measurements of the building by almost nine feet square," the inspector said.

"Old houses," said the assistant. "Probably never surveyed right to begin with."

"Well, that about wraps it up," said the chief.

They headed out the door past Finn.

"So how did we do?" Michael asked, following.

"Tell it to us straight," Tony said.

"We don't have great news," Angelo said to Finn.

"We don't have great news," the chief said to Michael. "Best case? You're looking at a half million dollars—minimum—to get this place up to code."

Both Tony and Michael gasped.

"Tell it to me straight," Finn said.

"What's *wrong?*" Angelo said to Tony. "Your face just went green."

"But that's not your most immediate problem," the chief said, shuffling down the staircase.

"Uh-oh," Michael said, galloping after him.

"Be right back," Tony said.

The inspectors started stringing yellow caution tape across the front stoop. "Your *immediate* problem," said the chief, "is that this town house shares its sidewalls—the only sound ones, by the way—with the buildings on either side. You'll have to get the approval of both your neighbors before we can authorize any sort of major repair work. But if either one objects that extensive renovation here will create a hazard to their own quality of life, we'll have no choice but to dismantle this property professionally."

"You mean tear it down?" Tony said.

The assistant stapled a big *Notice of Eviction* to the front door.

"Meantime," the chief said, "on behalf of the City of Boston, I hereby serve you, Anthony DiMarco, official notice that, in the interest of your own health and safety, you and your family have until six p.m. to vacate the premises."

Julia jogged up. She was obviously just back from a long run. "Now what?" she said, out of breath. Michael told her.

She burst into tears.

"This can't be legal," Tony said. "Where will we go?"

The chief handed Michael a pamphlet. "It's all in there," he said. "You'll be temporarily moved to a motel out at Revere Beach, pending a hearing on the feasibility of salvaging the building. In the event that Number Thirteen is condemned, you'll be given a small stipend to help you relocate to more permanent accommodations."

The twins wandered up from wherever they'd been.

"What's wrong with Mom?" Mikey said.

"'Notice of *eviction*'?" Angey said. "We're getting thrown out?"

Michael filled them in.

Mikey pivoted on his heels and stormed back out of the court, cursing a blue streak at Tony and Zio Angelo and Boston. This time Angey didn't follow. He was too curious to find out what would happen next.

Michael turned to the inspectors. "So how do we fight this?"

"Does Number Thirteen have any historical significance?" the chief asked. Michael shook his head; old town houses were pretty much a dime a dozen in the North End. "Shame," the inspector said. "This place could easily be saved from the wrecking ball by getting it listed as a historic site. Plus you could apply for funds to renovate it through the Historical Preservation Society." He told Michael he would be in touch about the date of the public hearing, once he'd contacted and interviewed the neighbors. Both inspectors wished the DiMarcos the best of luck, then climbed into their van and drove off.

Julia started to wail. She ducked under the caution tape and dashed into the house. Michael looked as though he was trying not to burst into tears himself. In a husky voice, he suggested that Angey and Tony start packing their rooms, then headed inside to console Julia.

"It's not your fault," Angey said.

"Thanks," Tony said, not so sure.

Angey went inside.

The curtains fluttered over at No. 15. Old Man Hagmann stared smugly out his bay window. As much as Tony wanted to chuck a rock at him—especially since he now had much better aim—he didn't see what good it would do. Michael was right; they had all better get packing.

So it was with a heavy heart that Tony trudged up to the attic.

Angelo, Solly, and Finn were still waiting for him on the bed.

"What the heck is going on?" Angelo said.

"Doesn't matter anymore," Tony said, sighing. "Sorry, but a Hagmann finally got the best of us. Game over." He grabbed one of the packing boxes still stacked in the corner. He strode over to the pawcorance and swept every last object on the spiral into it.

The boys on the bed vanished.

PART THREE
THE TREASURE

AN UNEXPECTED ALLY
SUNDAY, JULY 12, 2009

Tony knelt at the bookcase. He started to pack up all the trophies and memorabilia and mysteries on the shelves. He paused, though, when he got to Zio Angelo's scrapbook. He couldn't resist opening it and taking a closer look at what was inside.

The first page was blank, except for those little stick-on corner holders that framed the ghost shadow of a photo no longer there. He began to flip through the leaves. Angelo was always standing alone: Angelo in a pilot's uniform at the Eiffel Tower. Angelo in a wet suit on a tropical beach, holding up a gigantic oyster with a pearl inside. Angelo on a pack mule halfway down the Grand Canyon. Angelo in a pith helmet waving one of those archaeology picks in front of the Great Pyramid. Angelo popping a wheelie on a rickety old bike on the Great Wall of China. Angelo flying a kite in front of the Golden Gate Bridge. The Taj Mahal. The Colosseum. The Statue of Liberty. Flipping through the scrapbook's pages was sort of like watching time-lapse photography—Angelo transforming from the awkward teen Tony knew into a handsome young athlete, into a man Michael's age, into a rugged adventurer with salt-and-pepper hair.

The photo of Anders Fogelberg fluttered out.

Hang on a sec. Tony flipped back to the first page. The photo of Anders fit perfectly into the little stick-on corner holders. Angelo *couldn't* have been traveling alone. Somebody had to have traveled alongside him, taking all the pictures. Anders Fogelberg?

Tony flipped to the last page. Finally, Tony recognized the old man he had met last Thanksgiving in Ann Arbor in a photo of Zio Angelo, lying in the brass bed in the parlor of No. 13. Two things struck Tony as odd. The first was that Zio Angelo was wearing Ted Williams's cap, even though he was in his pajamas. The second was that somebody was finally in the photo beside him. Not Anders Fogelberg. A woman Julia's age, dressed in a white nurse's outfit. Beneath the photo was a business card: MARIA GOMEZ, RN. HOME CARE VISITS. Hang on a sec. Zio Angelo had had a visiting nurse? Since when? Tony pulled the card out. He tucked it into his wallet next to Hagmann's key. He wasn't quite sure why.

A thought struck him: *Ted Williams's cap!*

But then there was a rap at the door.

"Go away," Tony said.

Angey opened it a crack anyway. "You OK?" he asked. Tony shrugged. Angey slipped into the room. "Mom wants you and me to take those new tarps back to the hardware and exchange them for more packing tape."

"Where's Mikey?" Tony said. "The two of you are usually joined at the hip."

"Having a meltdown in his room," Angey said. "I was just talking him out of murdering you."

"Oh."

"Sometimes he can be pretty clueless," Angey said.

That totally surprised Tony. He had never heard Angey say one bad thing about his twin—*ever*.

"At least now you won't get stuck in this creepy room for the rest of your life," Angey said, looking around.

"It's not so bad," Tony said. "Once you get used to it."

"C'mon," Angey said. "The clock's ticking."

Tony nodded. He set the photo album back on the shelf. He stood. He followed Angey downstairs. *Ted Williams's cap.* He couldn't actually believe it, but he was going to miss this room. Not to mention all the thirteen-year-olds in it.

★ ★ ★

Coming out of the hardware store, they passed Ye Olde Curiosity Shoppe.

"So what's in there, anyway?" Angey said.

Tony shrugged a how-should-I-know?

"That's where you went when you ditched us yesterday," Angey said. "I saw you. I just didn't say anything about it to Mikey."

"How come?" Tony said.

"Like you need him on your back about anything else," Angey said.

"Just a bunch of junk," Tony said. "And books." But then he felt sort of guilty. As weird as Sarah Pickles was, she was also his friend—well, sort of. "Some of the junk is pretty cool," he added. "Interesting."

Angey told Tony to take a right. He knew a shortcut back to Hangmen Court. Tony shrugged and followed. He had been this way too. But he just couldn't remember when. The last couple of days had been sort of a blur. A couple of rights and lefts later, though, they were no longer in the usual maze of *caffès* and bakeries and butcher shops. Suddenly they found themselves on a grassy stretch at the harbor front called Christopher Columbus Park. Angey admitted he had taken a wrong turn somewhere; it was usually Mikey who led the way. But it was a nice park. A kid their age was in the middle, tossing a tennis ball to his German shepherd. The dog missed by a mile—there was something funky and mechanical about his back hip—and the ball rolled up to Tony's feet. Without thinking much about it, Tony picked up the ball and tossed it back to the kid. "Hey, do you know how to get to Hanover Street?" he asked. The kid told them it was easy; they just needed to follow the Freedom Trail back up North Street to Prince Street and take a left. Tony thanked him; then he and Angey followed the redbrick line in the sidewalk. A block or two later, Tony recognized where they were. North Square. A few doors down was the Paul Revere House.

"Who taught you how to throw?" Angey asked suddenly.

Tony shrugged. *I've been getting a few pointers from a future ex-outfielder for the Red Sox.* "I downloaded this video on YouTube," he said.

Angey poked his stomach. "Plus you've lost weight."

"Hello?" Tony said. "I've been on a crash diet since school got out? I've lost ten pounds. Well, OK, maybe eight." *Plus Zio Angelo and I now do calisthenics together while we're waiting around for a bunch of other long-dead thirteen-year-olds to turn up.*

"I'm not stupid," Angey said. "It's like you're suddenly leading this secret double life."

"No I'm not," Tony said.

Sarah Pickles stepped out onto the sidewalk dressed in her Colonial-maid outfit. She set a sandwich board at the front gate of the Revere House. NEXT TOUR STARTS HERE. "Hi, Tony," she said.

"Oh, hi."

"What did you mean by 'Case closed'?" she said. "Are you saying that sketchy Hagmann dude *didn't* murder your great-uncle after all?"

Angey stared at Tony, speechless.

"I'm not so sure now," Tony admitted. "He's on the warpath again. He just got a couple of Health & Safety inspectors to boot us out of the house."

"Ouch," Sarah said.

"I'm Angey," Angey said. "Tony's big brother?"

"Oh, hi," Sarah said. "Sarah."

"Her mom owns that curiosity shop," Tony said.

"So what are you going to do?" Sarah said.

"Nothing," Tony said. "We've got to be all packed up by six o'clock."

"You can't let him get away with this!" Sarah said. "That would totally suck."

"Tell me about it," Tony said. "They're moving us to a motel on Revere Beach."

"Ouch," Sarah said again. "Listen, I'm off work at three. Text me with anything you need me or Mildred to look up, OK?" A tour trolley pulled up, and a bunch of people climbed out. "I gotta go," she said. "Just don't give up, OK?" Tony nodded. Sarah told the tourists to shut off their cell phones, please, as a courtesy to the past. One of the first things they would notice on entering the courtyard was a gigantic bell to their right. Most people knew Paul Revere was a silversmith, but few were aware he also made bells and cannons and unpickable locks.

Tony continued down North Street.

"Freeze!" Angey said. Tony stopped walking. *Uh-oh.* "There is no way you are *not* going to explain what that was all about," Angey said.

"Why should I?" Tony said. "I'm suddenly supposed to trust you because you've been nice to me for, like, five minutes? This is probably the longest conversation we've ever had in our lives!"

"I'm not Mikey, you know," Angey said. "I'm a completely different human being on this planet."

It had never actually occurred to Tony that Angey might feel invisible too.

For some reason, he decided to go for it. He explained to Angey how he had strong reason to suspect Old Man Hagmann next door of foul play in the death of Zio Angelo. Sarah and her mother, Mildred, had been helping him figure out what Hagmann's motive might be. Turns out he came from a long line of murdering hangmen who would stop at nothing—including bumping off Zio Angelo—to lay their hands on No. 13. But Tony still didn't know *why*. It was definitely for something hidden inside the house. Old Man Hagmann had wanted whatever it was bad enough to frame Michael for Zio Angelo's death to invalidate his last will—why Michael had actually spent yesterday afternoon under police investigation and *not* shopping for Tony's new bed. When that hadn't worked, Hagmann had tried buying the place off Tony. And when even *that* hadn't worked, he had gotten it condemned so he could pick through the rubble after they were evicted.

"Shut up!" Angey said.

"You think I could make all that up?" Tony said.

They continued walking up North Street.

"Well, that girl Sarah is right," Angey said. "You gotta pin the murder on him."

"It's too late," Tony said. "He totally has the upper hand. If Hagmann objects to any major construction—and he will—the city is going to tear down Number Thirteen."

"Not if he's in jail," Angey said. "Then we just need to figure out a way of getting the place listed as a historical monument."

Tony walked a few more yards in silence. Angey had a point.

"There's still a big problem here," Tony said. "No murder, no crime. The cops already closed the case. As far as they're concerned, Zio Angelo died of natural causes."

"You've got nothing on Hagmann?" Angey said. "Nothing at all?"

Tony stopped. He pulled his wallet out of his back pocket. He fished out Maria Gomez's card. He handed it to Angey. "Hagmann claimed he was the only person looking after Zio Angelo. It was supposedly the big reason *he* deserved to inherit Number Thirteen, not me. Yet Zio Angelo clearly had a visiting nurse. Something doesn't quite add up."

Angey pulled out his cell phone. He dialed the number. Straight to voice mail. "Look, her agency's office is farther down Hanover Street," he said. "How about I just walk over there and ask her what the deal was? Meantime, go talk to Dad. He's gotta be able to dig up *something* historic about the house. He's a freaking historian."

They reached Hanover Street.

"Why are you being so nice to me?" Tony said.

"I don't feel like being homeless right now?" Angey said.

Tony grinned.

"I can't believe you already know people, even before Mikey and me," Angey said. "Especially cute girls."

Come to think of it, neither could Tony. How weird was that?

Tony found Michael in his study, filling crates with books.

"Careful," Tony said, handing his dad a roll of tape out of the six-pack he and Angey had just bought at the hardware store. "That bookcase looks like it's about to topple over."

"Not that it matters much." Michael sighed. "I can't believe I just got all these onto the shelves."

Tony had never seen his dad so down in the dumps. "Mom says lunch is make-your-own-sandwich out of the fridge," Tony said. "We gotta use stuff up."

"I'm not very hungry," Michael said.

"Me either," Tony said.

Michael held up a dog-eared manuscript. His unfinished dissertation. "Didn't get very far on this, did I?" he said. "Not that *that* matters, either. There's a big fat hole in my research, anyway. I was hoping to plug it this summer—a real live history mystery about Revere." Michael told Tony to take a load off for a sec, and he would explain. Reluctantly, Tony perched on the desk chair. The last thing in the world he cared about right now was Paul Revere. But he could plainly see his dad needed to vent.

Michael launched into a bit of history:

In 1779, four years after his Midnight Ride, Paul Revere was made Artillery Train Captain for something called the Penobscot Expedition. The goal of the campaign was to stop British forces from establishing a stronghold in Maine. But it was a total failure, mostly due to the incompetence of its commander, Dudley Saltonstall. Unfortunately, Saltonstall tried to foist all the blame on Revere by claiming he'd tipped off Loyalist spies about the campaign before leaving Boston, which ruined the surprise. Revere was dishonorably discharged.

Revere then did an incredibly risky thing: he requested his own court-martial. He could easily have been found guilty—it was, after all, his word against his commander's—but he was instead cleared of any wrongdoing before the case ever went to trial. It was Saltonstall himself who got dishonorably discharged in the end, and Revere's reputation as a hero was saved.

The history mystery was this: Why did the Continental Army suddenly decide to take Revere's word over Saltonstall's? What changed their minds about him tipping off the British? Michael still had no idea. And so far he hadn't been able to find a single clue in any of the books he was now packing.

Tony tried to keep his eyes from crossing. *Who cares?* They were about to be moved into a motel. They needed to get Health & Safety off their backs! He suggested to his dad that the answer might pop into his head if he turned his attention to something else—like, say, figuring out how to get 13 Hangmen Court listed with the Historical Preservation Society. Did Michael know, for example, that Hangmen Court was *the* court where real live hangmen strung people up? Wouldn't that be important enough to put No. 13 on the Freedom Trail?

Michael ruffled Tony's hair. It might be enough to get a

plaque bolted to the oak in the middle of the court, Michael said, but that was about it. All these town houses dated from the 1700s—not the 1600s—which was well after the last witch trial had ended. And though No. 13 did date from pre-Revolutionary times, Hangmen Court had played no real role in America's fight for freedom. It wasn't even on Revere's Midnight Ride route.

Ted Williams's cap.

"What if we finally got Ted Williams's cap appraised?" Tony said. "I'm pretty sure it's the real deal. We could probably sell it to some collector for a ton of money."

"Your mother and I thought of that too," Michael admitted. "For about two seconds. But we could never live with ourselves for making you part with such an incredible gift from your uncle. It's incredibly cool of you to make the offer, Tony. You're a star. But it's one hundred percent out of the question."

Another dead end. Disappointed, Tony made for the door, then paused. "Did Zio Angelo ever tell you he had a visiting nurse?"

"Birnbaum mentioned something about that at the wake," Michael said. "Zio Angelo hired her after he fell ill, I think. But then she quit. Why do you ask?"

"No reason," Tony said. "I just found a nurse's card, when all those canceled checks and bank statements spilled out of the metal cabinet in the basement. You don't happen to know who

Anders Fogelberg is, do you? I found a photo with his name on it at the same time."

"Haven't got a clue," Michael said. "Like I said, Zio Angelo was pretty tight-lipped about his life."

Funny, that wasn't Tony's impression of young Angelo *at all*.

"Too bad you didn't find an envelope stuffed with hundred-dollar bills." Michael sighed. "Even if we manage to save this place from the wrecking ball, we still don't have a half million to fix it up."

Hagmann's treasure!

"I better be getting back upstairs," Tony said.

Tony pulled the ball cap, mezuzah case, and claddagh ring out of the packing box. He set these, one by one, on the spiral of the pawcorance. Angelo and Solly materialized. And just in the nick of time! They were about to crash straight into each other. Both had been pacing back and forth in their own separate time periods.

"What the heck happened?" Angelo said.

"Sorry," Tony said. "I was a little freaked out. Wait, where's Finn?"

"Who knows?" Solly said. "One minute you're sweeping off the spiral, the next I'm sitting here talking to myself like a schmuck."

"What did you mean by *game over?*" Angelo said.

"It isn't over," Tony said. "But we're definitely down by a few runs at the seventh-inning stretch." He filled them in on the surprise visit by the Health & Safety inspectors, thanks to concerned citizen Benedict Hagmann.

"Don't worry," Angelo said. "It took a little doing, but Solly finally convinced Finn that the only way *not* to disappear forever when he's grown up is to never make any pacts about the Hagmanns with childhood friends, stay away from the track as an adult, and sell this house to Chester just as soon as he owns it."

"But that'll take ages," Tony said. "And by six o'clock tonight I'll be homeless. Sorry, we need to go straight to Plan B."

"Plan B?" Solly said. "What does that mean?"

"Find that treasure ourselves!" Tony said. "The very fact that one is hidden in these walls should be enough to get Number Thirteen listed on the History Mystery Tour and stave off the wrecking ball. If I promise to sell the treasure to Benedict Hagmann, he won't have any reason to object to us renovating the place. At the very least, I can use the money I make off the deal to hire Eddie Wong to repair the back wall and deck and bookcase in Dad's study—and whatever else—to keep this place from falling down around our ears while I'm figuring out how to raise the half million I actually need to get it up to code."

"So much for tweaking history to prevent Benny from killing me," Angelo sighed.

Oops. Tony had totally forgotten about that part.

"Wait, maybe there's a way to save Angelo *and* keep the treasure," he said. "What if, after we find it, we get Finn to show Cedric Hagmann it's already *gone*? Then Chester and Cyril—and even Benedict—will lose all interest in the place. No treasure to find, no reason to kill for it, right? I can just sell it to the highest bidder in 2009."

"Not bad," Angelo said, grinning.

"Except we don't even know what we're looking for," Solly pointed out.

"We're not going to get that out of any Hagmann," Tony said. "But at least we know the place to start *looking* for it is here in the attic." He told them about the inspectors' measurements—that No. 13's outside dimensions didn't sync up to the attic's inside floor plan by something like nine feet square. Plus they knew One-Eyed Jack had used the heart hook from the door knocker to get inside some sort of secret hiding place where he could eavesdrop on the Tailboard Thieves. Had either Angelo or Solly ever stumbled across an old hook latch or trapdoor or anything?

"I'm way ahead of you," Angelo said. "I asked Mama if she

knew about any secret rooms in the attic when she called me down to lunch."

"What did she say?"

"Typical Mama," Angelo admitted. "If there were any extra space, she said, she would have rented it out by now. But I didn't give up. I asked her if Solly's parents had ever mentioned anything strange about the attic when they sold it. Funny you should ask, Mama said. It was thanks to the attic that she and Papa were able to get this house instead of Cyril the Squirrel. Apparently, Cyril offered Solly's parents over double what my own folks could afford to pay for Number Thirteen. But the Weinbergs agreed to sell it to my folks anyway—on two important conditions, which they wrote directly onto the deed: The first was that Mama and Papa could never sell the house to a Hagmann; they could only give it to their first-born son on his twenty-first birthday. The second was that the son would have to sleep up in the attic until he was fully grown. Mama said she and Papa agreed to both conditions immediately. They hated Cyril Hagmann, and who knew if they would ever even *have* a son?"

"Which proves Antonio DiMarco *must* eventually marry your mama for love," Tony pointed out. "Since Number Thirteen could only ever go to you, legally. And your mama would surely have told him that, way before he proposed."

"You're right." Angelo grinned. "But listen, that's not the only weird thing about the sale. When the deed to Number Thirteen was finally handed over, Mama and Papa realized the house didn't even belong to Mr. and Mrs. Weinberg; it belonged to their son, Solomon."

Tony turned to Solly, surprised. "It's true," Solly said. "Number Thirteen's mine, as of this very morning."

"Start talking!" Tony said.

"Just after you vanished, there was a knock at my front door. Mameh and I got there at the same time. Somebody had slipped an old roll-up piece of parchment through the mail slot. Mameh's eyes went big as saucers when she started reading it. It's the deed to this house, she said; Finn McGinley has decided to give it away. My heart sank. Not to Chester Hagmann, I said. No, Mameh said; to *you*. She read me the last line: Finn had officially transferred ownership of Thirteen Hangmen Court to me, Solomon Weinberg, on my thirteenth birthday. But it was on condition that I not sell the place till I turned twenty-one—and *never* to a Hagmann—and that I sleep up here in the attic."

"It must have been Finn himself!" Angelo said.

"Do you think?" Solly said.

"Let's see that deed!" Tony said. "Benedict Hagmann accused my dad of stealing it out of Zio Angelo's desk. But now I'm wondering if *he's* the one who made it disappear, since it clearly bars every other Hagmann from owning the place."

"Mameh's still got it," Solly said. "She was worried there must be some mistake. People don't just give away houses. She took the elevated train over to Finn's house in Dorchester, to ask him in person. I didn't have the heart to tell her that neither she nor anyone else would ever get that chance again."

"It's sort of spooky, isn't it?" Angelo said. "As grown-ups, we obviously make sure this place goes to each other."

"I wonder if Jack gives it to Finn," Tony said.

"He does," Finn said, materializing at the door. "Look!" He took a seat on the bed. He appeared to unroll something in his hands.

"The deed!" both Angelo and Solly said at once.

"How come I can't see it?" Tony said. "Wait, I know why. Here in 2009, the deed has gone missing. It may no longer exist."

Angelo gave Tony the basic gist of what the parchment said. The property had been signed over to a half dozen owners through the centuries: Rodney McKeag, Thomas Willard, Nathaniel Tucker, Polly Pickles Tucker. The last two lines at the bottom were the most interesting: Tobias Tucker, upon his death, had deeded the house to Jack Douglass, on condition Jack sleep in the attic, not sell it until he was twenty-one, and never sell to a Hagmann. Jack Douglass had in turn deeded the house to Dolly McGinley for a dollar, as long as she gave the house to her son, Finn McGinley, on his thirteenth birthday, with the same conditions.

"Where did you get this?" Angelo asked.

"After everybody suddenly vanished, I decided I might as well head downstairs to celebrate Christmas Eve with my family," Finn said. "Mam had set this deed on the tree for me. She'd been keeping it a secret till she could finally give it to me. I wanted to run straight to the pub, even though it was late, to make sure Jack was OK, thank him for his amazing kindness, and invite him over for Christmas breakfast. Paddy told me there wasn't any point. He had actually stopped by the pub himself on his way home from buying presents—to repay Jack the money the Tailboard Thieves had stolen out of his register. Paddy had found Jack unconscious in the corner booth, completely ashen-faced. He'd rushed Jack to the Negro hospital over on Beacon Hill—none of the neighborhood infirmaries would see a black man—where the doctor soon discovered one of Jack's broken ribs had punctured a lung. In the meantime, Jack had slipped into a coma." Finn turned to Solly. "Do you know if he ever gets better?"

Solly shook his head. He laid a hand on Finn's shoulder. There was a somber moment of silence.

"I can't help you lads change history," Finn said. "It's clear from this here deed that Jack didn't want me to sell Number Thirteen to a Hagmann—for whatever reason he had of his own—and I'm not going to. I owe him that. I'm truly sorry for your troubles, lads, but that's final."

Tony assured him that was OK. None of them had ever felt comfortable with that plan. They had already moved on to Plan B—finding the treasure themselves—while Finn was celebrating Christmas, and he quickly explained why. With any luck, the treasure would now go to the highest bidder in 2009 without a Hagmann setting foot in No. 13.

"Count me in, then," Finn said, relieved. "Where do we start looking?"

"What if we conjure thirteen-year-old Jack?" Angelo said. "He obviously knows how to get into some sort of secret place where he hid as a runaway slave. If there's a treasure in there, he'd know about it."

Angey burst into the room. "Mission accomplished," he said.

"Angey!" Tony said, to alert the others. "What's up?"

"I just had a little chat with Maria Gomez, RN," he said, flopping onto the bed. "She didn't quit at all. Benedict Hagmann *fired* her." He filled in the details: Hagmann had told her that Zio Angelo was too embarrassed to let her go himself but that his savings had run out and he could no longer afford a private nurse. From now on, Hagmann would take over making Zio Angelo's meals, doing his laundry, helping him up and down the stairs, administering his medicine.

"What's happening?" Angelo said.

"Hang on a sec," Tony said. "*Hagmann* was in charge of Zio Angelo's daily meds? According to the coroner's report, there wasn't a trace of heart medicine in Zio Angelo's bloodstream. That's supposedly why his ticker suddenly seized up."

"Doesn't take Sherlock Holmes to put two and two together," Angey said. "Do we call the cops or what?"

Tony shook his head. "We don't have any proof. Hagmann could just say he *did* give Zio Angelo his pills, but Zio Angelo forgot to take them. The only way to nail Benedict Hagmann for murder is to get him to *confess* to withholding Zio's medicine."

"I knew it!" Angelo cried. "He *did* kill me, that rat!"

"Well, that ain't gonna happen," Angey said, sighing. "So how did it go with Dad? He wasn't in his office on my way up here. Was he able to dig up any sort of history angle on this place?"

Tony shook his head. "Right now he can't even figure out a way to plug the hole in his dissertation."

"So what do we do?" Angey said.

Tony appreciated the fact his brother was just trying to help. If it were any other time, he'd think it was great that they were finally making a real connection. But right now the clock was totally ticking, and Tony needed to get rid of him. "Maybe you could sneak onto Dad's computer, if it's still up and running," Tony said. "See if you can surf up anything historical about Hangmen Court from, say, Revolutionary times. Skip the witch trials. That's a dead end."

Angey slid off the bed. "Too bad this room *isn't* haunted," he said.

"Why do you say that?" Tony asked, startled.

"We could just ask the ghost of Zio Angelo why Hagmann would bump him off to get his hands on this dump," Angey said. "Knowing Hagmann's motive might at least lead us to some other proof besides a confession."

Mikey strode into the room. "I've been looking all over for you," he said to Angey. "Why aren't you answering your cell phone?"

"Out of juice," Angey said.

"What are you doing up *here*?" Mikey asked.

"Just getting more packing tape," Angey said. He hoisted himself off the bed. He grabbed a roll off the top of the dresser. He brushed past Mikey out of the room.

"I'm not talking to you!" Mikey said to Tony.

"Then get out," Tony said.

Mikey glared at him. But he didn't have a comeback, and he just left.

"Is he gone?" Angelo asked.

Tony nodded.

"So where were we?"

"Conjuring Jack," Angelo prompted.

"It's worth a try." Tony shrugged. "All we need is the right nine-ish object."

"It's got to be that heart hook thingy from the knocker," Finn said. "Jack had to turn it nine times with the clapper—remember?—before it would pop out."

Tony yawned. He volunteered to go down to the front stoop to fetch it. He needed some fresh air. Having just pulled his first all-nighter, he seemed to be going from moments of hyper-awareness to feeling like he was sleepwalking in a nightmare.

Tony sized up the knocker. What had Jack done to get the heart hook out? First he splayed the wrought-iron hands away from the heart. Next he pried the crown out of its slot on top of the heart with the screwdriver he'd pilfered from a toolbox on the workbench in the basement. He shoved the crown into the slot below the heart. He tried turning the clapper to the right. He couldn't get it to budge. The heart seemed to be rusted in place. Was he going to have to pry the entire knocker off the door and set it whole on the spiral?

"What are you doing?"

The hair on the back of Tony's neck went straight up. Old Man Hagmann. He was now standing at the bottom of the stoop, watching him. Tony flipped the Health & Safety notice back over the knocker. "None of your beeswax," he said. Beeswax might work, come to think of it. He wondered if there was any in the cleaning supplies.

Hagmann just stood there.

"What?" Tony said.

"I'd like a word with you," he said.

"Yeah, well, if you're here to rub it in, sorry, but we're all a little busy packing," Tony said. He tapped the word EVICTION with the screwdriver.

"Actually, I've got a proposition for you," Hagmann said. "A way out of your current housing difficulties."

It was all Tony could do not to fling the screwdriver, ninja-style, at Hagmann's heart. Instead he gripped the handle and counted to three. This might be his only chance to trick Hagmann into revealing what the treasure was, or where it was hidden. "Make it fast," he said. "We've got to start loading the car."

Tony was not expecting what came next.

"It's about that key," Hagmann said. "The one I lost at this house while I was looking after Angelo. The one that usually hangs around my neck with this triskele." He pulled the triple spiral out of his collar.

"The what?" Tony said.

"It's the Greek term for any object with three legs," Hagmann said.

"What's it for?" Tony said.

"Who knows?" Hagmann said. "It's probably Druidic. An ancestor of mine brought it over from England. He helped John Winthrop settle Boston."

By hanging all the Indians who were already here.

"No. I mean, what's the *key* for?" Tony said. "What does it open? A door? A chest?"

"I doubt anyone remembers," Hagmann said. "It's just a keepsake, really. But we Hagmanns are a sentimental lot. And I'd like it back."

Yeah, right. "Cut to the chase," Tony said.

"All right, I will," Hagmann said. "This house is coming down, one way or the other. You won't get a red cent if the city dismantles it as a safety hazard. And the final decision about that rests with me. They're waiting for my call. On the other hand, I am still prepared to make you a modest offer for the place—enough to get your family comfortably settled elsewhere—if you find that key and return it to me."

"I'll need more time," Tony said. "Health & Safety are escorting us out of here at six o'clock. Maybe you could get them to hold off on evicting us for a day or two. That way I can make a thorough search of the house."

"You don't need to search the house. I'm certain I lost the key either in the kitchen or in the parlor where Angelo moved his bed."

"Still," Tony said.

"You have until Health & Safety get here at six," Hagmann said. "Otherwise, the city will throw you out as planned, then raze this house to the ground. I'll just pick through the rubble for that key—and whatever else I want—*and* get myself a bigger rose garden in the bargain."

Without another word, Hagmann returned next door and disappeared inside.

Tony lifted the eviction notice. He slipped the screwdriver through the loop of the knocker. He grabbed both ends and, channeling all his pent-up rage, tried turning the clapper to the right. Slowly, it started to move. One, two, three turns. *You have until six.* Four, five, six. Yeah, well, with any luck Tony would have that treasure by six. Seven, eight, nine. The wrought-iron heart popped out of the middle of the knocker into his hand. There was indeed an old-fashioned hook at the end of it, just as Finn had predicted. Now they just had to figure out what it—not to mention the key in his wallet—opened.

★ ★ ★

Tony set the heart hook on the spiral. Behind him the other boys waited in tense anticipation. He hovered his hand. Prickle of static. Echo of the word *riddle.* "Riddle?" he muttered to himself. "You could say that again." He leaned closer and whispered, "Where is *your* heart?"

Jack materialized almost immediately. In fact, he was standing right beside Tony, having just placed the very same heart hook on the mantel. Jack startled when he noticed Tony with his good eye. He was even more surprised when he whirled around to find himself surrounded by a gang of white kids his own age.

Something about Jack's lithe body, ready to leap and flee, reminded Tony of an antelope. Jack's animal totem? Tony wondered again which animal he resembled to the other boys. If his own totem was indeed a hamster, he was more determined than ever to drop those twenty-five pounds and trade it in for something better.

"You're Jack Douglass, right?" Tony said.

Jack shook his head no.

"But you must be One-Eyed Jack," Finn insisted. "You're wearing a patch."

"I am Jack. But I don't have a last name."

To Tony, Jack's English sounded straight out of some late-night cable movie like *Gone with the Wind.*

"But you *did* just turn thirteen," Solly prompted.

"I—I don't know," Jack stammered, terrified. "Are you slave catchers?"

Tony did his best to explain—as he had done three times before—who they were, how the pawcorance worked, and why they had all ended up in the same room: They had reason to believe a half dozen Hagmanns throughout history would stop at nothing—including the murder of poor Angelo here—to get their hands on a treasure stowed in the attic someplace. And the only way to prevent Angelo's death was for them to find that treasure first.

Jack just stood there.

"You have to believe us," Angelo.

"I do," Jack said. "The Hagmanns are definitely after that treasure."

"We're almost positive it's in the secret room you've been hiding in," Solly said.

"It is," Jack said. "Tobias told me so himself."

"How do we get inside?" Finn said.

"You just use that heart hook on the spiral," Jack said. "I'll show you."

"And then you'll lead us to the treasure?" Tony said, excitedly.

"Sorry. I can't," Jack said.

"Why not?" they all cried at once.

"I don't know where it is," Jack said. "In fact, I was hoping—if you're really from the future—that you'd show *me* where it's hidden."

"Wait, *you're* looking for the treasure too?" Solly said.

"For most of the night," Jack said. "I have to find it before Tobias's next-door neighbor, Horatio Hagmann, turns up at daybreak with slave catchers and the constable. I need to buy my own freedom with it. Otherwise the constable will arrest Tobias for harboring a fugitive slave, and the slave catchers will drag me back to North Carolina in chains. If only I knew my letters!"

"What's that got to do with anything?" Angelo said.

"For the riddle," Jack cried.

"What riddle?" Finn said.

"And who's this Tobias?" Solly added.

"Better start from the beginning," Tony advised.

And so Jack did.

JACK
How Jack Saved William Lloyd Garrison's Life

SATURDAY, FEBRUARY 9, 1839

With his good eye, Jack searched the door of every house in the Negro neighborhood of Boston called the New Guinea. He was looking for his next station along the Underground Railroad to Canada. He would know it by a brass knocker in the shape of a heart flying out of a crown. Jack had run away from a tobacco plantation in North Carolina six weeks ago. He could no longer feel his fingers and toes. He hadn't eaten in three days. His left eye socket ached horribly under its patch.

The eye itself was gone. Master O'Connor had gouged it out during a beating. Jack had stolen a pumpkin so that Auntie Sukey could make the slaves a Christmas pie. The master had wanted to set an example. Lucky for Jack, Auntie Sukey was slave row's resident healer. She had packed the socket with a poultice of herbs, then covered it with a flannel patch. It was Auntie Sukey who had arranged for Jack to join the next band of fugitive slaves headed north on the local liberty line. He had fled the plantation while the master was celebrating New Year's Eve.

Six weeks had never felt more like six years. Jack had thought more than once he might freeze to death without a winter coat or pair of waterproof boots. Most of the stations northbound had been barn lofts and root cellars, so Jack had barely slept. Food had always been scarce and rarely hot. But fear had gnawed at Jack's belly more than hunger. Always the threat of being tracked down by bloodhounds, dragged back in chains, dangled by a noose from the eaves of Master O'Connor's front porch— an even sterner example. Jack's only comfort had been the other runaways in his band, all dreaming of the same thing: freedom. But even they were gone now. They had all split up in Providence, to take separate lines to the Canadian border.

Where was that knocker? Jack was just about to give up hope when he stumbled into a small side court of brick row houses built around a giant oak. At the far end he spied an iron knocker with a heart at its center. But it wasn't right. It was in the shape of two hands clutching a crowned heart—just like the ring Master O'Connor wore. And the person sitting wrapped in a buffalo robe on the front stoop wasn't black, like the other safe-house operators Jack had encountered after crossing into the North. It was an elderly white gentleman smoking a clay pipe.

Disappointed, Jack saw little choice but to turn around and keep looking.

"I don't suppose you go by the name of Jack?" the old man said.

Jack nodded, utterly surprised.

"Thirteen, are you?" he said.

"Thereabouts," Jack said. "I don't know my birth date."

The old gentleman suddenly broke into a grin. "I'm Tobias Tucker," he said. "Well, it *must* be today. I've been waiting here a long time to wish you a happy birthday."

To Jack's continued surprise, Tobias stood. He converted the knocker behind him into the very flying heart Jack had been hunting for.

Tobias cranked the clapper nine times to the right, then pulled it out. It had an odd hook on the end of it. "Better get ourselves inside," he said, and winked. "Before my busybody next-door neighbor, Horatio Hagmann, sees what we're up to."

Tobias led Jack up to the attic, which he declared to be his bedroom. Jack watched him use the heart hook to open the back of the fireplace. Tobias ushered Jack through a secret passage into a tiny room. He lit a hurricane lantern and hung it from the eaves. "This is where you'll hide," Tobias said, "until we make contact with the local stationmaster about which liberty line you should take to Canada." A rap at the front door echoed up the stairwell. Tobias frowned. "Be back as soon as I can," he said.

He ducked through the fireplace and sealed Jack inside.

Jack surveyed his surroundings. In one corner, a mattress had been laid across several small casks. This was made up with blankets and a pillow. Beside it there was a chamber pot, and a washbasin and an ewer of water. Jack took a seat on the mattress. From three more upturned kegs a makeshift table and two chairs had been fashioned. There wasn't really much else to look at, apart from a piece of parchment nailed to the wall. This was inked with five lines of writing.

Jack fell almost immediately asleep, the deepest sleep of his life.

Eventually Tobias returned and woke him up. He was carrying a plate of sausages and potatoes, and a mug of cool water. He set these on the table. Jack wolfed the food while Tobias told him it had been his neighbor, Horatio Hagmann, at the door. Hagmann was getting suspicious. He swore he had heard someone bumping around in Tobias's attic the week before, and echoes of voices coming through the walls. Tobias had tried his best to calm Hagmann's suspicions by informing him he'd been interviewing for an apprentice to take over his silversmithing business. He had then ushered Hagmann out of his house with the excuse he was late for an appointment in town. From now on, though, neither Jack nor Tobias should speak above a whisper, and Jack would need to keep quiet as a mouse up here.

"But why would a rich white man like you ever risk getting arrested just to help runaway slaves?" Jack blurted.

"Everyone deserves to be free," Tobias said. "Why do you think we fought the Revolution? For the freedom to be yourself. And in my opinion, that means regardless of race, color, or creed. But enough about all that. I have a little surprise for you." Tobias ducked out to his bedroom. A moment later, he returned with a pair of boots, some trousers, a shirt, and a coat. "Put these on," he said. "We're going out."

"But that's against the rules!" Jack said. "Once in hiding, stay in hiding till you hear from the stationmaster about where to go next."

"That's why we're going out," Tobias said. "To make contact with the stationmaster. Hagmann's already suspicious. So the sooner you leave, the better. But we may as well have a night out on the town while we're at it—to celebrate your birthday!"

"But I don't know if it's my birthday," Jack said.

"It is, it is," Tobias said. "Now get dressed."

Reluctantly, Jack donned his new clothes. He hesitated at the threshold of the secret room. What if someone recognized him as a runaway? Tobias reassured Jack he would be fine—as long as he talked and walked and held his head high, like he had always lived in Boston as a free man. Easier said than done for someone who had been a slave all his life! Jack nonetheless tried his best not to quake in his new boots as he left the house, walked out of the cobbled court, and ambled side by side with Tobias through the North End, Quincy Market, Scollay Square, and Beacon Hill. Eventually they joined a stream of black and white folk entering a brick building.

"The African Meeting House," Tobias told him. "The Massachusetts Anti-Slavery Society invited a guest orator tonight. And it's not just *any* speechifying abolitionist, apparently. It's the publisher of *The Liberator* himself—William Lloyd Garrison."

Tobias installed Jack in one of the only free chairs, near the speaker's podium. Jack should stay put and not draw attention to himself while Tobias searched the crowd for the local stationmaster. Hopefully he'd get word about which liberty line Jack should take north before Garrison stood to speak. With that, Tobias disappeared into the crowd.

"I'm Freddy," said the young black man sitting next to Jack.

Jack froze in panic. It was also against the rules to speak with anyone besides your safe-house operator.

"It's OK," Freddy said. "I'm a runaway myself, from a plantation in Maryland. But I'm working as a caulker at the New Bedford shipyards now."

"I go by Jack."

"I cannot wait to hear Garrison speak." Freddy grinned. "It was actually one of his articles in *The Liberator* that gave me the courage to toss aside the invisible shackles that bound me and begin my walk toward freedom."

"You can *read*?" Tobias said, shocked.

"The master's wife taught me in secret," Freddy admitted. "And then the master gave me a heck of a beating when he found out. But at that point it was too late. There was no unlearning my letters."

"Well put," said a distinguished-looking white gentleman now standing next to them. He extended his hand to Freddy, who shook it. "I'm William Lloyd Garrison," the man said. "And I would be very much obliged if you would tell your story to the crowd, then introduce me as this evening's speaker."

This Freddy did. The audience soon grew enrapt by Freddy's vision of an America that might one day exist. And when he introduced Garrison, it was to a thunder of applause. But as Garrison began to speak, Jack noticed out of the corner of his good eye a white man pulling a revolver from his topcoat. The man aimed it directly at Garrison's head. Without thinking, Jack tackled him. Freddy leaped to Jack's aid and wrestled the gun out of the would-be assassin's hand. More men joined the fray to subdue the man, then bound him in ropes. Tobias suddenly appeared from nowhere. He grabbed Jack's arm and dragged him out the back door. The stationmaster hadn't had time to reveal Jack's next safe house, Tobias said, before the meeting had ended in mayhem. So they still didn't know which liberty line Jack should take. All they could do was hightail it back to the North End through the dark alleys of Beacon Hill, Scollay Square, and Quincy Market.

More bad luck. Tobias's nosy neighbor, Horatio Hagmann, was just returning home himself as they reached the front stoop of the house.

"What's this, then?" Hagmann said.

"My new silversmithing apprentice," Tobias lied. "I hired him this very afternoon."

"Silver thief, more like," Hagmann said, sneering.

"I'll have you know Jack, here, comes from a long line of freemen from over Beacon Hill way," Tobias insisted.

"No doubt," Hagmann said.

"Now if you'll excuse us, we have an early start tomorrow," Tobias said.

"As do I," Hagmann said.

Tobias ushered Jack inside.

He was in complete despair by the time they reached the secret attic room. "I should never have tempted luck by taking you out!" he said. "I'm a Jonah. Cursed. Bedeviled by bad luck.

Always have been. It's why I've never married or had a family. Once a Jonah, always a Jonah!"

"Maybe your neighbor believed you," Jack said. "That I'm your new apprentice, I mean."

"Hagmann? Not on your life!" Tobias said. "He'll go straight to the constable at daybreak. He would love nothing better than to see me arrested for breaking the law about fugitive slaves."

Auntie Sukey had already explained to Jack about the risk safe-house operators were taking—even in the North, where slavery was abolished—by harboring and not returning runaway slaves to their masters.

"Mark my word," Tobias continued, "Hagmann will turn up on our doorstep at daybreak with the constable and half the slave catchers in Boston."

"To get the reward on me?" Jack said.

"To get his hands on Number Thirteen!" Tobias said.

"I don't understand."

"The Hagmanns have been after this house ever since Horatio's father, Ian, first realized what was hidden in this very attic: a treasure so valuable, he would gladly give both eyes to possess it. With me safely in prison, Horatio would be first in line to bid on Number Thirteen as soon as the city confiscated it and auctioned it off."

Jack couldn't help but peer around the room. A treasure?

Where? All he saw was a bunch of dusty old kegs. His eyes rested on the parchment nailed to the wall.

"That's a riddle," Tobias said. "I wrote it myself when I was your age."

"A riddle about what?" Jack said.

"I can't tell you." Tobias sighed. "I made a solemn vow never to reveal the answer. Only the right person is meant to find it and solve it." Suddenly, his eyes brightened. "Maybe all is not lost! Maybe you'll turn out to be the right person in the end. I wouldn't be breaking my vow if you were to solve the riddle on your own, would I? And if you did, trust me, you would be more than able to save yourself from Hagmann's slave catchers."

"But—" Jack began.

"I'll say no more on the subject," Tobias said, standing abruptly. "As soon as I fetch the pistol I've hidden in my bedroom, I'm off to the front stoop to await Hagmann's arrival at daybreak. I'm not about to give in to any Hagmann—ever—without a fight. Meanwhile, you have until dawn." With a wink, Tobias ducked through the hearth and sealed Jack inside the secret room.

Jack spent a sleepless night staring at the parchment hanging on the wall. Tobias had clearly meant for him to understand that the riddle written upon it revealed where the treasure was hidden, and that once he found it, he could use it to buy his own freedom. Unfortunately, in his excitement, Tobias had overlooked an obvious flaw with his plan: Jack couldn't read. Few slaves could. Unlike Freddy, he had never encountered a kind white person on his plantation in North Carolina to teach him how.

Just before daybreak, Jack decided to let himself out of the secret room. If he gave himself up voluntarily to the slave catchers, the constable might not arrest Tobias. Jack closed the passage and set the heart hook on the spiral of the fireplace mantel while he looked for a place to hide it. Come what might, he was *not* going to lead Horatio Hagmann to the secret room, or anything hidden in it. Hagmann would just have to make do with the bounty on Jack's head.

Suddenly he heard the echo of a soft voice whispering *Where is* your *heart?* He turned to discover the room was full of white boys his age, clamoring for the treasure.

A RIDDLE
SUNDAY, JULY 12, 2009

Well, *we* can all read!" Finn said. "Just show us how to open up the back of the fireplace grate with the heart hook, and *we'll* solve the riddle."

"Except for one small problem," Tony said, clearing his throat. "I don't see any fireplace in the room. Just some crappy paneling behind the bookcase."

"What bookcase?" Jack said.

"What paneling?" Finn said.

"My parents put that up," Angelo said. "When I was born. The fireplace made the room really drafty. And they didn't want me to catch pneumonia in my crib."

"Well, the heart hook fits into the center slot of another iron knocker bolted to the chimney," Jack said.

"There's a *second* claddagh?" Angelo said.

"I don't know what that is," Jack said. "But there's another knocker, just like the one on the front door, that opens the back grate."

"I don't see another knocker," Finn said. "I see the fireplace, but nothing else besides a smoke-stained brick chimney with a crack in it."

Tony shoved the bookcase aside. He turned to Angelo. "The two of us need to get rid of this paneling," he said, "so we can see what everybody else is seeing."

"How?" Angelo said. "It's a two-man job, and we're not actually standing in the same room at the same time. We can't use the same tools. We can't even help each other lift or move stuff."

Definite problem.

Suddenly Jack looked alarmed. He raced over to the dormer window and flung it open. "It's Hagmann," he said. "He's down in the street with a couple of slave catchers and a policeman, just like Tobias predicted. He's accusing Tobias of escorting a young Negro boy named Jack, wearing an eye patch, into this house last night. He's saying I must be the very same one-eyed Jack who's in all the morning papers *and* on all the bounty posters around town." Jack raced for the attic door.

"Wait, show us how to get into the secret room first!" Angelo said.

"There's no time," Jack said. "If I don't turn myself in, they'll arrest Tobias!"

"But everything will turn out OK," Finn said. "I know for a fact you win your freedom somehow. You end up owning this house, giving up silversmithing to run the corner pub, giving *me* a job washing dishes."

Jack flung the door open and bolted out, vanishing into the past.

"Well, *that* didn't go so hot," Tony said.

"Now what do we do?" Angelo said.

"Look what I found!" Angey said, striding into the room. He was holding up an old Ouija board.

"Oh hi, Angey," Tony said, to telegraph his arrival.

"Not him again!" Angelo said. "Now what does he want? We're in the middle of a crisis here!"

"It was in a cupboard down in the parlor," Angey said, "with a bunch of other lame games like Parcheesi. Maybe we can use it to conjure up the ghost of Zio Angelo."

"I don't really think you can talk to the ghost of Zio Angelo with Ouija," Tony said, to fill the others in. "People just push that little arrow thingy around the board to scare one another at parties."

"That's why we're both going to hover our fingers *over* it," Angey said, handing Tony the Ouija board. "If the thingy moves on its own, then we know it's Zio Angelo."

"Wait, I see it now!" Angelo cried. "It's the one Mama bought for her boarders, even though they prefer Parcheesi." He turned to Tony. "Put it on the bed and play along with whatever I tell you. Maybe I can get you some demolition help."

"Genius!" Tony said to both at once. He laid the Ouija game on his comforter, climbed up onto the bed, and told Angey to take a seat on the opposite side of the board. They both hovered their fingers over the arrow thingy. "Wait, I don't remember the rules," Tony said.

Angey quickly explained: You set the arrow in the exact middle of the board, which had all the letters of the alphabet printed on it, plus the answers *Yes*, *No*, and *Good-bye*. Then you asked the board questions. Supposedly, whichever spirit was in the room caused the arrow to spell out the answers. You knew the round was finished when the arrow landed on *Good-bye*.

"Ready?" Angey said.

"Ready," Tony told Angelo.

"Ask the board if I'm in the room," Angelo said.

Tony asked if Zio Angelo was present. Angelo moved the arrow to *Yes*. To Angey, though, it totally looked like the arrow was gliding on its own.

"Awesome!" Angey said. "Ask him if Old Man Hagmann next door murdered him to get this house."

This Tony did. Angelo slid the arrow straight to *Yes*.

"Why?" Tony asked aloud, catching on.

Angelo spelled out the word *T-R-E-A-S-U-R-E*.

Solly and Finn clamored to know what was going on. They couldn't see the Ouija board, of course—and wouldn't have known what it was if they could have. Angelo explained as he went along.

Tony asked the board where the treasure was hidden. Angelo spelled out *A-T-T-I-C*. Tony asked where. Angelo spelled *S-E-C-R-E-T-R-O-O-M*. Where? *P-A-N-N-E-L-I-N-G*.

"'Panneling'?" Angey said.

"It must be behind that paneled wall over there," Tony said, "even though Zio Angelo spelled it wrong."

"Oops," Angelo said. "Spelling's my worst subject."

"Maybe we can pry it up somehow," Tony said. "Go see if there's a crowbar in the toolbox on the workbench down in the basement."

"I'm on it!" Angey said, dashing out of the room—

Just as Jack materialized at the door and strode in, smiling.

"Finn was right," he said. "I'm no longer a slave. I was just set free!"

"I told you," Finn said.

"How did that happen?" Solly said.

As it turned out Jack never got the chance to turn himself in. In fact, he didn't even make it to the front door. Because William Lloyd Garrison himself had suddenly arrived on the scene. Jack had hung back at the coffin corner while Garrison informed the slave catchers there was no need to search the house for a one-eyed slave named Jack. When they demanded to know why not, Garrison said, "Because the boy is no longer a runaway. I own him."

Garrison had also seen the morning papers. He had immediately gone calling on the members of the Anti-Slavery Society to collect enough money to buy Jack. As the slave catchers could plainly see, he held a thousand dollars cash in his hand, which he planned to send by an express rider to Jack's master in North Carolina.

Horatio Hagmann objected, of course. The sale couldn't possibly be official without Master O'Connor's consent. Garrison calmly pointed out that the going rate for prime field hands was half that sum—and Jack was, after all, a half-blind child—so there should be no reason to assume O'Connor would dispute the sale, and every logical reason to consider Garrison as Jack's new owner. Garrison gave the slave catchers his word as a gentleman that he would immediately contact the constable should he hear otherwise from O'Connor. Neither the slave catchers nor the constable was about to take on William Lloyd Garrison. They merely bade Garrison, Tobias, and Hagmann a good day and strolled off. Hagmann stormed into his own house and slammed the door. Garrison and Tobias burst into laughter. Garrison told Tobias he would now like to see his new "property."

Jack bounded down the remaining stairs and thanked Garrison, his new master, for saving his life. Master O'Connor would surely have hanged him back in North Carolina as an example. "A fair trade, I think," Garrison said, "since you saved mine last night. I guess that makes us even. So I hereby grant you your freedom."

Garrison then invited Jack to stay in his home—as his guest—until Jack could find a more permanent situation. Tobias cleared his throat. It just so happened he was still looking to take on an apprentice in his silversmithing business. If Jack was keen to learn a trade, he could stay on at No. 13 for as long as he liked. Jack nodded happily. "Well then, it's settled," Garrison said, smiling. "Jack, you should start thinking about which last name you would like to appear on your manumission—your certificate of freedom. Tobias, you should tell the local stationmaster to start looking for a new safe house. And I must get over to the express delivery office. After which I will be taking Jack's new friend, Freddy, out to breakfast."

Whereupon Jack had raced back upstairs.

"Mr. Garrison said Freddy has a fine career as an orator ahead of him," Jack concluded to the others. "He said the world hasn't heard the last of young Frederick Douglass."

"Frederick Douglass?" Tony said. "Are you kidding? He turns

out to be one of the most famous men in American history!"

"I guess I'll be taking Douglass for my last name after all," Jack said. "Anyway, now I can show you how to get into that secret room!"

"Not until my brother gets back with a crowbar," Tony said. He explained how Angey had turned up with a Ouija board, how Angelo had come up with the genius idea of posing as his own ghost to ask for Angey's help to rip out the paneling in front of the fireplace, and how he had just sent Angey down to the basement for the tools.

"Oh rats, I just realized something," Angelo said. "The paneling's still gonna be right there in my time. I won't get to see the secret room."

"We'll totally do a play-by-play for you," Tony said. "Meantime, while Angey and I are tearing out that paneling, maybe Solly and Finn can have a look around the house for the other claddagh, the one that's supposed to be hanging on the chimney. Angelo can't go anywhere, in case Angey wants to ask the board more questions. And Jack may as well just hang out, since the claddagh isn't missing for him."

Everyone dispersed. Tony weathered a moment of intense fatigue. Or hunger. He wasn't sure which. But then Angey raced back into the room. There hadn't been anything like a crowbar in the toolbox. All he could find was an old fireplace poker.

"It'll have to do," Tony said.

"Move that junk off the shelf," Angey said, pointing to the cap, mezuzah, claddagh ring, and heart hook.

Think quick! "Mind if we work around that stuff?" Tony said. "They're good-luck charms. And we sort of need all the luck we can get right now."

"Whatever." Angey shrugged. He set to work prying up a corner of the first plank. Tony grabbed hold and pulled. Together they wrenched it from the wall.

"You're not as big a wimp as I thought," Angey said.

"And you're not as big a jerk as *I* thought," Tony shot back.

They attacked another plank. Tony called a time-out and pulled the cell phone out of his pocket. He set it next to the objects on the shelf, so he could keep track of the time. T minus an hour and a half before Health & Safety arrived. If he didn't find that treasure soon, he would have to hand over Hagmann's lost key. Speaking of which, he added his wallet—where the key was still stashed—to the pile so he could move more freely. Back to work. Their progress was slow, but he and Angey were determined.

"Hey," Angey said. "There's a fireplace back here!"

Sure enough, an old brick fireplace emerged, plank by plank.

Meanwhile, Angelo and Jack sat cross-legged on the bed, watching Tony. He seemed to be very busy and, at the same time, not really *doing* anything. Eventually Solly returned to the attic—empty-handed—and joined Angelo and Jack on the bed. "How's it going over there?" he asked Tony. Tony told him they had uncovered most of the fireplace. But the back of the hearth was a solid plate of cast iron. Angey said he didn't need a play-by-play; he could see for himself it was just a fireplace. Tony told Angey he was just trying to keep the ghost of Zio Angelo posted. He continued to muse aloud: Above the slate mantel there was a long vertical slot in the brick chimney. There were holes bored into the bricks on either side. So that must be where the missing claddagh went.

"What claddagh?" Angey said.

Think quick! Tony pointed to the heart hook on the spiral. "That looks just like the heart from the claddagh knocker on the front door. But I found it up here in the attic when I was moving in. I'm guessing it belongs to another claddagh just like it."

That's when Finn returned to the room. He was also empty-handed. But he was grinning from ear to ear. He had just had a word with Paddy, who had fallen asleep on the sofa down in the parlor. (It was now past midnight of Christmas Eve in their time.) Paddy knew exactly where the second fireplace knocker was. He hadn't liked the fact the heart was missing from the middle when he'd first moved into the attic. He was sure it meant bad luck. So he had taken the hands and crown down and stowed them.

"Where?" Angelo cried.

"Hang on a sec," Tony said. He turned to Angey. "Maybe you should double-check that Mikey can't hear what we're doing up here."

"Good idea," Angey said. "Be right back."

"All clear!" Tony said, as soon as Angey was gone. Finn dove beneath the bed. The other boys followed him. Finn pried up two loose floorboards. A secret compartment! In it were hidden Paddy's personal treasures—a few girlie postcards (fairly tame, Tony thought, by modern standards), some stale cigars, a half-full bottle of whiskey. Jack was disappointed he couldn't see any of it. Meanwhile, Finn pulled out a pair of wrought-iron wings and a crown.

"Better double-check we haven't missed anything," Tony said. He reached into the compartment and fished his hand around.

"There *is* something else in here. It's tucked way in the back corner." He pulled out a length of rotting rope, looped at the end. They could *all* see that.

"You think maybe it's a lasso?" Finn said.

"Looks more like a noose," Jack said with a shudder.

"It is a noose," Tony said. "Maybe it's, you know, *the* noose."

"How do you think it ended up *here*?" Angelo said.

"What are you doing under the bed?" Angey said, returning to the room. Tony crawled out, leaving the noose behind. "I thought I heard a rat," he said. "It was just a couple of loose floorboards. But look what I found under them." He held up the claddagh pieces. "I bet all this stuff fits into those holes and slots above the chimney. Maybe if we put it back, it'll open the fireplace grate somehow."

"What makes you think that?" Angey said.

"I read something similar in one of my mysteries," Tony bluffed.

"We don't have time for fiction," Angey said. "Fire up that Ouija game. Ask Zio Angelo what to do next."

Tony pretended to reconjure Angelo with the Ouija board. He asked how to open the back of the fireplace. Angelo shrugged and turned to Jack. "I think it's your turn to be the ghost," he said. Jack told Tony what to do, and Tony relayed the information over to Angey at the fireplace: Place the wrought-iron hands and crown into the corresponding bore holes to form a claddagh. Turn the hands outward, so they crank the metal pulleys and gears inside the flue. Place the heart hook on the mantel in the catch of the vertical slot.

Jack vanished.

"Now what?" Angey—and all the other boys in the room—cried.

Tony tried not to panic. He took a good long look at the chimney. And he totally winged it. He told Angey to turn the heart hook nine times to the right with the clapper. This Angey did, though it wasn't easy. Next he told Angey to pull the heart hook down through the slot. As Angey did so, there was an ear-piercing screech of metal as the iron plate at the back of the hearth slowly rose. The secret passageway! Tony gave Angey one last instruction: Put the heart hook back on the spiral.

Jack reappeared. "Follow me!" he said, leaping off the bed. He ducked through the fireplace grate, with Solly and Finn right behind him.

Tony told Angey to follow him.

The room contained just what Jack had described: a moldy old mattress laid across several casks on their sides; a chamber pot, washbasin, and ewer; three upright casks arranged like a table and two chairs; several more casks lined up against the wall, all branded with the letters *VOC* topped by a little star.

Tony made straight for a piece of parchment nailed to the wall. He read the riddle aloud:

> *When after his Midnight Ride*
> *Paul's treasure I was taskt to hide*
> *Pluckt I the 9th of 13 stars*
> *From a 4th of heav'nly bars*
> *To keep freedom yet ringing inside.*
> *—J.J. 1779*

"What's that supposed to mean?" Angey said.

"It's a riddle," Tony said. "Maybe it tells where the treasure is."

"But it doesn't make any sense," Angey said.

"It's not supposed to," Tony said. "It's a *riddle.*" He pondered it for a second. "The only stars in this room are the ones branded on all the kegs above the *V* in *VOC*," he said. "I guess you could say a *V* is made up of two touching bars."

"What's going on?" Angelo wailed from the other room.

"Maybe the treasure's in one of those dusty old kegs," Tony said.

Jack piped up that looking in the casks was the first thing *he* had thought of during his long sleepless night. But they were all nailed shut, and he hadn't had anything to open them with.

"Wait, how many kegs are there?" Tony said.

The boys quickly counted them. Thirteen!

"Thirteen," Angey confirmed.

"Four of them are lying on their sides to make the bed," Tony said. "They aren't numbered, are they?" He pulled the mattress off. The side of each cask was indeed scratched with a slightly smudged inventory number. The fourth one was number 9! Tony stood it up while Angey grabbed the poker from the other room and pried off the lid.

"What's that?" Angey said.

Crumbly brown dirt. Like sawdust, only with an oddly

fragrant and familiar smell. Hardly the cascade of gold dou-bloons Tony had been imagining. Tony plunged both hands into the cask. He fished right to the bottom, causing some of whatever was in there to spill over the sides. He pulled out a handful of the gunk to show the other boys.

"What's that?" they all said at once, including Angey.

"I don't know," Tony said, shoving it into his pocket. "But I doubt it's what the Hagmanns have been after."

"Somebody tell me what's going on!" Angelo shouted from the other room.

Solly shouted back that all they had found so far was a baker's dozen of casks full of funny-smelling dirt.

"Rats!" Angelo said.

Angey suggested he and Tony hop back on the Ouija board and ask Zio Angelo what the poem meant.

"But what if Zio Angelo doesn't know the answer to the riddle?" Tony said.

"I don't!" Angelo cried from the other room.

"Tobias does," Jack said. "He told me he wrote it himself when he was thirteen."

"You're right," Solly said. "We can conjure him. All we need is something that connects Jack to him."

Tony knew what that was! But first he needed to get rid of Angey. He suggested his brother sneak back onto Michael's computer and surf for the meaning of *VOC*. Maybe he could find some connection to the riddle. Or maybe the brown gunk, whatever it was, was actually valuable. Meanwhile, Tony would have a word with Zio Angelo on the Ouija board. They needed to start multitasking now, or they were toast. Reluctantly, Angey agreed. He ducked out of the hearth passageway. Tony waited until he heard his sneakers clomping down the stairs before pulling the riddle off the wall.

The thirteen-year-olds trooped back out of the fireplace, where Angelo was waiting for them at the slate shelf—which was, in actual fact, a mantel. "It's kind of weird to watch you all walk out of the paneling like that," he said. Tony showed him the fistful of brown flaky dirt in his pocket. "Time for Plan C," he said, pointing to the 9 in the *1779* dating the riddle. He told Jack to place the parchment on the spiral, since he had the closest connection to Tobias. This Jack did. The others all crowded around, waiting in suspense.

Nothing.

"Maybe you should read it aloud," Tony said.

"I can't," Jack reminded him.

Oops. Tony read the riddle, line by line. Jack repeated the words. There was an echo in Tony's ears of someone else reciting the poem along with Jack.

A boy their age suddenly stood at the fireplace. He was bent in concentration over the spiral, scratching out the 9 of *1779*. Tony couldn't actually see what he was writing with, but it had to be a quill pen. Because the boy had long golden hair tied in a ponytail, and he was dressed in britches and a billowy homespun shirt. "Which animal does he look like to you?" Tony whispered to Angelo.

"A wild colt?" Angelo said.

"That's what I thought," Tony said.

"What made you ask *that*?" Angelo asked.

"I'll tell you later," Tony said.

Tobias looked up—having obviously overheard them—to see that he was not alone. "Crikey!" he said.

"Tobias?" Tony asked.

Tobias backed away in terror.

"You *are* Tobias Tucker," Tony insisted, "and today *is* your thirteenth birthday—isn't it?"

"And yet I'm clearly *still* a Jonah," Tobias said, sighing. "I have the blackest luck."

Once again Tony launched into the complicated tale of who they were and how they had conjured him with the pawcorance. They could prove they were from the future because they knew about the secret room behind the fireplace—they had just been inside—and they also knew about the riddle Tobias had just written. They were pretty sure it was a riddle that revealed the location of a treasure. And they were almost positive the treasure *wasn't* in any of the barrels. Tony showed him the fistful of brown flaky dirt. "All we found is this," he said.

"Tea," Tobias said. "But you can't arrest me for that. The Tea Act was repealed last year."

Tea? "We don't care about tea," Tony said. "We want the treasure."

"I'll never tell you where it's hidden!" Tobias cried. "The fact that you know about it only proves, in my mind, that you're Tory spies working for the Hagmann family!"

He was clearly not getting the "we're from the future" part.

Tony tried again. He assured Tobias that, in spite of how oddly they might be dressed, they were all patriotic Americans from the future. Not only that, but they hated the Hagmanns as much as Tobias did. In fact, their sole purpose in being there was to prevent a Hagmann from getting his hands on the treasure.

"So you're with Revere?" Tobias said, relieved. "I'm a future American too. And a patriot. Does Revere want to take the chest with him after all?"

"No," Tony said, "You don't understand. We're actually from—"

Angelo stepped on Tony's foot. "Revere," he interrupted. "You're right. Revere did send us to collect that chest. That's why we know it's in the secret room behind the fireplace; Revere told us himself. Now if you'll just show us where you hid it—"

"Not so fast," Tobias said, still suspicious. "If Revere sent you, you'll know where he's headed and why."

Clearly, Angelo was drawing a blank. Spelling was not his only weak subject.

"Wait," Tony said. "It's 1779, right?"

"When else would it be?" Tobias said.

"The Penobscot Expedition," Tony said. (Thank God Michael *had* collared him about his unfinished dissertation earlier that afternoon.) "Revere is Artillery Train Captain under Dudley Saltonstall," Tony said. "He's headed for Maine to keep the British from establishing a stronghold in Penobscot Bay."

Tobias slapped him on the back. "You can never be too sure, what with all these traitors about," he said.

"What's in the chest?" Tony said. "Revere was in too much of a hurry to tell us what we're actually picking up for him—or why *you* have it to begin with."

"I helped him forge it," Tobias said. "I'm an apprentice in his shop. He hired me back in seventy-three after I showed him where to hide all that tea. Little did he realize I'd bring such terrible luck to his house. I was born a Jonah, you see—"

TOBIAS

How Tobias Rescued Paul Revere's Treasure
from the Clutches of a Traitor

SATURDAY, JULY 24, 1779

In 1773, Tobias was sweeping the ashes out of the grate in the parlor when he heard an unexpected rap at the front door. He dusted off the knees of his britches and headed for the stairwell. For though he was only seven, this was his lot in life: cleaning fireplaces, lighting and snuffing candles, answering the door. His mother had died giving birth to him. His father had been trampled to death at the Boston Massacre a few years later. He was now a Jonah in everyone else's eyes. Cursed. Bedeviled by bad luck. What more could he expect than to toil as a servant for the only aunt who would take him in?

It was Paul Revere at the door.

The silversmith was no stranger at Aunt Polly's house—Uncle Nathaniel had also been a Son of Liberty, like Revere, before he was shot (as opposed to trampled) at the Boston Massacre—though Revere was, Tobias had to admit, strangely dressed at the moment: in war paint, a feathered headdress, and buckskin. But like any good footman, Tobias didn't ask why. He just went to fetch Aunt Polly.

"Is there a masquerade ball tonight?" Aunt Polly asked Revere.

"We need a place to hide a baker's dozen of tea casks," Revere said. "They're sitting in a wagon directly out front."

Aunt Polly peered over his shoulder. The items in question were indeed stacked on a wagon at the bottom of her stoop—on top of which sat a half dozen similarly clad Sons of Liberty. "I'm afraid I can't help you," she said. "It's plain by the *VOC* brands on the barrel staves that they've been smuggled from Holland to evade the Crown's tax on English tea."

"Your late husband would have been all too glad to protest such blatant taxation without representation," Revere exploded.

"Yes, well, patriotism aside, there's simply no place in this entire house to hide thirteen barrels," Polly insisted.

"What about the secret room?" Tobias said. "Up in the attic where I sleep?"

"Secret room?" Revere said.

"What secret room?" Polly said.

"The one behind the fireplace," Tobias said. "I felt a cold

draft coming through the hearth last winter. While I was trying to block up the gap at the bottom of the grate, I noticed there was a little room behind it."

To Aunt Polly's dismay, Tobias led everyone upstairs to prove his point.

Revere immediately recognized the iron ornament on the chimney—two hands clasping a crown—as a very old and very clever lock. He claimed it was designed by Irish pirates of yore to safeguard their booty, back when Hangmen Court was their favorite lair. An accomplished locksmith himself, Revere soon worked out that the back of the grate could be raised by pulling the heart of the ornament through a slot in the mortar of the chimney. His companions duly stowed the casks of tea inside the secret room and resealed the grate. Revere then manipulated the ornament's iron parts to remove the heart—which was actually a sort of hook—and tucked it into his pocket. "And now we have a pressing engagement on the waterfront," he said. Whereupon he and his companions trooped out of the house, climbed aboard the empty wagon, and rattled off into the night.

The next morning all Boston was abuzz with the news of a so-called Tea Party at which the Sons of Liberty, disguised as Mohawks, had sneaked aboard three cargo ships and dumped casks of British tea into the harbor, with very un-Mohawk-like cries of "No taxation without representation." The daily papers wryly observed that spoilage of so much English tea would hardly present an inconvenience to any patriot refusing to buy it; there was plenty of contraband Dutch tea around to brew.

About a week later, Revere returned to Aunt Polly's—dressed in his customary frock coat and three-cornered hat—with a strange gift: a door knocker of two hands clasping a heart fashioned out of wrought iron. An exact replica, in fact, of the chimney ornament in the attic. Aunt Polly thanked Revere for his thoughtfulness. Though her family was indeed of Irish origin, wasn't the knocker a bit . . . elaborate?

"The perfect disguise," Revere said. He attached it to the front door, explaining how, positioned in its original shape, it indeed represented Irish feudal loyalty to royalty. But repositioned in the shape of a heart flying out of a crown, it represented freedom from the tyranny of King George—and would serve as Revere's signal to Aunt Polly that he had another delivery of tea to make.

Revere then turned to Tobias. "Your late father would have been proud. Few people know it, but when he was crushed at the Massacre, he was actually on a secret mission for the Sons of Liberty. He's an unsung hero of the Revolution, and I would be honored to take his son on as an apprentice silversmith. What do you say, Polly?"

Aunt Polly saw little choice but to agree. It would be one less mouth to feed. And Tobias wasn't all *that* good at sweeping hearths. Plus Polly had already hired out her eldest daughter, Abigail, to the Reveres as a housemaid.

Tobias moved into Revere's house that very day, marveling at his good fortune—the very first of his life.

For the next few years, Tobias virtually forgot he was a Jonah. He loved apprenticing for Revere. Partly that was because Revere was a kind and patient teacher, partly because Revere was given to reciting riddles and off-color poems as they worked. But mostly it was because Revere thought Tobias had a real talent for smithing.

Which was why, when Royal Magistrate Benedict Hagmann commissioned Revere to forge a handbell for the high court, Tobias was immediately put on the job. (Ironically, the bell—which was to be cast in the finest silver—would be rung at the trials of Patriot traitors and tea smugglers to pronounce them guilty. Which wouldn't be very often. Because, even more ironically, the royal magistrate had himself been one of the so-called Mohawks at the Tea Party.) Unfortunately for Tobias, Hagmann's son, Ian, was also hired to help out. He claimed to be keen on silversmithing as a trade.

Tobias took an instant dislike to Ian. Though both boys were the same age—born, in fact, on the very same day—they were nothing alike. Ian was a snob, claiming to be descended from one of the Puritan families that had first settled Boston. He was also lazy, refusing to do any of the more menial tasks and foisting them all on Tobias. Ian much preferred gossiping with Tobias's cousin Abigail, who often sat in a corner of the workshop to do the household mending or peel potatoes, since she too liked listening to Revere's colorful stories and poems.

Progress on the bell was slow, especially when Revere started riding to New York and Philadelphia as a messenger for the Sons of Liberty. Tobias and Ian had little choice but to turn their attention to a backlog of teapot and candlestick orders. It was in fact during one of Revere's absences that Ian first showed his true colors. He brought Francis Hopkinson, a distant cousin visiting from Philadelphia, into the workshop.

"What are you stitching?" Francis asked Abigail.

"'Tis nothing," Abigail said, flushing crimson. "A way to amuse myself with odd ends of cloth in my spare moments."

"Go on then, hold it up!" Ian said. Reluctantly, Abigail held up a rectangular banner of red and white stripes. On a blue field in the upper-left corner she was affixing five rows of white stars.

"You're making a flag?" Ian said. "What on earth for?"

"Every new country needs one," Abigail said, shrugging.

"What do you think of it, Francis?" Ian said. "I'll have you both know Francis is an amateur draftsman *and* songwriter."

"Stars and stripes?" Francis said. "The design scheme isn't very original. Nor is the color palette. It's the exact same as England's."

Abigail flushed an even deeper crimson.

"It's all a new country would ever want in a flag," Tobias reassured her.

Abigail rewarded him with a grateful smile.

"The Colonies won't, in any case, be needing their own banner," Ian said. "The Sons of Liberty are trying their best to work out their differences with King George through diplomacy rather than violence."

"News to me," Tobias said. Revere was quite vocal about the fact that the Sons of Liberty soon planned to tell King George exactly what he could do with his taxation without representation. "Which side are you on, anyway?"

"Why, the right side, of course," said Ian.

He and Francis left the shop.

"What do you suppose he meant by that?" Tobias asked Abigail.

"I could hardly care less," said Abigail.

As the months passed, Tobias forgot about Ian's odd reply. The two boys toiled away at casting and etching the bell to Revere's exacting specifications. Finally Revere declared the bell finished—April 18, 1775—a night Tobias and the rest of the world would never forget.

★ ★ ★

Tobias was actually wiping away the last bit of polish from the bell when a messenger from the Sons of Liberty suddenly burst into the workshop, looking for Revere. War was upon them! The British had somehow gotten word that Patriots were stockpiling weapons in Concord. General Gage had just dispatched several troops of Redcoats up the Charles River to arrest John Hancock and Samuel Adams in Lexington, before marching on to Concord to confiscate the secret arsenal. The sexton at the Old North Church had already sent a lantern signal to Charlestown from his steeple that the Redcoats were mobilizing by water. Revere needed to ride at once to Lexington to warn Hancock and Adams that the British were indeed coming. En route, he should rouse every available Minuteman out of bed to grab his musket and defend that arsenal.

"Abigail!" Revere called into the house. "Fetch me my overcoat and hat!"

"Wake the countryside with this!" Tobias said, handing Revere the bell. "It would be better used to rally Patriots to arms than to sentence them to the gallows."

"You can't!" Ian gasped. "My father commissioned that bell for the Crown. It belongs to King George. If it's used to incite rebellion, they'll surely arrest Papa for treason."

"The bell belongs to *me*," Revere said. "King George has yet to pay for it. And your father can hardly be accused of treason against the Crown if the Colonies are no longer ruled by one. Now run home and tell your papa to take up his musket. It's time for all good Patriots to reveal themselves!"

Ian shot Tobias a murderous glance before removing his apron and dashing out the door. Meanwhile, Abigail brought Revere his coat and hat. Revere slapped Tobias on the back and made for the river.

No word from Revere the entire night. Still no word the following day, though there were alarming reports of bloody skirmishes between the Redcoats and Minutemen in both Lexington and Concord. Ian was furious with Tobias for giving Revere the bell and wouldn't speak a word to him. It was only after dark the following night that Revere returned home, exhausted and bedraggled—but triumphant. He set a small chest on his workbench. He pulled the bell from the pocket of his overcoat and handed it to Tobias.

And then Revere commenced his tale:

"I did indeed ring the handbell all the way to Lexington, calling every available Minuteman to arms. I was able to warn Hancock and Adams in time that the British were after them. Mission completed, I set off for the Concord arsenal with William Dawes—who had roused Patriots along the Boston route—as well as young Samuel Prescott, who came along for the lark of it. But we were soon stopped at a roadblock by

British guards. Prescott jumped his horse over a stone wall and escaped into the woods. Dawes tried to follow, but he fell and was captured. Meanwhile, the guards clapped a pistol to my own head and threatened to blow my brains out if I tried to escape. They were resolved to escort me straight to the jailhouse in Lexington. But as soon as my captors heard shots ringing out from Lexington Green, they stole my horse and left me to my own fate. In truth, I never got the chance to see the skirmish myself. Hancock asked me to take a metal chest of secret papers back to Boston. Unfortunately, I was bucked off Hancock's horse in Cambridge when a musket ball whizzed past my shoulder. To my surprise, Ian, your father emerged from behind a tree. He had just seen a Redcoat taking aim at my heart, he said, and had fired himself to divert him. Needless to say, I thanked Benedict for saving my life. I then remounted and rode straight back here to the North End with Hancock's chest."

"And the bell?" Ian said. "Did anyone recognize it?"

"General Gage is apparently mad as a hornet." Revere chuckled. "We'll have to hide it for the time being. But not here. It's the first place his men will look."

"Give it to me," Ian said. "I'll stow it away at my house."

"Now that your father has revealed himself as a Patriot, the Redcoats will no doubt be searching your home as well," Revere said. "In fact, he and I are both off to Doc Warren's in

Cambridge to lie low. Another battle is brewing at Breed's Hill. Gage's attention will soon be occupied by that."

Revere plucked a small key from his waistcoat pocket and opened the chest containing Hancock's documents. These he would bring straight to Doc Warren. He pulled a wadded silk handkerchief from his topcoat pocket, took the bell from Tobias, wrapped it in the handkerchief, set the bundle in the chest, and locked it up. "I designed this case myself, based on an old pirate design," he said. "It's virtually unopenable without the key." He handed this to Ian, telling him to guard it with his life. Ian pulled a simple silver chain from the neck of his shirt. He threaded the key onto it, promising Revere he would find a clever spot to hide the chest, elsewhere in the North End, where the British would never find it. "That won't be necessary," Revere said. "The most clever thing to do is keep the key and chest separate, since one is useless without the other." Revere pushed the chest toward Tobias. "Hide it at your Aunt Polly's," he said with a wink. "Then have yourself a nice strong cup of Dutch tea."

Tobias ran straight there. At the front door, he tucked the heart hook from the knocker into his pocket. Inside, Polly and her brood were madly packing to flee to the family summer cottage on Martha's Vineyard. So she barely noticed the chest he was toting up the staircase. "It's a pity you and Abigail will have to stay behind at the Reveres'," Aunt Polly said. "But you're both under contract. And there's no room for you in the carriage." Fine by Tobias! He wouldn't want to miss all the excitement. He continued his way up to the attic and stowed the chest among the dusty casks of tea. And just in the nick of time. Redcoats were at that very moment pouring into Boston to occupy the city. The Revolution was on!

The next morning, Tobias was delivering a teapot to a customer on Beacon Hill when he was nearly sideswiped by General Gage's own carriage as it pulled up in front of British Command. To Tobias's astonishment, it was Benedict Hagmann who stepped out, not the general. Two Redcoats standing guard at the front door nodded a salute as Hagmann was ushered inside. Wasn't Hagmann supposed to be *hiding* from the Redcoats with Revere in Cambridge?

Tobias didn't tell anyone about the incident—especially Ian—until Revere returned to the workshop two days later.

"I wish I could say I was surprised," Revere said, sighing. "Hagmann insisted while we were all lying low at Doc Warren's that he must go to Boston on urgent business. He would not be deterred. All we could do was ask him to bring back medical supplies for our wounded. A day later, though, Hagmann returned to Doc Warren's empty-handed. He claimed he had been captured by Redcoats at Boston Neck. They had dragged him in chains to British Command, he said, where Gage himself interrogated him. Hagmann swore he admitted to nothing, which is why Gage finally let him go. A harrowing tale to be sure. But he had more likely been sipping tea with the general and having a nice chat about upcoming Patriot plans."

"You think Benedict Hagmann is a spy?" Tobias said.

"With the help of his son Ian," Revere said. "Benedict relays whatever Ian overhears in this very shop to British Command. Which is no doubt how Gage caught wind of the arsenal we were storing in Concord."

"I'll strangle him," Tobias cried. "After I get that key back."

"You'll do no such thing," Revere said. He advised Tobias to continue making teapots and candlesticks alongside Ian, just as though nothing had happened. Now that Revere knew for certain the Hagmanns were Tory spies, he could use the situation to his advantage. He would just fill Ian's head full of misinformation for the remainder of the war. Meanwhile, the chest containing the bell was perfectly safe at Aunt Polly's house.

Safe until today, that was. July 24, 1779. Tobias's thirteenth birthday.

★ ★ ★

Revere returned to the workshop at midday with surprising news. He would set sail for Maine in three days' time. He told the boys about his commission under Commodore Saltonstall to Penobscot Bay.

"You have my word, sir, that in your absence I'll carry on here in the shop—with Tobias's help, of course—and that your treasured bell will continue to be safe with us," Ian said.

"That won't be necessary," Revere said. "I'm closing the smithy until the end of the war. You should return home to your family in Garden Court Street. And Tobias should ask his aunt to take him back in at Hangmen Court."

"But Aunt Polly is still on Martha's Vineyard," Tobias reminded him.

"All the more reason to look after the place," Revere said.

As soon as Ian departed, Revere asked Abigail to begin packing his own trunk at once. He would leave for Maine that very afternoon. Hopefully the Patriots would already have secured Penobscot Bay before Gage acted on the false information the Hagmanns would soon be supplying him. Tobias wished Revere the best of luck. Revere told Tobias to protect the new nation's liberty bell with his life.

The very first thing Tobias did when he got to Hangmen Court was to check on the safety of the chest in the secret room. To his relief, it was still collecting dust among the casks of Dutch tea. Nervous about Ian, Tobias devised a special hiding place for the chest, then sealed the secret room.

Just in the nick of time. Ian Hagmann suddenly burst into the attic brandishing a pistol. "Give me that chest," he said. "Or I'll happily blow your head off."

"You Hagmanns are nothing but Tory spies!" Tobias said.

"Of course we're Tories!" Ian laughed. "It's perfectly obvious the Colonies should remain loyal to the Crown, with a proper British class system in place and a strict social order. Not everyone is equal, nor should they be. You have no idea how utterly humiliating it's been for me to work alongside the likes of *you*—an orphan from the gutter with no family lineage. Thank God my family is fleeing to Toronto, a Loyalist stronghold, for the remainder of the war. In fact, my father is picking me up in the family carriage in a matter of moments. So fetch me that chest and be quick about it. We Hagmanns will return to Boston once this uprising is quashed. My father will resume his position as royal magistrate. And he will indeed ring that bell, just as he planned, to sentence traitors like Revere to the noose!"

Tobias charged Ian before he could get a shot off. He wrenched the pistol out of Ian's hand and knocked him over the head with it. Ian crumpled to the floor in a dead faint. Tobias tore up strips of sheeting from the bed. He bound, blindfolded, and gagged him, then dragged him into the secret room. It was only as he caught his breath at the slate mantel afterward that Tobias began to shake with fear. Of all the rotten luck. He should have known: Once a Jonah, always a Jonah. What should he do now? Seal Ian inside? Ian's father, Benedict, would be there any moment. And if Benedict managed to kill Tobias, how would Revere know where he had hidden the chest?

Tobias quickly composed a riddle on a piece of parchment—his own awkward attempt at the type Revere was fond of reciting—one that would lead him straight to the bell. But as he scratched out the last 9 of the date with his quill, he realized he was no longer alone in the attic.

STARS AND STRIPES FOREVER

SUNDAY, JULY 12, 2009

You mean Ian's *still* in there?" Tony said, pointing to the secret room.

Tobias nodded, ashen-faced.

Tony peeked inside. Sure enough, a boy their age now lay hog-tied and passed out on the floor, dressed in Colonial clothes similar to those Tobias had on. One by one, the others had a look while Tony conferred with Angelo. "I wonder why you guys can suddenly see Ian in there," Angelo said.

"He turned thirteen today," Tony said. "He's the exact same age as Tobias."

"Yeah, but we didn't conjure *him*," Angelo pointed out.

"Maybe we got a two-for-one with the riddle," Tony said.

"But there's nothing that connects Ian to the riddle," Angelo insisted. "Tobias wrote that *after* he knocked Ian out."

Tobias interrupted them. "Someone is downstairs," he said. "It must be Benedict Hagmann, wondering where Ian is." He reached into a hidden niche in the bricks just behind the slate mantel. A pistol materialized in his hand—the very one he must have wrestled away from Ian. (One that must still be hidden there more than two hundred years later, because every single thirteen-year-old, including Tony, could see it plain as day.) Tobias strode with determination toward the bedroom door. "Are you lads with me?" he said. "There are enough of us to overpower him."

"Right behind you," Tony said. He pretended to follow Tobias. But Tobias vanished, of course, as soon as he left the room. "Quick," Tony said, turning back. "We've only got a few minutes to find that bell!"

"But what about Tobias?" Solly said.

"Finding it might be the only way to save him—not to mention the rest of us—from the Hagmanns," Tony said. He explained his thinking: If they solved the riddle and located the chest, they could open it with the key around Ian's neck. Tony could then show the bell to Health & Safety in his own time to prove No. 13 was a historical site worthy of rescue from the wrecking ball. Meanwhile, Benedict and Tobias would return to the attic to find the chest empty. Tobias would no doubt tell the Hagmanns that four boys working for the Patriots had found it and taken it to Revere in Maine—leaving the Hagmanns with no good reason to harm Tobias now, or any future Hagmanns to menace the rest of them.

"Worth a try." Angelo grinned.

"Don't just stand there," Tony said, ducking through the hearth. "Help me drag Ian into the main room."

The thirteen-year-olds all sprang into action. They grabbed Ian's inert body and half carried, half dragged him through the hearth to flop him onto the brass bed. Angelo, who could now see him, promised to stand guard and shout if Ian started to wake up. The rest of them returned to the secret room, where Tony recited the riddle aloud:

"When after his Midnight Ride
Paul's treasure I was taskt to hide
Pluckt I the 9th of 13 stars
From a 4th of heav'nly bars
To keep freedom yet ringing inside."

The boys all turned to Tony, expectantly.

Tony shrugged. He was stumped. And tired. Really, really tired. He gazed around the room. Nothing but kegs. No point in prying any more of them open with the poker. They were just full of moldy old tea.

"The first two lines and the last tell you that Tobias has hidden the handbell Revere used to rouse the Minutemen," Solly prompted.

"The third and fourth lines must tell you where," Finn said.

Tony shrugged again. He sat on the lid of the nearest keg. He yawned. He could barely think straight. He stared up at the rafters. What had those two guys from Health & Safety joked? That the roof was now so sketchy, you could probably see stars through the gaps in the rafters at night.

Stars.

"Stars and stripes," Tony said, suddenly. "That's what they called the first American flag in 1777. Mildred Pickles has one of the originals, hanging in her shop. Thirteen stars and thirteen stripes, one each for the first thirteen states."

"So?" Solly said.

"Look at the slope of the roof. Thirteen wide planks, just like the flag. The planks are knotty pine, and most of the knots are in the upper left-hand corner—where the stars of a flag would be."

Tony was right! Not only that, but there were exactly thirteen of them.

"Sarah Pickles told me the ninth star is Massachusetts,"

Tony continued. "And the ninth pine knot up there is definitely in the fourth roof plank."

"Which has been cut crosswise in two places," Finn pointed out.

He and Solly rolled a cask over. Tony climbed onto its lid for a closer look at the sawn plank. The patch at the ninth knot pulled out fairly easily. Tucked up in the eaves beneath the roof shingling was a small metal chest. Tony handed it down to the others. "Bring it out to the main room," he said.

They all ducked back through the hearth passage. "You found it!" Angelo cried.

"Grab the key from around Ian's neck," Tony said.

Angelo reached into Ian's shirt. He pulled out the chain. No key. Just that odd triple spiral that some Hagmann ancestor or other brought over from England. Ian must have gotten it just today. The rest of the boys pounced on the spy. They searched every single pocket and seam of his clothes. They pulled his shoes off and checked inside.

"He didn't bring it with him," Angelo sighed.

"Why risk having Tobias end up with both the key and the chest?" Solly said. "The Hagmanns may be evil, but they're not stupid."

"Ideas?" Angelo asked Tony.

Tony broke into a huge grin. He retrieved his wallet from

the fireplace mantel. Out of the credit-card slot he pulled the little key. He explained how it had fallen off Benedict Hagmann's chain while he was supposedly looking after Zio Angelo. Tony had found it in the parlor before Zio Angelo's brass bed had been moved back up to the attic. No wonder Hagmann was so desperate to get it back. It had been handed down from Hagmann to Hagmann—along with the secret of the chest it opened—for generations.

"Wait—where did Ian go?" Finn said, alarmed.

All the boys looked over to the bed. It was empty. Ian had vanished.

"Stay calm—I bet he's still there," Tony said. He took the key back to the mantel and placed it on the spiral. Ian reappeared. "The key obviously has nine-ish energy," Tony said. "I must have conjured Ian with it while it was still in my wallet." He held it up.

The little loop in its handle *did* make it look like a nine.

"So it really *was* a two-for-one," Angelo said.

Tony took the key off the spiral, causing Ian to vanish again. He ambled over to the chest and inserted it into the lock. It was a perfect fit. He raised the lid. He pulled out a silk handkerchief. He unwrapped it.

They all marveled at America's *first* liberty bell, the bell that had rung in a new era of freedom from British tyranny.

"Three cheers for Tony!" Angelo cried.

"Not so fast," said Tobias, standing in the doorway. He was pointing Ian's pistol directly at Tony's head. "It wasn't Benedict Hagmann at the door after all," he said. "It was my cousin Abigail. Revere is sending her to Aunt Polly in Martha's Vineyard while he's away in Maine. She came back to the house to pack up a few things. She wanted to give me the flag she designed, to use as a bed quilt. She said she just needed to mend it first. I told her about Ian. She promised to tell Benedict Hagmann, as soon as he gets here, that Ian ran straight home to Garden Court Street with a small chest."

"Tony found the treasure!" Angelo crowed. Obviously.

"You're not with Revere, are you?" Tobias said. "You really are from the future."

They all nodded.

Tobias cocked the trigger of the pistol.

"But Tony solved the riddle, fair and square," Angelo said.

"That only proves it was a bad riddle," Tobias said. "I can't let you take Revere's bell to the future any more than I can let Ian have it. So I'll need Tony to put it back in the chest, please. Now."

Tony tried to reason with Tobias. Technically speaking, Tobias wasn't breaking his promise in the time anomaly. He *owned* this house—they all did—and everything in it. Plus Revere would obviously give the bell to Tobias outright at some point. Because in 1839, Tobias would tell Jack it was still hidden in the house. In fact, Tobias would virtually give Jack permission to try and find it.

"That may well be the case in 1839," Tobias said. "But for me, it's still 1779 and the bell is still Revere's. I promised Revere I would protect the nation's first liberty bell with my life. And that's what I aim to do."

"I totally understand," Tony said—to everyone's surprise. "That's what I would do too, if I were in your shoes."

"No!" Angelo said. "Tony is going to take the bell downstairs and hand it over to his parents so they can hire a builder to stop the back wall from collapsing on top of the back porch that already did collapse, not to mention keep the bookcase in the library, and whatever else, from crashing down around their ears. Tobias is going to show Ian the empty chest when he wakes up, then turn him in as a Tory spy. The Patriots will hang both Ian and his father as dirty double-crossing traitors to the Revolution—an excellent tweak of history if ever there was one—and the rest of us will head back to our own times, happy as clams."

"Except Ian, of course," Tobias said.

"So?" Angelo said. "He deserves it."

Tobias disagreed. As much as he disliked Ian personally, and as much as he hated the Loyalists, he was not sure anyone deserved to go to the gallows merely because their beliefs were different from his own. Ian actually believed he was doing the *right* thing by stealing the bell back for the Crown. That was just war. When you really thought about it, the Colonists were fighting a Revolution so *everyone* would have the right to believe what they wanted and grow up to be what they wanted. Which was why Tony was going to put the bell back in the chest, why they were all going to disappear, and why Tobias was going to rehide the chest in the secret room, then set Ian free—without returning his pistol, of course—as soon as he came to.

"Don't do it," Angelo said to Tony. "We can take him. It's four against one."

"No, Tobias is right," Tony said.

"Are you crazy?" Angelo said. "Think about what will happen to all of us because of a Hagmann. Jack will slip into a coma. Finn will disappear during the Molasses Flood. Solly will get booted off the Red Sox. And *I'll* get murdered! We've been able to turn back time with the pawcorance, just like you said. Now we've got to finish the job and tweak history—just like you said—to prevent all that from happening. Too bad if Ian ends up dangling from that old oak out front."

"Yeah but, think of what *won't* happen if we do," Tony said, quietly. "There's a huge problem with my whole tweaking-history hypothesis. Something I never thought of till just now."

"What?" Angelo said, exasperated. "I don't see a problem!"

"We can't tweak just one tiny part of history, can we?" Tony said. "Not without changing a whole bunch of other stuff. It's all interconnected, like the Hagmanns' triple-spiral charm." Tony went on to explain. Every thirteen-year-old in this attic had had some sort of brush with an important historical figure. And that had been *because* of a Hagmann. So any change they made to their individual Hagmann stories—even the smallest—might well result in a major historical shift. Jack might not save William Lloyd Garrison's life or inspire Frederick Douglass to become an orator, for example. Finn might not help Honey Fitzgerald get reelected mayor by catching the Tailboard Thieves, which would mean his grandson, John F. Kennedy, might never get elected president. Solly might not convince Finn to save No. 13 from the Great Molasses Flood with a claddagh. (OK, so Solly might also not inspire Finn to *cause* the flood to begin with; but that was only if Finn did blow up his own tank. Maybe he didn't. Maybe it *did* just burst in the unusually warm weather.) As for Angelo himself, he might not encourage Ted Williams to stick out his rookie season with the Red Sox and become the greatest left fielder of all time. And that was all in totally random years ending in nine. What about zillions of the other important historical events to come? Were they really willing to risk all that?

A long, quiet moment.

"Put the bell back in the chest," Angelo said, sighing. "Lock it up. Tuck it into the rafters. Let Ian go. Let history play out like it should."

Tobias lowered the pistol. "What a relief," he said, crossing the room. "I emptied out all the gunpowder after I tied Ian up." He shoved the pistol back in its niche behind the fireplace.

Tony placed his hand on his future great-uncle's shoulder. "I'm really sorry Benny Hagmann will end up bumping you off after all," he said. "But at least you're pretty old when it happens."

"I'll just try and lead a superinteresting life beforehand," Angelo said.

"But you do!" Tony said. He set the bell on the lid of the chest. He went to the bookcase and pulled out the dusty old scrapbook he'd found in the basement. He sat next to Angelo on the edge of the bed.

"I can't see whatever you're holding," Angelo told him.

"It's a scrapbook of your life," Tony said. "You may inherit this house when you turn twenty-one, but you don't live in it. Your mama does. *You* set off to have tons of adventures all over the world!" Tony began leafing through the scrapbook, describing the sort of life Angelo would lead as soon as he got those contact lenses: Air Force pilot in France. Pearl diver in the South Pacific. Archaeologist in Egypt. Visitor to the Grand Canyon, the Great Wall of China, the Golden Gate Bridge.

"All by myself?" Angelo said skeptically.

"Of course not," Tony said. He flipped to the front of the album and tapped the photo he'd inserted there. "It's a picture of your faithful sidekick, Anders Fogelberg," he said. "The two of you travel the world together, until his untimely death in 1979."

"Anders Fogelberg?" Angelo said. "Who's that?"

"I don't know."

"Well, what happened to him?"

"I don't know. But *you* don't return to Hangmen Court until a few years later, when your mama dies."

"I hope my life turns out to be that exciting when I disappear," Finn said.

"Um, lads?" Tobias said. "Better hurry. I think Ian is starting to come round." They all looked over. He was not on the bed, of course, because the key was still in the lock and not on the spiral. Only Tobias could actually see him.

Tony closed the scrapbook. He set it on the floor. He turned to address the other boys. "It was really cool meeting all of you, and hearing your stories."

"Well, you are one heck of a sleuth, Tony DiMarco," Angelo said.

Tony smiled. He *was*, darn it. He was good at history. So what if he needed to drop twenty-five pounds? He was a rock star, just like Julia had said. "Truth is, we were all totally awesome when we joined forces to find the treasure," Tony said. "That's what the *real* American Dream is about, if you ask me—united we stand, divided we fall—and I'll never forget that, even if I end up losing Number Thirteen an hour from now."

They all agreed.

"Shouldn't your brother Angey be getting back soon?" Solly asked.

"You're right," Tony said. "Before he does—and Ian wakes up—we should make the pact: never to mention these past few days to anyone, not even to one another when we're grown-ups and we meet the kid versions of ourselves on our thirteenth birthdays. It's the only way to make double sure that history plays out the way it should."

Tony went over to the pawcorance. He laid his right hand on the spiral. The others joined him. They all swore a vow of silence.

"Egads," Tobias whispered. "Ian's beginning to thrash around. And his blindfold is about to come loose."

Tony put his finger to his lips. He returned to the chest. He took up the bell and began to rewrap it in Revere's silk hanky. A white cloth star fluttered out of the folds.

"What's that?" Angelo said.

"It's from the flag Abigail designed," Tobias said. "I noticed the star for Massachusetts was missing when she gave it to me.

It's what she wanted to mend before laying it on my bed. She told me she had plucked the star off the night of Revere's Midnight Ride and tucked it into his pocket—for good luck—before handing the coat to him as he set off. Revere never mentioned finding the star. She just assumed he'd lost it along the way."

While the other boys speculated whether the flag that would soon adorn Tobias's bed was, in fact, the very *first* American flag, Tony slipped the star into his pocket—a harmless souvenir, he thought, of these past few days when everything that had happened would start to feel more and more like a dream, one he had made up in a sleep-deprived state. Tobias cut short the debate over the flag. Ian was now trying to call for help through his gag. Tony placed the snugly wrapped bell back inside the chest. He closed the lid, then locked it with Ian's key. He tucked the key into his wallet, which he shoved into his back pocket. He told the others to wait for him at the pawcorance while he stowed the chest in the knotty-pine compartment in the eaves of the secret room.

Just as Tony was getting back to the others, there was yet another rumble like an earthquake. A huge crash echoed up from the stairwell. The wrecking ball? Tony checked his cell phone. Couldn't be. The DiMarcos still had a half hour before Health & Safety booted them out. Probably just more of the house caving in.

"Better make our good-byes," Tony said.

"Thank you for putting the bell back," Tobias said. "Letting Ian go is the right thing to do. And thanks for your kind words about me, even if I'm still a Jonah. I promise to find some way of repaying you." Tobias took his riddle away from the pawcorance and stuffed it into his shirt. Though the parchment remained there on the shelf for the rest of the boys, Tobias himself vanished into his own time to deal with Ian.

It was Jack's turn next. He stepped up to the pawcorance, pulled the heart hook away from the spiral, and disappeared with a wink and a smile—a free man. Next, Finn stepped up. He contemplated his brother's ring—a vow of fidelity—then placed it on his finger. He faded away. Solly's turn. Solly shook both Angelo's and Tony's hands, wishing them the best of luck with their baseball careers. He placed the mezuzah case in his pocket—to carry his faith with him wherever he went—and returned to 1919.

Just Angelo and Tony left, now. "Thanks for a peek into the future," Angelo said.

Tony nodded sadly. He thanked Angelo back for the exercises and dieting tips. Even Angey had noticed he was now officially losing weight. Plus he had finally gotten his own room, even if it had been for only a short time.

They hugged each other tight.

"You don't look anything like an owl," Tony said. "If Benny Hagmann ever calls you Hootie again, punch him in the face. Your animal totem is definitely an eagle—the noblest of birds."

"*What* are you talking about now?" Angelo asked, laughing.

Tony explained what Sarah had told him about animal totems and vision quests.

"Wow, an eagle!" Angelo said, pleased.

"So which animal do I remind you of?" Tony asked.

"Lion," Angelo said without hesitating. "Courageous. Fearless. A born leader."

Tony hugged Angelo tighter. "I will avenge your death," he whispered into his ear. "I will find a way to bring Benedict Hagmann to justice somehow. I promise."

"See you in about seventy years," Angelo whispered back.

Embarrassed, they parted. Angelo took the ball cap off the spiral and jammed it onto his head. "Anders Fogelberg, huh?" he said. He faded away.

Tony waved his hand over the objects on the shelf. No static shock. No echo of voices. Just a ball cap, mezuzah case, claddagh ring, heart hook, and riddle written on a piece of crumbling parchment. And a cloth star, in his pocket.

He raced downstairs to find out what the most recent disaster at 13 Hangmen Court might be.

CONDEMNING A
HANGMAN

SUNDAY, JULY 12, 2009

Tony found the rest of the family in Michael's study, staring at the remains of the built-in bookcase, now smashed
to bits on the floor. Michael pulled a biography about Revere
out of the wreckage. Its spine was cracked in half. "Lucky I
already packed most of these up," he said, sighing.

Angey turned to Tony and whispered, "I was just sitting
down at Dad's computer to find out what *VOC* meant when
Mom called me down to the kitchen to bring a bunch of boxes
to the car, which took forever. I only made it back up here a few
minutes ago. But then I heard this weird groaning noise behind
me. When I looked around, half the wall was teetering over. If
this desk were another foot to the left, I'd be a goner."

"What's that?" Tony said, pointing to where the bookcase

used to be. Stuffed into a niche in the bricks was a sheaf of yellowed parchment.

Michael stepped over to have a look. "I think it's a letter," he said, leafing through the brittle pages. Julia suggested Michael set it aside. Right now he should salvage books. After that, the car would still need to be packed before Health & Safety turned up. As Julia and Mikey began to sift through the pile of splintered shelves, Angey handed Tony a Post-it note: *Vereenigde Oost-Indische Compagnie*. "That's what *VOC* stands for," Angey said. "According to Wikipedia, it's the name of the Dutch trading company that smuggled tea to the Colonies during the Revolution. That brown gunk in the barrels must be tea. Not much of a treasure."

"About that treasure," Tony said. "I think we should just forget about—"

"Oh my God!" Michael gasped. He was still over by the bookcase, reading that old letter.

"Now what?" Julia said.

"It's from Paul Revere!" Michael said. "To a thirteen-year-old named Tobias Tucker who lived in this house. The dateline at the top says it was sent from Maine in 1779."

"So?" Mikey said.

"So it's about what happened to Revere after the Penobscot Expedition!" Michael said. "Revere is writing to thank Tobias for sending a testimonial to Army Command, swearing it was an apprentice in Revere's shop—a Tory spy—who tipped off the British about the expedition, not Revere himself. Tobias claims Revere was actually feeding the spy false information so that the British would arrive in Maine three days too late. Revere is certain that it was Tobias's testimonial—along with Tobias's detailed account of Revere's patriotism during his Midnight Ride—that convinced the military tribunal in Maine to clear him of any wrongdoing. Basically this Tobias, whoever he is, saved Paul Revere's career!"

Which means he's not a Jonah after all. He's totally good luck.

"So?" Mikey said again.

"So it plugs the hole in Dad's dissertation," Tony said.

"Far more than that," Michael said. He quoted a passage near the end of the letter. In it, Revere thanked Tobias for offering to bring the chest hidden at 13 Hangmen Court to Penobscot Bay. But Revere would no longer need to sell the treasure inside to pay for his legal defense, since there wouldn't be a court-martial after all. In any case, Revere would not be able to open the chest without the key. Tobias should instead leave it hidden at 13 Hangmen Court. Revere strongly suspected the key would turn up in Boston again one day soon. And there might come a day when Tobias would need the treasure himself. It would be Revere's gift to Tobias for saving his life. Meantime, the mere memory of what they had forged together—and the freedom from tyranny it represented—was sufficient to sustain Revere until he returned home to Boston.

"There's a treasure hidden in this dump?" Mikey said. "Like what?"

Michael had no idea. It might be long gone by now. But the *possibility* that Revere had hidden something valuable in these walls—especially if he had forged it himself—was more than enough to convince Health & Safety to call off the wrecking ball. The City of Boston would no doubt insist the house be X-rayed and sonogrammed, room by room. And if they should be lucky enough to *find* that chest, No. 13 would definitely be a shoo-in as the next site along the Freedom Trail. Michael suggested Julia get on the phone to Health & Safety with the news, then contact the Historical Preservation Society and whoever was in charge of the Freedom Trail. While she was doing that, Michael would head straight over to the Revere House with the letter, to verify its authenticity. In the meantime, the boys could tidy up the mess, since it looked like they would now be staying. Julia gave Michael a massive *my hero!* hug. Michael dashed out of the room with the letter. Julia picked up the phone and dialed 411.

Mikey turned to Angey and shrugged. "I guess we should head down to the back patio to fetch the push broom from the last disaster."

"Get it yourself," Angey said. "It doesn't take two of us. And I've got something I need to discuss with Tony in private."

"What is up with you lately?" Mikey scowled. He stalked out of the room.

"You dog!" Angey said to Tony once they were alone. "You know where it is, don't you? I can tell by the look in your eye. Did Zio Angelo tell you on the Ouija board?" Tony nodded. "Well don't just stand there—let's go get it!"

Why not? There was nothing stopping Tony. By stuffing this letter behind the bookcase—knowing it was about to collapse in 2009—Tobias had kept his promise of returning the favor: He was basically giving Tony permission to "find" Revere's liberty bell, more than two hundred years later, in his time of need.

An unexpected twist in the way history had finally played out.

"OK," Tony said to Angey. "But we have to do it my way." He dug his cell phone out of his pocket. He dashed off a quick text message and handed the phone to Angey. "What I'm about to ask you to do next may seem a little weird," he said.

Angey shrugged. "Absolutely everything you've said and done since your thirteenth birthday has been totally off-the-charts weird," he said.

At exactly six o'clock, Tony rapped on the door of No. 15. As soon as Old Man Hagmann answered, Tony dangled the key in front of his nose. "Follow me," he said. "I'm pretty sure I've found what you're looking for."

Hagmann hurried after him.

Tony led him up to the attic of No. 13. But he didn't take the old man into the secret room. Instead, he pulled the locked chest out of the hearth. He told Hagmann that that was where he had found it, while tearing out the ugly paneling behind the bookcase. He placed the key in the lock. Should they have a look inside? Hagmann lunged for the lid, barely able to contain his excitement. Tony sat on the lid. "First we need to make a deal," he said.

"Get off it!" Hagmann said.

"Nope."

"Get off it, you fat little toad, or I'll drag you off it," Hagmann said.

"Not unless you do what I say," Tony said.

Hagmann raised his hand to strike Tony but then thought better of it. He took a deep breath instead. "My modest offer for the house still stands," he said. "I'll discuss the price with your father, but I promise it'll be enough to get your family settled elsewhere."

"That's not enough," Tony said, crossing his legs. "We want to live here."

Hagmann clenched his fists with rage. Actually, it took him

a couple of moments to control himself. "I can't imagine why, but fine," he said. "I'll call off Health & Safety *and* write you a check to get you started on the renovations."

"That's still not enough," Tony said.

"What else could you possibly want?" Hagmann shouted.

"A confession," Tony said. "That you murdered Angelo DiMarco and tried to frame my dad for it."

Hagmann looked startled but quickly recovered. "You can't be serious!"

"Dead serious," Tony said.

"But Angelo was my best friend!" Hagmann scoffed.

"He hated your guts."

Hagmann frowned. His eyes narrowed. He sized Tony up. "That's hardly a reason for me to kill him," he said.

"Maybe, but it sure raises a lot of questions," Tony said. "Like why Zio Angelo would suddenly decide to leave this place to you—his worst enemy—right after he fell ill. Especially since his last act alive was to make sure Number Thirteen *didn't* go to you. The very house your family has been trying to get its hands on for generations."

"Who has filled your head with these preposterous notions?" Hagmann said.

"Then there's the question of why you suddenly took it upon yourself to fire Zio Angelo's visiting nurse," Tony said.

"According to Maria Gomez, that was so *you* could start giving Zio Angelo his daily meds. Except that the coroner's report clearly shows he died of coronary arrest because there wasn't a trace of heart medicine in his veins."

"You have no real proof of that," Hagmann said. "Any of it!"

"You're right," Tony said, switching tactics. "Anyway, it's all water under the bridge now. Truth is, I barely knew the guy, and I never understood why he left me this dump to begin with. I like solving mysteries—it's my hobby and I'm planning on becoming a detective when I grow up—and I just want to know if I'm right."

"Never," Hagmann hissed.

"Then get your bony old butt out of my house," Tony said.

"Horrid, spoiled little monster," Hagmann said, beginning to pace the room. "Just like Hootie Saporiti when he was the same age. No respect for his elders. No regard for the class system. No sense of his rightful place in society. What we Hagmanns have had to endure! Rubbing elbows with the likes of the DiMarcos and Saporitis. Not to mention kowtowing to Jews and Irishmen and blacks. What I've sacrificed! Never marrying, never having a family, never producing an heir to carry on the quest. You can't imagine the burden! And now this. It's too much to endure."

Was it Tony's imagination, or was Hagmann sort of coming unhinged?

"So are you going to fess up or not?" he said.

"And then you'll give me the chest?" Hagmann said.

"As long as you call off the wrecking ball and write me a big fat check."

Hagmann returned to his pacing. "What have I got to lose?" he muttered to himself. "What's the worst the kid can do to me—call the police? I'll just deny everything. It'll be his word against mine."

Yup, Hagmann was definitely losing it.

"Hurry up," Tony said. "Or I'll just haul this piece of junk over to Ye Olde Curiosity Shoppe and sell it to Mildred Pickles."

"No!" Hagmann cried. "Don't do that!"

"Well?" Tony said.

Hagmann took a seat on the bed. He began to laugh—that weird hyena giggle—then stopped suddenly. "I knew I was running out of time," he said. "Angelo and I were getting old. If we both died, the secret of the treasure would be lost forever. I couldn't bear the idea of it. But what could I do? He wouldn't even let me in the house!

"Then one day, while I was out pruning my roses, his visiting nurse stopped by for a chat. She said Angelo had suffered a stroke after Thanksgiving. She told me he'd lost his ability to speak and was too frail to get up and down the stairs. Suddenly I knew: It was now or never."

And so Benedict Hagmann revealed his whole diabolical scheme:

After Angelo's nurse had come and gone the next afternoon, he broke into the bulkhead door behind No. 13. He tiptoed up the basement steps, through the kitchen to the staircase and up to the parlor, where he found Angelo dozing in his bed. It was easy enough to knock Angelo unconscious and strap him to the brass rails, given his weakened state and inability to cry for help. This left Hagmann free to ransack the attic for the chest. But all he found, even after a full night of searching, was a dusty old bookcase, dresser, and chair. So when Angelo finally came to the next morning, Hagmann threatened to smother him with a pillow unless he revealed the whereabouts of the treasure. Angelo's shakily written reply on his notepad: *No idea what you're talking about.* Before Hagmann could menace him further, though, he heard the rattle of a key in the front door. It must be the visiting nurse on her rounds!

Hagmann intercepted Maria Gomez in the front hallway. He explained how their chat the day before had prompted him to pay an overdue call on his oldest and dearest friend. He and Angelo had conducted a wonderful heart-to-heart chat via

Angelo's notepad. Unfortunately, Hagmann now had a delicate matter to discuss with her on Angelo's behalf. Could they take a cup of tea in the kitchen? That was when he promptly fired her. What could she do? She reminded him to give Angelo his daily dose of heart medicine, then handed over her set of house keys.

Which was when Hagmann realized what he must do.

He gave Angelo an ultimatum, while he was still strapped to the bed: Angelo would never see another drop of heart medicine unless he revealed the whereabouts of that chest. Angelo merely scratched out a feeble question mark on his pad. Finally, Hagmann had to consider the very real possibility that Angelo didn't know anything about the treasure.

So he switched gears. He went through all of Angelo's paperwork in the rolltop desk of the parlor until he found what he was looking for: the original deed to 13 Hangmen Court and Angelo's last will and testament. As for the deed, he just burned it. It barred every Hagmann for all time from inheriting the place. And as for the will, he quickly typed out an addendum on Angelo's old-fashioned typewriter that revoked Michelangelo DiMarco as inheritor and named himself instead. He then presented three copies of the addendum for Angelo to sign, pointing out that he was basically a goner without his medicine. If Angelo refused to sign the addendum, Hagmann would merely forge his signature and get the house anyway. But if he did sign, Hagmann swore he would regift No. 13 back to the DiMarcos as soon as he found what he was looking for. Surprisingly, Angelo agreed to sign. On one condition: Hagmann box up an old Red Sox ball cap before his very eyes and hand it to the postman—also before his very eyes—to be sent, along with a card he'd scrawled, special delivery to his great-nephew Anthony DiMarco for his thirteenth birthday. An odd request, to be sure, but Hagmann quickly carried it out. Once the postman left, Angelo signed the addendum in triplicate—one copy for Hagmann, one for Angelo's lawyer Birnbaum, and one for Angelo's desk.

Of course Hagmann had no intention whatsoever of regifting the house to the DiMarcos. As soon as Angelo was dead, he intended to tear the place apart, brick by brick if necessary, until he found the chest. And his plan would have worked, too, if it hadn't been for Michael's unexpected visit.

Luckily for Hagmann, Angelo still used an old-fashioned answering machine. So they both heard Michael's voice echoing through the parlor as he left a message for his uncle: He was just getting into Boston for his history conference; he would stop by for a visit first thing in the morning; he would let himself in with his own key. The thought of rescue must have been too much for Angelo. He gasped, clutched at his chest, then slipped into a coma. Which was why Hagmann decided to untie him and leave him alone in the parlor while he himself waited out the night in the kitchen. With any luck, Michael would arrive the next morning to discover Angelo stone-cold dead in his bed while Hagmann innocently pretended to prepare Angelo's breakfast downstairs.

Except that Angelo must have faked the coma. Because he somehow managed to stumble over to his desk during the night, hand-revise his copy of the will, and stuff it into an envelope addressed to his lawyer. In fact, Angelo was far from dead when Hagmann confronted Michael for "breaking in" the next morning. More alert than he had been in weeks, Angelo was scribbling an alarming note to his nephew: *Trying to kill me.* Lucky for Hagmann, it was Michael who offered him a plausible explanation: that Angelo's medicine made him paranoid. Frowning, Angelo scribbled another note for Hagmann: *Make tea.* Hagmann invited Michael to join him down in the kitchen. But Angelo emphatically wrote: *He stays.* Hagmann saw little choice but to leave Michael alone with Angelo while he put the kettle on. Which was when Angelo must have handed Michael the will to mail off.

Hagmann had already told Tony the rest. Michael stuffed the envelope into his pocket and left for his history conference.

Alarmed, Hagmann raced back to the parlor to find out what Angelo had given him—only to discover Angelo dead. Dead with a big grin on his face. At that point, all Hagmann could do was call 911. He ransacked the parlor before the ambulance got there. That's of course when he discovered the will was now missing from the desk. To make matters worse, the key to the chest must have broken loose from the chain around his neck in the mad search—a fact he hadn't noticed in all the mayhem until yesterday at the hardware store.

"But now you've found it," Hagmann concluded with a yellow grimace. "And what it opens. That's made all of our lives easier."

"Except Angelo's," Tony said.

"He was old and dying," Hagmann said. "You just admitted yourself that you barely knew him."

"You still killed him," Tony said.

"Who says?" Hagmann sneered. "There isn't a single witness to confirm this conversation ever took place."

"Except me," a voice said from behind him.

Hagmann whirled around to find Angey emerging from the hearth.

"I heard the whole thing, loud and clear," Angey said.

Hagmann blinked rapidly a half dozen times. He stood. He began to cackle again. "It'll never stick," he said. "You're just a couple of snot-nosed kids from the melting pot with overactive imaginations. I come from one of the oldest and most distin-guished families of Boston."

"You do not," Tony said. "You come from a long line of murderers, traitors, double-crossers, and thieves. Thirteen gen-erations of racist, sexist jerks who think they have more rights than blacks, or the Irish or Jews or Italians, just because you happened to sail over on an earlier boat."

Hagmann stopped cackling.

"I've got news for you, dude," Tony said. "It's diversity that makes this country great. And a hangman is still a hangman, even if you move the *n* from the middle of your name to the end."

"Besides," Angey said, holding up Tony's cell phone, "I took the added precaution of recording every single word of your confession on the voice mail of Tony's friend Sarah."

"And anyway I'm here in person as backup," said Sarah, duck-ing through the chimney. "Not to mention to settle an old score between my great-great-greats and yours."

Hagmann slumped onto the bed, speechless. He mopped his face, which had gone very gray. He had finally been bested—by a thirteen-year-old, no less—and he knew it.

Angey dialed 911. He told the operator he'd like to report a murder.

"At least let me see it," Hagmann whispered to Tony. "Just once."

Tony stood. He opened the chest. There was nothing like a silver bell inside. Instead, he pulled out a rotting hangman's noose. "I guess this belongs to you," he said. "And I think you just used it on yourself."

THE END?

MONDAY, AUGUST 24, 2009

Tony jumped out of bed as soon as he heard the alarm. It was the morning of his first day of eighth grade at Boston Latin. He pulled on a new pair of jeans—two sizes smaller than the ones he had worn when he'd arrived at Hangmen Court, thank you very much—and his favorite Red Sox jersey. He checked himself out in the mirror. All in all, it had been a pretty good summer.

Just as Michael had predicted, the letter from Revere to Tobias was more than enough to get 13 Hangmen Court off Health & Safety's demolition list. As soon as Tony "found" the treasure chest in the attic's secret room, No. 13 easily qualified as an exciting new site for the Freedom Trail, since Revere's handbell proved it was an important part of his Midnight Ride, and the *VOC* casks proved it was the Sons of Liberty's hiding place for smuggling tea prior to the Tea Party. As an added bonus, No. 13 also qualified for the Black Heritage Trail, seeing how the secret room itself was a heretofore unknown station of the Underground Railroad. Plus when Michael sold the letter to the Revere House, he got a good enough price for Eddie Wong to make all the emergency repairs necessary to allow the DiMarcos to remain safely in the house until a full restoration could begin the following summer—to be funded by the Boston Historical Preservation Society.

The DiMarcos would, of course, have to move temporarily when construction got under way. But that would only be next door, to No. 15. As it turned out, Benedict Hagmann hadn't been as well off as he had pretended—he hadn't been paying his back taxes for years—and he had desperately *needed* that bell to get himself out of some serious debt. (So basically, if he *had* written Tony a big fat check for the place, it would have bounced.) Anyway, the City of Boston had confiscated Hagmann's home, and it now served as temporary housing for any families evicted by the Health & Safety Department. Much more comfortable than a motel room at Revere Beach.

Benedict Hagmann certainly wouldn't be needing No. 15 any time soon. He had been charged with the murder of Angelo DiMarco and was now sitting in Walpole Prison awaiting trial.

Rumor had it that Hagmann's lawyer planned to plead not guilty by reason of insanity.

As for Michael's dissertation, he was in final revisions now—thanks again to that letter. A major New York publisher had offered to turn the whole thing into a book you could actually buy and read. Not only that, but Harvard had offered him a teaching job in January, when one of their history professors was to retire.

Meantime, Michael had attended a bunch of Red Sox games with Tony and Angey over the summer. (Tony had worn Ted Williams's cap to every game, for luck. In the end, he had never bothered to get it appraised; he knew for a fact it belonged to Williams. And anyway, it wasn't for sale.) Mikey hadn't joined them much on their excursions to Fenway Park. He continued to be a die-hard Tigers fan. Actually, Mikey had pretty much given Angey the cold shoulder after all that had happened. It had bummed Angey out at first, but then he just started hanging out with Tony and Sarah. As luck would have it, Sarah was starting tenth grade at Boston Latin this fall. The three of them focused instead on perfecting their throwing arms at Christopher Columbus Park so they could all try out for JV baseball in the spring.

Which meant Tony had spent a lot less time online in virtual reality, and a lot more time in, well, reality. And the pounds kept melting away.

Speaking of the Pickleses—

Mildred was overjoyed when Tony jangled into Ye Olde Curiosity Shoppe and set the cloth star on the spiral of the slate countertop for her inspection. Needless to say, it was a perfect match to all twelve of the others on the Stars and Stripes hanging overhead—thereby proving, at least to them, that the first American flag's quincuncial design was neither a Hopkinson nor a Ross, but a Pickles. Mildred had seen no need to prove this fact to anyone else. The flag was still not for sale. There was a big difference, she had said, between an artifact and a keepsake, though both could be curiosities.

And finally, the fate of Revere's silver handbell. Since Tony hadn't really needed to sell it to help his parents pay for the renovations (and since he had the front door knocker, also forged by Revere, as a secret backup), he had decided to donate it to the Smithsonian Institution in Washington. As America's first and *original* liberty bell, it now sat in good company alongside other treasures such as Old Glory, Thomas Jefferson's Bible, Abraham Lincoln's top hat, Lewis and Clark's compass, and Thomas Edison's lightbulb.

"Tony, get a move on!"

Angey, calling up from the third-floor landing.

Tony glanced over at the slate fireplace. He had never put the paneling back up. He liked having access to the secret room, now that the tea barrels had been donated to the Boston Tea Party Ships & Museum. He wandered over to the pawcorance and placed his hand on the spiral. He wondered what Angelo and Solly and Finn and Jack and Tobias were up to right now. Though he loved having his own room, he had kind of gotten used to sharing it with five other thirteen-year-olds for a while.

The distant echo of other voices from other times in Boston history, beyond Revere and the Revolution, reverberated in Tony's head. He listened intently. What were they trying to say? Sounded like the word *noose*.

Reluctantly, he pulled his hand away. If he didn't hoof it down to the kitchen, he wouldn't have time to wolf his breakfast yogurt, granola, and juice. He would just have to ignore the voices and leave that hangman noose hidden in Paddy's secret compartment beneath the bed. Right now, he had the rest of ordinary old 2009 to get on with. Then again, who could say who he might cross paths with today, or how he might unwittingly change the course of history just by being himself?

I can't think about that right now.

Tony didn't want to be late for his first day.

What's Story, What's History

SUMMER OF 2009

Story: As a fiction writer, I love the idea that story is being made out of history all the time—every single day of every month of every year—in spite of the fact that you may only remember a handful of dates like 1776 and 1812 and 1945. That's kind of why I set Tony's extraordinary tale in 2009—what might be considered one of the more ordinary off years in recent U.S. history. I specifically chose years ending in 9 because, frankly, I just like the nine-ishness of that number.

History: Mid-July of 2009 was, in fact, fairly quiet in Boston. America was in full economic recession, and the unemployment rate was at 9.5 percent with a loss of 467,000 jobs. President Barack Obama was valiantly trying to end two unpopular wars on terrorism—one in Iraq, another in Afghanistan—and not making much progress with either. Apart from that, there were a couple of noteworthy world events taking place while Tony was busy conjuring thirteen-year-olds: The big news was probably the funeral of legendary pop singer Michael Jackson, who died of an overdose in late June. Alaska's governor Sarah Palin (the unsuccessful vice presidential candidate for the Republicans in 2008) announced her resignation, shocking most Americans with the declaration she was leaving presidential politics for good. (We'll see.) India repealed its ban against homosexuality, declaring antigay laws to be a violation of human rights. Oh yeah, and the Red Sox swept a four-game series against the Royals at Fenway, though they ultimately ended the season eight games behind the Yankees.

13 HANGMEN COURT

Story: I wouldn't bother looking for a cul-de-sac with that name in the North End. I thought long and hard about whether I would want a bunch of people knocking at *my* door asking to see Tony's pawcorance in the attic. I immediately made up a fake address. Just as fake, actually, as the names Hagmann and Hangman. Neither family (nor the Pickleses, for that matter) figures prominently in Boston history for thirteen generations.

History: You might, however, notice the resemblance of Hangmen Court to *Henchman* Street, which does exist. That was named after Captain Daniel Henchman, who came to Boston as an indentured servant in 1666. However colorful his name, Daniel seems to have been a fairly upstanding—and busy— citizen before he moved to Worcester: militia captain, banker, lawyer, farmer, and brewer. But what if he really had been some sort of henchman? Or better yet, Boston's original hangman? See how stories are hatched?

TED WILLIAMS

Story: This legendary left fielder for the Boston Red Sox never walked out of that series with the Tigers during his rookie season—which actually took place in Detroit, not Boston, in May of 1939. Nor would his doing so have ruined the career of number 27, Solomon Weinberg, because I made Solly up. In 1939, the Red Sox uniform numbers stopped at 26. (Note, however, that when you add 2 + 7, you get a 9. . . .)

History: Ted Williams *was* of Latino descent on his mother's side, though he wasn't ever allowed to talk about it to the press. Williams didn't get along at all with team manager Joe Cronin, who was by all accounts an unabashed racist. Cronin, who later became the general manager of the Red Sox, never traded for a single black player, and he refused to sign the young Willie Mays. But here's something for the weird-but-true category: Williams was, in fact, cryogenically frozen when he died, to allow for the possibility of being brought back to life by future relatives. So I personally think he would have liked making a guest appearance in this book.

PAWCORANCES

Story: The spiral carved into Tony's pawcorance comes straight out of my imagination, though it is based on a number of spiral pictographs and petroglyphs found in ancient Native American ruins throughout North America. Working with modern tribes, anthropologists have guessed their meaning to be the universe, a portal to the spirit world, or the coiled nature of time—and many others. And I've totally made up the link between spirals, pawcorances, and vision quests.

History: A word or three about pawcorances themselves: These mysterious stone markers have been found the entire length of the eastern seaboard. Their original purpose remains a mystery. It was actually Captain John Smith, settler of the Jamestown Colony in Virginia, not Myles Standish, settler of the Massachusetts Bay Colony, who described pawcorances in his memoirs. (I pulled a quick switcheroo because I thought the information coming from a Massachusettsian made my story spin a little tighter. . . .) Smith asserted pawcorances were indeed stone markers and altars identifying places where the Algonquians had encountered spirits. According to Smith: "As you travel past them, they [local tribesmen] will tell you the cause of their erection, wherein they instruct their children." Algonquian tribes gave the pawcorances of New England their name. Some sources claim that *pawcorance* was also the word for a small bird—of unidentified species—sacred to the Algonquians. It was believed to be inhabited by ancestral spirits, since it only ever appeared at dusk and dawn to sing. I've made the pawcorance a mockingbird for this story; I like the fact that mockingbirds mimic the languages of many other animals. Speaking of Myles Standish—he was, in fact, invited to a welcome feast of boiled lobsters and roast cod by the Massachuset sachem Obbatinewat. I have no idea if they discussed pawcorances, since Standish didn't actually write a memoir titled *Of My Amazing Exploites in the New Worlde*.

VISION QUESTS

Story: The vision quest rituals I attribute to the Massachuset tribe—though based on a number of Algonquian traditions—are also made up. This is partly to protect Native American privacy. Many tribes prefer to reserve their cultural and religious practices for members of their own community. The Massachusets would certainly not link spirit encounters with the notion of time anomalies, as Hermann Minkowski (a real person) did in 1909 with his block universe theory (his honest-to-God hypothesis). It is true, though, that there was no word for *time* in Algonquian until the arrival of Europeans in North America.

History: Vision quests aren't, by the way, solely a North American practice. The ritual can actually be found in nearly every ancient culture on the planet. If you're interested in learning more about Native American practices, Google "Grandfather Stalking Wolf." He was an Apache elder who traveled North and South America, distilling a wide range of rituals and philosophies—including the vision quest—to their most common roots.

THE GREAT MOLASSES FLOOD OF 1919

Story: No one by the name of Finn McGinley ever rented that derelict tank in the Purity Distilling Company's yard (a real molasses factory) or planned to make rum with what was stored in it. I based that part of Finn's tale on persistent rumors that Purity itself was trying to get rid of all evidence of rum making prior to the official effective date of Prohibition in 1920. What Purity *officially* made was industrial alcohol, which was then used in the production of munitions.

History: The Great Molasses Flood itself *sounds* like a fake event, I agree, but it's totally true. It killed 21 and injured 150. It took volunteers 87,000 hours to clean some 2,300,000 gallons of molasses off cobblestone streets, buildings, and automobiles. Boston Harbor was said to have run brown until summer. Local residents brought a class-action suit against Purity Distilling for the disaster. Purity tried to claim the tank was blown up by anarchists protesting the outcome of World War I. But it did ultimately pay over $6 million (by today's standards) in out-of-court settlements.

MAYOR JOHN F. "HONEY-FITZ" FITZGERALD

Story: Honey-Fitz's spectacular arrest of Stevie Wallace at the Charter Street Bank never took place. (I bet, though, that

Honey-Fitz would have loved the tale—especially the part about them blowing open the safe as a Christmas gift to the poor Irish in the neighborhood.) A well-known champion of multiculturalism many decades before such a word was envisioned, Honey-Fitz did love the North End, where he grew up. He considered all its inhabitants, regardless of their race, color, or creed, as his "dearos." Here's a story that might actually be true: When Honey-Fitz finally convinced President Cleveland to veto an anti-immigration bill, his archenemy in Congress, Henry Cabot Lodge, was said to have shouted, "Impudent young man, do you think Jews or Italians have any right in this country?" and Honey-Fitz was said to have replied, "As much as your father or mine. It's only a difference of a few ships." It's pure fiction, though, that Honey-Fitz (or his Red Sox fan club, the Royal Rooters) headquartered in a North End bar. Honey-Fitz was, as Jack points out, a teetotaler.

History: Honey-Fitz did indeed get reelected mayor in 1909 on a platform of reform. His gift of gab (known as Fitzblarney), and the fact that he sang "Sweet Adeline" at every campaign rally, certainly helped him to win—though no one knows who actually came up with *that* idea. Honey-Fitz did bring Irish mobsters Stevie and Frank Wallace under control with a few minor arrests. But it didn't put an end to their shenanigans. It just prompted them to change their mob's name from the Tailboard Thieves to the Gustin Gang and become Boston's premier bootleggers. (Others claim that that title went to John F. Kennedy's other grandfather, Joseph Kennedy.)

FREDERICK DOUGLASS *and* WILLIAM LLOYD GARRISON

Story: Though many threats were made against William Lloyd Garrison's life over his long and controversial career as an abolitionist, the assassination attempt at Boston's African Meeting House is pure fiction, as is his collection of $1,000 to buy the freedom of a one-eyed runaway slave named Jack.

History: In 1839, Frederick Douglass did hear Garrison orate in Boston about the abolishment of slavery for the first time, causing Douglass to state: "No face and form ever impressed me with such sentiments as did those of William Lloyd Garrison." In 1841, Douglass went to hear Garrison again in Bristol and was unexpectedly asked to speak. Impressed, Garrison sang Douglass's praise in *The Liberator*, which more or less launched Douglass's career.

PAUL REVERE

Story: Paul Revere never rang a handbell to rouse Minutemen to arms. Nor did he forge such a bell for royal governor

Thomas Hutchinson—though he did indeed own a bell and cannon works. (I admit it: I also made up the part about Revere learning how to make unopenable locks by copying North End pirate designs.) I actually got the idea for the handbell from a couple of inaccurate illustrations of Revere's fabled Midnight Ride. Utterly missing from my story is the fact that Paul Revere Junior—a fine silversmith in his own right—held the shop together while Paul Revere, an excellent rider, delivered messages up and down the eastern seaboard for the Sons of Liberty.

History: Revere didn't really become famous for his role in the American Revolution until 1860, when Henry Wadsworth Longfellow published a poem about the Midnight Ride in the *Boston Transcript*. There can be no doubt of Revere's patriotic commitment to American independence. He created one of the first (and most famous) engravings of the Boston Massacre. He was indeed one of the Mohawks shouting "No taxation without representation!" at the Boston Tea Party. He even wrote his own detailed account of his Midnight Ride—which you can actually read online just like I did. (In it, in fact, you'll hear about the exploits of a Tory traitor and spy named Benjamin Church who served as inspiration for my totally fictitious characters Ian and Benedict Hagmann.) That Revere requested his own court-martial to clear his name of any wrongdoing in the Penobscot

Expedition is a fact. What caused the Continental Army Command to dismiss the case before it ever came to trial is less clear, since military tribunal proceedings were, for the most part, oral and not well documented.

THE U.S. FLAG

Story: As you have no doubt guessed, I made up the fact that Sarah Pickles's great-great-great-plus grandmother Abigail was the real, true designer of the American flag. No one knows for sure who came up with the very first stars-and-stripes motif. Legend has it that George Washington handed seamstress Betsy Ross a pencil sketch of *his* idea—a circle of thirteen white stars in a blue field, resting on thirteen alternating red and white stripes. But there is no hard evidence that such an event ever took place. Truth is, many variations of the Stars and Stripes were in use during the American Revolution before the Second Continental Congress adopted the horizontal (or quincuncial) version as the official U.S. flag on June 14, 1777.

History: Though this official version of the flag has often been cited as the handiwork of Francis Hopkinson, there's no documented proof that he actually designed it. About all we know for sure is that Hopkinson billed Congress a quarter cask of public wine for having done so. But he was never paid.

ACKNOWLEDGMENTS

Writing a book is a very solitary task. For me, that means sitting alone for about a year and a half, waiting for the words to come, with only my imagination to keep me company. But *making* a book—now, that's an entirely different story. *13 Hangmen* simply wouldn't exist without the help of dozens of generous and supertalented people. For providing me the time and space to sit alone: Timothy Horn, Chima, Michael Martinez, Beverly Donofrio, Nada Hermitage, the Corporation of Yaddo. For helping to shape early drafts and representing the final one: Albert Zuckerman at Writers House. For bringing this novel so beautifully to print at Abrams: Howard Reeves (editor extraordinaire), Jim Armstrong (top-notch managing editor), Maria Middleton (fabulous book designer), Jenna Pocius (conscientious editorial assistant), and Jason Wells (marketing genius). Special shout-outs go to Renée Cafiero (copy editor) and Rob Sternitzky (proofreader), who went above and beyond the call of duty to help me pin down all the facts and weave this story in and out of history.

ABOUT THE AUTHOR

ART CORRIVEAU holds an MFA in writing from the University of Michigan. His writing has received great reviews from *School Library Journal, Booklist, Kirkus Reviews,* and many others. *Booklist* praised his first middle-grade novel, *How I, Nicky Flynn, Finally Get a Life (and a Dog)* (retitled *How I Finally Got a Life and a Dog* in paperback) for its "vividly drawn" characters. He lives in Vermont.

Keep reading!

How I Got a Life and a Dog
Art Corriveau

ISBN 978-1-4197-0015-6